SINGLING OUT THE COUPLES

STELLA DUFFY

Virago

VIRAGO

First published in Great Britain in 1998 by Hodder and Stoughton,
a division of Hodder Headline PLC, as a Sceptre paperback
This edition published in 2006 by Virago Press

A CIP catalogue record for this book
is available from the British Library.

ISBN-13: 978-1-84408-333-6
ISBN-10: 1-84408-333-0

Typeset in Bembo by M Rules
Printed and bound in Great Britain by
Clays Ltd, St Ives plc

Virago Press
An imprint of
Little, Brown Book Group
Brettenham House
Lancaster Place
London WC2E 7EN

A member of the Hachette Livre Group of Companies

www.virago.co.uk

For Jase, the sweetest Prince ever to give his heart away

Acknowledgements

Thanks to Yvonne Baker, Shelley Silas, Carole Welch, Andrew Paine, Stephanie Cabot and Antonia Hodgson.

One

Once upon a time in a land both far away and remarkably close there is a truly happy people and ruling over them all in justice and joy there is a queen and a king. He is a king of remarkable loveliness and she is a queen of good counsel. They are loving and loved and to them is born a daughter, long limbed, bright eyed and perfect in every way.

To the Naming Ceremony of the precious daughter are invited the great and the good, the fair and the fancy, the wise and the wild. Their gifts are prized above all else and they give them willingly for, as everyone knows, to give to the Princess is of itself an uncommon blessing. To the sweet baby daughter they give gifts of great beauty, special charm, intense attraction, enviable wisdom and courageous passion. And the daughter grows strong in her gifts, full in these favours and with seasons and time and much sunshine and just a little fierce rain, she becomes a renowned beauty, famed scholar and fabled wit.

Then one day she leaves the land that is far distant and very close and journeys to our land and walks among us.

And I see you for what you are.

Then she laughs aloud. For in her own land she would only ever be a princess. Which would be such a terrible waste of talents and fortune. Here she shall be Queen.

And the Princess is perfect in every way, every direction, every point – except for the gift that was forgotten. For while the daughter has beauty and charm and elegance and wit and wisdom, she has no compassion. The Compassion Fairy was stuck on a tube and her gift was missed at the Naming. Missed but not noticed, for the charms of the Beauty Fairy were so glowing, the laughter of the Comedy Fairy so loud and the intellect of the Clever Fairy so bright, that no one even noticed the Compassion Fairy had failed to arrive. And she sat fuming and forgotten in the dirty underground cave.

To the daughter then, everlasting love is an obscene myth and sweet tenderness a rotting peach, a kiss just a maggot wriggling at its heart. To the daughter the parents are a nuisance and the mother is an obstacle in ambition's path, she would be Queen and she will control. Eventually. But no matter, for now she is beautiful and funny and gentle and sweet – and her cruelty exquisitely encased in the finely wrought and delicate shell that are her perfect eyes, nose, mouth, hair, arms, legs, breasts, feet, torso and cunt. And she knows us and we love her and only the Compassion Fairy sleeps a troubled dream.

Two

I live in an ivory tower. Dark ivory. Ivory wrenched from the face of a bleeding elephant. Ivory held down and ripped off and hewn and hacked and beaten about and made into a thing of beauty, pooled blood glistening just below the surface. I live in Notting Hill. My place is a palace – extra 'a' to soften the created symphony of what is in reality, just another seventies block of cold concrete. A pedestal containing small hallowed hollowed caves of passion, sixty homes in seventies housing. Mine is by far the finest. I have furnished it in par-adisal blues and greens, soft floating clouds pass my balconied windows and peek in at what they are sure must be the sky kissing the sea, walls bend to the smooth wooden floor, skirting boards flirting with the glistening slivers of varnished tree trunks. Forests were murdered to fashion the ground on which I walk. Daily I appreciate their sacrifice.

Sometimes, when I am alone, I reach my perfectly pointed foot to my full bow lips, close my big bright eyes and kiss me. A row of kisses planted like pearl seeds on a shiny neck. I run my tiny palest pink tongue along the instep, taste sweet skin and salt body sweat, nibble at the baby softness that is the ball of my foot, twirl my lips around the beautifully shaped toes. Sometimes I marvel so much at my beauty that I can only fully appreciate it when it's in my mouth. It is the taste of me that tastes so good. My flesh is manna and mama and more.

Notting Hill is not a wilderness, though after forty years I may not feel the same. I chose Notting Hill for the people. There are many people here. The choice is wide, the selection vast. There are real people and there are tourists and passing trade and passing maids and workers and shoppers and so many and varied, the happy, hippy shoppers of the Saturday afternoon stroll, the Sunday morning brunch, the misters and missuses, the mses and sirs. There are the heads that turn as I walk along the street. I walk in a glow of self-reflected light, I am the passion that illuminates my presence and they cannot help but notice it, be warmed by it, want it. There are pavements full of sprained ankles as I walk by in seeming unknowing. And then, surprisingly oblivious, there are the hand-holding elite in their in-love in-lust halo glow.

I spot the couple from my eyrie, clouds pass to clear my view and my trained eye zooms in. I spy them, note them, follow their coarse course of meet greet kiss and fuck. And then the plans and then the plotting, my house, your house, our house, our home. My name, your name, our name, play the game. The wedding day, the wedding dress, the bedding dress, the heaving chest. And each time, every time, every one the same time, the same old, same old, same old story. I do, I will, I am, I have. I am half, make me whole. I am nothing, make me real. I am not. Make me I am.

I fucking hate the couples. Their smugness, their sweetness, their names and games and charm and we not me, and they not he or she. I loathe the couples. I despise their giving

4

over, giving in, giving up the sin and the pleasure and the delight and the whole lies and the half-truths. I abhor the 'he knows me inside out', 'I could never lie to her'. I detest the taunt of 'I'm a grown-up now, my one is two.'

I'm not. I don't want to be.

But you know? It isn't enough just for me to be free. I pity them, wish for them my unadulterated freedom. I am a true liberationist. So I let them out. I save them from themselves. Open the gilded cages, break the chains, set fire to the tissue paper handcuffs and bite clean through the gold ring, to where the cheap brass shines through.

I am the world's most alluring woman and with love and charm I bestow my attention on all, drop a little touch of honeyed allure on anyone who passes me, makes passes at me. But only a drop. Because I'm saving myself. I have a duty to save myself, save my charm, keep it fresh and undiluted, pure and unpolluted. I cannot simply sit here and be ravishing. I can't just accept the showering gifts of love and continue as if I didn't have a care in the world. No. For I am burdened by my knowledge and weighed down by my responsibility. Every single person who touches me takes a little of my love away with them, but even mine is not a bottomless well of charm, a constant flow of giving. My gifts are costly. I do not single out just anyone to receive them. That would be importunate. I'm only singling out the couples. Because I hate the couples. The fucking couples. The fucking, kissing, smiling, simpering, love you, love me, make our baby, we'll be a family, couples.

And then, from my window, at a north by northwest through two o'clock I see them. A He and a She. Hands touch, electricity runs from his palm to hers. They'll do. They're done. I've only just begun.

Three

Sally and Jonathan are getting married in March. Today it is September. Late summer September, London clinging to an August of hot clear weeks broken by sultry days, damp and often windy as the equinox whips itself back into place. The warm wind stirs the ubiquitous McDonald's cartons and they dance in a frenzy of discarded activity, jay-walking the pedestrian crossing outside the little café in the High Street. Sally and Jonathan don't notice the weather though. Or the litter. Or the passing traffic. They hold hands. Tiny, pretty, blonde Sally gazing adoringly into big, dark Jonathan's pacific blue eyes. They are planning. They have been planning for six months. Listing, plotting, shopping, sorting and ordering for the last half year. The Big Day approaches and Saturdays and Sundays are parcelled up into whole hours of this shop or that, this gym or that, this way or that way and always together.

Sally holds Jonathan's big hands in hers, sometimes pausing mid-speech to wonder at the size of his hands, to kiss his smooth nails, so glad she has a man with nice hands, the hands of a real man. A really nice man who might be big and strong but knows enough to scrub his fingers before they touch her, to douse himself with proper perfume before he kisses her. Before Sally Jonathan was just an aftershave boy, now he is re-educated in the ways of male perfumes and can CK with the best of them. Jonathan looks at Sally intently, because he loves her he automatically understands her need to keep Aunty Sybil away from Uncle Fred at the reception, knows why she so much wants his mother to like her father. He loves Sally and leans across their empty, stained coffee cups to kiss her furrowed brow, to touch his lips to the tiny scar just under her left eye. Jonathan is aware with the raw nerve endings of emotion and remembers that Sally is self-conscious about the scar she has had since she was thirteen. In his unquestioning adoration Jonathan means to spend the next fifty years kissing that self-consciousness away. Kissing the scar away.

Neither of them notices the waitress arrive, not even the third time she stands before them and asks for their order. They barely notice when she slams the cold plates on the table. They don't really taste the food, Sally nibbling at the lollo rosso remembering more the taste of Jonathan's skin late at night, fresh from the shower, the taste of soap and kissing, of dead cells and hair. Jonathan sips the cool coffee and remembers his surprise when he first realised the taste of Sally was daily changing. They don't notice the waitress when she picks up the twenty pound note left for their £18.96 bill and snarls after them. Their bill wasn't too much for wine and water and a three course meal and two filter coffees. Cheap, had it been for two people. But Jonathan and Sally are so nearly one, so clearly one, that they ordered together. Will easily survive on a diet of shared dinners and joint breakfasts and air. Air in which kisses are born. Jonathan and Sally are clearly in love. Dearly in love.

Very nearly out of love.

Sally met Jonathan at her friend's house. Susie's boyfriend Jim knew a bloke Sally might like. A tall bloke, a dark bloke, a handsome bloke, a good bloke. Jonathan met Sally at his mate's house. His girlfriend Susie had a girlfriend Jon might like. A sweet girl, a neat girl, a nice girl, a good girl. Sally and Jonathan met just the once and before you could say second date, joint mortgage, married person's allowance, council tax deductions and the approval of all society, they were off and planning. Susie feels disgruntled and quite left out. Jim still hasn't proposed to her and it's been eighteen months. They've been living together for nearly a year and still she sports no shiny ring. She will not wear a ring she has to buy herself and so her hands remain bare. Sally has tried to make it better by offering Susie the runner-up role of chief bridesmaid, but Susie isn't certain that even the modern bridesmaid's dress of elegantly plain purple silk will do the trick. She has actually confided after a margarita or eight that perhaps Jim just isn't the marrying kind. Sally frowns her pretty little head into a crease and promises she will talk to Jonathan and ask him to have a word with Jim. In the throes of perfection she knows that her man can do anything, surely he can help with this? It would be so lovely if they could announce Susie and Jim's own wedding at their reception. Or maybe Jim might propose when he makes his best man's speech? Wouldn't that be romantic? Jonathan looks fondly down at his bride to be and, over takeaway pizza and a half-bottle of once-chilled chardonnay and in front of *When Harry Met Sally*, he breaks it to Sally that he just doesn't think Jim is the marrying kind. He's a good bloke, but not a marrying bloke. In her heart of hearts Sally knows this to be true. And though the room is warm, she snuggles up closer to Jonathan anyway, confident in the knowledge that she, Sally Withers, has done it. Found the one. Found herself a real diamond, fine cut and ready – the hard-to-find marrying kind of bloke. Sally and Jonathan The Gem watch the video. They are more smug than Billy Crystal.

When Cushla walked into the plain grey and matt-black office the next morning, Jonathan couldn't believe his eyes. It was her, the one perfect girl he'd been dreaming about since he was sixteen, when he began to know what women were, when he formed the first picture of what his future could hope to be. The picture that had faded and blurred and been reprocessed and reprogrammed by reality so many times in between. The picture that had been replaced altogether by the truth of Sally. Sally who would never be five foot ten with a size eight body and impossible breasts. Sally who didn't speak soft and slow. Sally who giggled too much to be cool. Sally who didn't have brown eyes, red hair, smooth honey skin covering long cool limbs. Sally who couldn't be his dream woman but might just be his real girl. Sally who loved him. Sally whom he loved.

And yet here She was, in his very own office. That woman. The Woman. The woman he'd described in detail to Jim, to Mick, to Bill, to every mate he'd ever had, talking late into the drunken night about their fantasy lives, fantasy wives. And he knew the dream girl wasn't real, couldn't be real. He thought Jim stupid to wait for the dream girl, thought Jim foolish and silly and told him so and Jim had agreed yes, he was stupid, but that's the way it was. Susie just wasn't his dream girl and though he loved her, Jim would wait. Just in case. If the dream girl never showed then, as long as she allowed him, Susie would do. But only as the girlfriend, never as the wife. Jim would marry the dream or not at all. Jonathan scoffed at Jim's *naiveté*, taking reality for

9

his guidebook and fate into his own hands. From where it was a small step to the wedding finger. And, knowing his dream girl would never, could never materialize, Jonathan had proposed to Sally and he did love her and he was looking forward to the honeymoon, to the house, to the babies, to their life together. He was happy. Was happy.

And now, she present and he tense, the Dream Girl was standing in front of him. Cushla. That woman. Asking if she could help him. Telling him she was here to help him. That was her new job. To look after him. The new secretary, girl Friday, girl Monday. The new girl.

Four

I do so like the red-hair jobs. I adore the chance to stand out. Far too often I'm called upon to be blonde. The blonde Bond girl, the bimbette, the Ford Fiesta of the romance world. Every second girl is blonde, it's an easy hour's work to become blonde, even the black girls are blonde these days. But red hair is another matter. When I'm red I carry with me the added blessing of freckled skin, skin that changes with the seasons, skin that blossoms and comes alive in summer sun, skin newly encoded in secret morse messages, skin to chameleon shimmer through thin cotton. There are statistics to enhance the red-hair jobs. Only one person in seven has red hair. That's in the Western world, add China and you're down to about one in twenty-three. There are few Chinese with naturally red hair.

There are also specific tricks to the red-hair jobs. To the danger of red. You can ask him to count your freckles. Once you get close enough. Offer a forearm and he knows how much further that skin goes. The counting, the peering, the tiny, nail-tip touching. It's an intimate beginning to an intimated end. And then the hair itself is so fine, finer than any other. Finer and softer. In the red-hair jobs I am a baby. Knowing baby. Fine delicate skin, soft hair. That's why I prefer to do red work with brown eyes. Blue eyes or green eyes would be too much of a cliché, and therefore too soft, too pretty. After all, under the hair and the eyes and the skin, there's still me down here, hiding in the newly formed body. I can't give in too much to the surrounding flesh. I might become like them, become gentle. Might return the love – and that would never do.

And of course the red hair makes me stand out. He won't miss me, can't miss me. How clever of Jonathan to know all along that the Right One would be a redhead. So much easier to pick out in a crowd. And I know what it does to his brain, his pituitary gland, his lymph glands, know how it spins the serotonin throbbing through his veins. He has bought all the myths, paid well over the odds for every one. A hidden look and he knows I'm a fiery beast under the cool mottled exterior. He knows for certain that my long soft limbs are violent geometric explanations of the working of male-female joining. Deep down in that primeval part of him, where considerations of fair play are tossed aside and from whence he smothers his reality with gentlemanliness and charm and perfume and elegance and fixed rate mortgages and bank loans and mummy and daddy and morning suits and white satin dresses with blue velvet sashes, deep down there in the groaning panting moaning X and Y undeniable DNA of himself – he knows, he just knows I'm a good fuck.

And he's right.

Five

Jonathan couldn't believe his luck. Not only had Cushla agreed to go out to lunch with him on the first day she'd started work, but also the second, and then the third. In three different restaurants, they nibbled at their possibilities across Europe from modern English through to old French and finally bastard Italian. And then, after the third lunch of Mr Freud's special spaghetti vongole with asparagus tips, followed by a teaspoon-shared creamy peach pie dripping warm amber juice from her fingers, she'd asked him for a drink the next night after work. Just a drink. She'd even said 'a quick drink'. And what was the harm in that? People had drinks all the time didn't they?

Though not usually Jonathan and Sally. Saving for the house.

Jonathan spread-sheeted his way through the afternoon, avoiding Cushla's cool gaze, diverting calls and rationalising his qualms out of existence. He ignored the warnings and didn't even whisper the truth to himself. The fact that he hadn't told Sally about the new secretary should have been caution enough. The fact that he hadn't mentioned the three lunches, this quick drink. The fact that he'd actually lied when Sally offered to pick him up the next night, they had a wedding list to complete, a dinner service to choose and it was late-night shopping. But Jonathan was tired, busy, distracted with work for the new account. Sally understood didn't she? And of course Sally understood. It was her job to understand. She intended to devote her life to understanding Jonathan, to loving Jonathan, to helping him through whatever came his way, because after all, his way would be their way. Just as her way would also be theirs. Sally had no doubt in her post-feminist, ideology-free way, that for every sacrifice she made, Jonathan would one day make an equal and easily offered sacrifice for her. Sally understood so well that she arranged to go shopping with Susie instead. They would make a shortlist, choose the three or four best, then Jonathan wouldn't have to help. Wouldn't need to muddy his busy brain with silly little things like the particular pattern they'd be asking for on the wedding list. Silly little things like the plate he'd pick his dinner from every night for the rest of his life.

Jonathan kicked himself for cheating Sally, hated himself for lying to Sally, berated himself for deceiving Sally. And then, as Sally showered herself clean of their every morning sex, he put on his best suit for work, with clean socks, red silk boxers and spent the day counting down the minutes until five past six. Cushla left the office half an hour before Jonathan as planned. He sprayed on the perfume of the new man and then followed her flesh scent out into the streets.

When Jonathan walked into the little bar in Covent Garden, the surprisingly quiet and dark bar where Cushla had suggested they meet, he knew he had already signed his life away. He looked across the small dim room to the corner where Cushla sat, lit by the reflection of candlelight as it

14

spun iridescent through her hair. She was leaning back against a pile of tapestried cushions, a bottle of mineral water in front of her, idly running her finger up and down the bubbles of condensation collected on the outside of the bottle. Cushla felt Jonathan's eyes colonise her the minute he walked in the room. She kept her own gaze on the glistening bottle and flicked back her hair, took a gentle breath, pulled in her stomach, pushing out her perfect breasts and slowly raised a glistening, dripping fingertip to her mouth. By the time he had taken the five steps necessary to be standing in front of her, she had her lips parted and her fingertip just touching the moist corner of her dark mouth. She knew Jonathan was at the edge of the table, the side of her chair, finally at her elbow and only then did she look up, facing him with a small half-smile, the smile of a child caught out but knowing they wouldn't, couldn't be told off.

She ran her finger along her lower lip, backwards and forwards, 'Woops, you caught me.'

Jonathan frowned, his own guilt startled at the word 'caught', 'I'm sorry?'

'I couldn't wait. I started without you,' she licked her finger fully now, 'I do hope you don't mind.'

Jonathan didn't mind. Didn't mind that he was so obviously being played with, didn't mind that Cushla was flirting with him more like a Charlie's Angel than a secretary, didn't mind that Cushla held all the cards in her long, fine, manicured hands. He didn't know enough to mind. Jonathan didn't know he had a right to mind. He still thought he knew what he was doing. A last fling. The sowing of the final wild oats. Just to prove the Dream Girl doesn't exist. One last time before I give myself over to Sally for richer for better forever and ever. Amen. Jonathan didn't mind because, as yet, he had no idea that the Dream Girl really was

15

a truth. But that her existence would be confined to sweaty, troubled nightmares.

They had a glass of house white each and then another glass of house red each and then they graduated to a shared bottle of the more expensive recommended red and Jonathan told Cushla all about his childhood in Swindon and the football team he played in on Sundays in the park and the way his mother had managed to dry out the Sunday roast every week and the way his dad had mowed the lawn once a fortnight, summer and winter, rain or shine. And Cushla told him nothing, but she let him think they were having a conversation. And they were of sorts. He talked. She listened. He talked some more and she nodded, frowned, patted his arm, caressed his knee, stroked his shoulder. He talked in English and she conversed in body language. Though the words came only from one, it was certainly a two-way communication. While he talked Jonathan munched his way through two packets of cheese and onion crisps, the warm garlic potato wedges with hot chilli salsa and a fat piece of carrot and orange cake with extra cream cheese icing. He didn't taste a single mouthful. Just kept on talking and when he wasn't talking he was filling his mouth, cramming his mouth full of food and wine and still more wine. Another bottle was opened. More food was brought. Opening his mouth minute after minute for food or wine or words. Opening and closing and chewing and talking and accumulating spit and mushy garlic potato at the corner of his mouth, wiping it in a clumsy action that landed a glob of cream on his designer tie. Just moving his mouth, propelling it, filling it, cramming it full. Anything so he didn't do what he longed to do, what every molecule of his flesh ached to do. Anything to stop himself reaching out and taking her hand, the hand she ran through her golden

16

hair, the hand that adjusted the thin silk skirt across tender thighs, the hand that toyed with her own unsullied lips. He longed to reach out and grab that soft girl hand and stuff it into his mouth, to eat her hand, her arm, her shoulder, her breasts. Jonathan ached to consume the whole heaving, breathing body displayed before him. Cushla was spread out like an untouchable feast where the only rules were the ones he himself had created and the only reason to be on a diet was because the world said so.

Not a good enough reason.

Whether he got drunk so he could ask her to do it, or maybe the drink loosened his tongue, or perhaps she forced him to the moment with her deep dark eyes, Jonathan next took Cushla's hand in his, clumsily kissed each finger in turn and then suggested leaving. Together.

'To your place, Jonathan?'

He shook his swaying head, 'No! Oh, I mean, um, my place isn't, you know . . .'

'Available?' Cushla, who was available, whispered and smiled and finished his sentence.

Sally finished his sentences too, but not usually while running her free hand across the very top of his left thigh.

Jonathan choked on a last greedy fingerful of carrot cake icing, slurring his words still more in an attempt to slur them less.

'Yeah. Whassit, I mean, whass . . . the, you know . . .'

'My place Jonathan? Would you like to come home to my place?'

The way Cushla said home, it sounded like brothel. Yes. Jonathan would like to come home.

Jonathan went home. All the way home, wagging his tail behind him.

Six

Today Jonathan is discovering another London. Uncovering a new city. Jonathan knows the London he shares with Sally. The Pizza Hut London. The movie and a daringly late curry London. The fifteen tube stops to get to Leicester Square London. Suburban London. The outer city London to which his family migrated when he was fifteen, where he and Sally spent thrilling teenage nights, where their parents still live, just high streets from Sally and Jonathan's maisonette. Where for a decade of Saturdays they have shopped in the local supermarket, willingly bought passion-free cucumbers (EC regulation straight) and perfectly rounded, soulless Dutch peppers. This is the London where they work 'in town' but take lunches they have made at home – lunches they have made for each other. Lunches nibbled as they sit in the pub, nursing half a pint with the friends from the office. Extra-spicy chicken tikka sandwiches for hardy Jonathan, tuna salad for Sally's more delicate constitution and more easily fattened thighs. Since the engagement they have made once monthly trips 'up to town' to look in the windows and compare prices, not for potential purchase but for Sally to note with glee how much cheaper she could get that nice floral-print duvet cover from her catalogue. Trips that give both of them the chance to complain about the crowds, the fumes, the noise. To hurry back on the grateful tube to the outer reaches of the metropolis, to the tasty frozen supermarket pizza offering them much-needed sustenance. Once it has been microwaved with the oven chips. And swallowed down with the Belgian beer they buy for the look not the taste.

Saturday after Saturday they have parked their car in the neatly lined parking space and hop skipped past the private privet and up the stairs, laden with bags and boxes and unloaded their new acquisitions into their perfectly fake, newly built, brick-façade maisonette. They have settled down for a night with the lottery and a rented video. An action movie for Jonathan, a romantic comedy for Sally, or a bloody thriller to excite the unvoiced parts of both of them. A night of pre-connubial bliss. They are happy. They have no reason not to be.

Yet.

Sally sits on the sofa, her head on Jonathan's shoulder, warm fizzy glass in her hand and, as the pizza heats itself into a botulistic mess of melted plastic mozzarella, she reviews her plans. She knows that one day they will move to a larger place, a whole house of their own, with the small garden that Jonathan will pave over, so much better not to have to mow the lawns. Jonathan is not his father, he has made changes. Maybe they will have a pond. They will buy a gas-fired barbecue and invite their like-minded friends over for long summer evenings of imported beers and easy Australian whites. The future is so rosy and bright, so warm that Sally could keep her ever-cold toes snug, wrapped in a blanket woven of their plans. Sally knows that the house will have a nursery. She knows this deep in the uterus which she sweetly calls a womb. Blessed be its fruit. She plans to paint the whole room Mothercare lemon picked out in eggshell white. Jonathan once suggested real egg yellow – egg yolk eggshell. But there were too many eggs for Sally's crowded ovaries, her uterus complained at the early, unplanned intrusion and they settled for the safety of lemon and white. Sally is more of a lemon-meringue girl anyway. She knows that one day her nursery will be full of the sweet smells of Ideal Baby, a catalogue baby, selected with care and accuracy and so much cheaper than the very same thing from Covent Garden or Oxford Street. Soft and quiet and sleeping and perfect. Sally's daughter will never smell of shit or cry from midnight until dawn, and Jonathan's son will not vomit bitter milk stains down his grandma knitted lemon-yellow cardie.

Thus the London of Jonathan and Sally's pale reality is a big city with room for all to live out their exemplary lives in perfectly ordered, easy-clean, low-ceilinged homes with Sally's kitchen and Jonathan's garden shed and double glazing and loft conversions for all.

Jonathan though, is now trawling through that other London. The London that is a divine arena for wickedness. This huge, ramshackle city that was cobbled together from village overflows and fat-brat towns and is linked by multi-coloured underground lines and pink painted taxi cabs and dank, pitted sewer networks. Where there are rounded corners too soft for safety and narrow alleys and secluded green lockgated gardens. The haughtiest hotels and the seediest bars. Disturbingly frequented by people Jonathan is stunned to see in the corner table, people who always wear black except when the fashion pages dictate that brown or grey are the new black and then the only change is a hint of muted colour in the lining of another perfect suit. People real in the fluorescent light of the plush office becoming uncertain gossamer in the sharp re-focus change as the retina shifts comprehension from onstreet daylight to rooms of perpetual evening. He meets Cushla in the dark, quiet restaurants hidden in alleyways and dead-end streets, where intimacy is encouraged and fat oysters are to be found jostling baby clams, dripping in warm sweet butter just seconds away from turning to rancid oil. These are the restaurants that do not see the light of the sun in Soho, shunning wide street angles and curling themselves into small paths, dark clubs, basement entrances. This is also a London of miniskirts and bare flesh in winter, of sex for quick sale, no refunds, no returns, bodies stalking on long legs ascending to a haven that may be male or female and Jonathan has no way of knowing which, much less an educated discernment to help him decide. Converging sides of the multi-faceted city that he has until now simply driven through, eyes averted from what might turn his head. Or his cock. Streets with soft beds to rent where fast fucks are paid for by the hour, getting faster by the minute. Jonathan did not know about this city. But he is happy to learn.

And he will of course, pay for rather more than just one hour.

Jonathan leaves work quickly at lunchtime, just ten minutes after Cushla's hasty departure – tongues will start to wag if he is not more careful. Cushla's wagging tongue is flesh-pink enough for him. He slams half-finished files in the wrong coloured folders and checks his minted breath against his sweaty palm in the empty reflecting elevator. He hurries to the appointed meeting place. Jonathan braves buses and heedless cycle couriers to fly to omnipotent Cushla. She greets him in the small Soho room, meets him two floors above the street full of advertising men and marketing

21

women, two floors up where the windows are shut tight to keep in their moans.

Cushla is not shut tight. She welcomes Jonathan in, receives him ardently, a long kiss at the door, another anointing him on the stairs. Her lips and teeth hold fast to his tongue as he struggles to remove his tie – she breaks away to breathe in his ear that he need not bother, she will have him fully clothed. With one deft hand she undoes the buttons of his fly and in a swift and expert moment descends to the floor. There is a hiatus of perhaps five still seconds. Cushla is an artist. She looks up at Jonathan from her knees. He stands above her, parted feet planted on the swaying step, one hand stretched out in front of him grasping at what he believes to be possible. The other hand rests lightly on her head, her red hair, ready to grip, to wrench her locks. Here is a man who swallowed all the myths, who is at this moment seeing himself the star of his own pop video. Jonathan does not have quite enough imagination to stretch to a full length feature. Cushla knows the effect she is having on Jonathan. She recklessly holds it two long seconds more. Cushla adores her own glorious power. Knows she looks her best here, dark eyes wide above a white stretched neck, breasts full and heavy, reddened nipples half-covered by her classic black silk gown. Cushla smiles up at Jonathan in self-adoring piety and he swells with pride and strength. She bats her eyelashes for him and he actually believes she really is kneeling before him.

Cushla sucks supplicating, takes him in her mouth and quite simply takes him in. She swallows him whole and he gulps. And Jonathan still thinks he's in charge.

Worse, he still thinks he can stop when he wants to.

Seven

Guilt is making Jonathan a less than charming partner. He is treating Sally like shit. Sally puts it down to pre-wedding nerves. Jonathan is being cold and callous and then over-whelmingly gentle and soft. Sally blames pressure of work. He brings her home new perfume and body lotion, large sizes, very expensive and in ten minutes has stormed out to the pub on the slightest provocation. Sally blames herself. Which annoys Jonathan all the more.

'God Sally, it's not your bloody fault. I'm just in a crap mood. Why can't you just accept that? It's got nothing to do with you!'

Jonathan is looming over her and shouting into her face. Sally finds it a little hard to divorce herself from feeling that if not the cause, then at least the effect, must have something to do with her.

Silence might be the more sensible tactic but Sally is not a skilled war games tactician, 'Try me. I know something's wrong darling. Just tell me Jon, let me in?'

Sally is sweet and quiet, a gentle hand on Jonathan's tight

fist. He could melt now. Tell her all. Go through the sordid details, the passionate kisses, the exquisite sex. Sally is his partner but she is also his friend. He actually wants to share his dilemma with her, she is the one in whom he confides, now who is there to talk to? Jonathan may not always respect Sally's opinion but he has used it to shore up his own many times in the past. He could do with her support here.

He pictures her acquiescence, 'Yes darling, it's fine for you to sow wild oats. I understand darling, of course you need a final fling. Go ahead. Fuck with my blessing.'

Jonathan could do with hearing all this. But it's impossible. Sally would never say fuck. Instead he violently shakes her hand from his, dismisses her attempt at truce and storms out of the maisonette. Cushla has told him she cannot meet him tonight so he goes to the pub alone, telling his third pint what he can't tell his wife-to-be. The fourth pint he shares with Jim. There is man-bonding and there is football and there is music and then there is truth. Jonathan can easily explain the flesh of her, the lust for her, what is harder to convey is the why.

'So . . . but . . . yeah, you know . . . I just . . .'

'Fancy her?'

'Sure, yes, of course, but more. Much more. She's it mate. She's it.'

'What do you mean, it?'

'She's the one. I'm having an affair with the perfect woman. I found her. Too late, but I found her.'

Jim is unnerved by this, it upsets the double couple balance. It also reminds him of how he too yearns for the perfect unreal. He tries to force Jonathan into a backtrack, 'Yeah, but you wouldn't leave Sally for her would you?'

In vino veritas, in real ale reality. The pint is drained and Jonathan looks across the beery table to his oldest friend, school friend, best friend. He endeavours to be more honest than ever before. His shoulders shrug themselves and his body language is more easily heard than his words, 'I don't know, I do love Sal. I do. And I don't want to hurt her and I know this would kill her but the thing is, the whole damn thing is, Cushla just is perfect. She's perfect. It's simple and it's a real fucking mess. I just don't know what to do. But Sally isn't enough and to be honest, I don't think she ever will be.'

Jim has no reply and goes to get the next couple of pints. The conversation moves haltingly away from reality and on to work and weather in a slow, becoming-more-pissed swing. There is no discussion of the need for secrecy, the promise of absolute discretion is a given. The two men can hold secrets in their drunkenness but both of them know that a whispered word to Susie would translate to an epic tale to Sally and then it would all be over. Jonathan doesn't want it all to be over. He just wants it all.

Sally discusses the situation with her mother. To be completely honest, Sally's mother has never really liked the man, she actually hoped her elder daughter might achieve a little more with her life than simply attaining the pinnacle that is to be Mrs Jonathan. But with the reception hall and caterers booked, the dressmaker already working on the flower girl's outfit and the invitations on their way back from the printers, Sally's mum isn't going to feed any doubts right now.

'Don't be silly darling. Of course Jonathan loves you.'

Sally flicks back a blonde curl from her forehead. This is a new and irritating habit she has developed in lieu of biting her nails. Bitten nails do not make for a great photo of the wedding ring.

'I know he loves me, Mum. I just think . . . I don't know what to think. He's just not acting like he loves me.'

Sally's mother sighs. She wants to explain to Sally that actually Jonathan has never acted like he loves her. Never acted like he knows how to love. She dusts her hands with white self-raising flour and continues rolling out the short crust pastry. Sally's father loves apple pie. Garden-grown apples, homemade pastry, an hour or so to create and devoured in five minutes flat.

'Listen Sal, it's all about compromise. That's what marriage is. Do you think your father and I haven't had our ups and downs?'

Actually Sally had thought her parents' marriage was the one perfect constant, but she shakes her head, agreeing with her mother in the hope that the maternal wisdom to come will nullify her aching doubts.

Sally's mum turns the pastry over, sprinkles more flour on it, rubs her hands together, the sound of dusty hands making Sally's skin crawl quicker than unbitten nails on a blackboard. Her mother rolls out the pastry in the opposite direction, flattening indecision in the process.

'You know, your Dad and I haven't had a perfect marriage by any means. We had a terrible time at first, living with his parents,' she places the pie dish over the pastry and carefully cuts around the edges, rolling the spare pastry into a ball to use for decoration, Sally absentmindedly picks at the pastry ball, her mother slaps the grown woman fingers in little girl action, the revelations continue, 'His mother was an absolute tartar, treated me like dirt . . .'

'Nana Irene?'

Sally is shocked. Nana Irene died when Sally was eleven. Nana Irene was a tiny little old woman who was only an inch taller than the eleven-year-old Sally herself. She used to sneak her humbugs behind her parents' back. She liked Sally more than little sister Janey. She was Sally's ally.

'Yes, lovely Nana Irene. She couldn't stand the sight of me. Used to tell your father he'd be better off without me, even after we were married, let alone all the times before. And then when we moved out, when I was carrying you, I thought it would be different but it wasn't. She kept on with her attacks, just a few streets away instead.'

Sally's mother uses her becoming-arthritic forefingers to crimp the pastry around the edge of the dish, pricks it several times in the centre with a fork and shapes the nibbled spare pastry into a two-dimensional apple and three perfect leaves. She lick-sticks them to the centre of the pie and places it carefully in the oven. Sally is confused and hungry, she eats three rich teas in quick succession.

'But she wasn't like that when I knew her. She was really nice when Janey and I were little, we loved going to her place. What happened?'

Sally's mother puts the kettle on. Should she tell Sally about Granddad Mac's will? The last will and testament of a man dying too young of liver cancer, in which he bequeathed a whole thousand pounds to his unnamed mistress, a woman he had stopped seeing more than twelve years earlier. Only Sally's mum and dad and Nana Irene ever heard the reading of that will. The solicitor took care of the bequest. Nana Irene never knew who her husband's mistress had been. She said she never wanted to know either. Only the three of them knew the secret, and Sally's mum rather thought her husband had forgotten all about it. She spooned instant coffee into the second-best mugs and left the truth unsaid.

'Granddad Mac died and she needed us. Actually, she needed me, your Dad was never very good with her. Never really knew how to talk to her. She needed me to look after her and I did.'

'But why? If she'd been so horrible to you?'

'It was my duty Sally. It's what you do. You make a choice and you stick with it and you keep going even when times are hard. That's the point. Times are going to be hard anyway, love. For all of us, no matter what. You've really only ever got yourself to lean on, we're all alone in the end. Just like Grandma Irene was. So you might as well get some companionship while you can.'

Sally took the proffered coffee and smiled at her mother. A decent, hard-working woman. A woman who could dispense sound advice while rosemary roasting a leg of lamb and baking an apple pie with homemade pastry all at the same time. They talked about nothing until Sally finished her coffee and went home to Jonathan, a tupperware container of mother-made biscuits in a supermarket plastic bag. So she would love Jonathan and get on with him despite his moods and she would make a home with him. She would have him for her companion as long as she could. She would make it work.

Sally's mother smoked a guilty cigarette, dropping ash into her pile of wish-perfect apple-length peelings. She wondered if perhaps she should have told her daughter the truth. That Nana Irene had been right all along, right not to trust her. Known that Sally's mum had been having an affair when she married Sally's dad. Not that Nana Irene had known who with. Sally's mum had always been more careful than that. But Nana Irene had known what was going on. Had startled Sally's mum just the day before the wedding, coming into her bedroom at her own parents' house and pleading with her not to marry her boy, not to trap him in a loveless marriage. Nana Irene had begged Sally's mum to come clean, to own up to the affair she'd been having and let Sally's dad off the hook.

What Nana Irene didn't know of course, was that the man Sally's mum was having an affair with was already married himself. Sally's mum couldn't tell the truth or she would be alone. He'd never leave his wife for her, he'd told her that, he loved his wife and Sally's dad loved her. So she was going to go through with it and marry Sally's dad and give up the affair and she would be happy because she determined she would and even if it wasn't really love, what did that matter? Who knew what love really was anyway? She sent Grandma Irene away and got on with ironing her petticoat. She'd have a life companion and that would be enough, she would make it be enough. She and Sally's dad might not start out with two-sided love but they'd grow into it. That's what people used to do all the time, wasn't it?

And she had learnt to love her husband, eventually. Love him dearly in the end. And of course, the thousand pound legacy had come in very handy too.

Eight

I am not perfect by chance. This purity of form is through expert design. There is aim, method, conclusion, creation. Created in recreation. I swim, I run, I play and each apparently chance movement is intentionally linked to a body function, a muscle group, an organ, a joint, pore, cell. Everything I do is contrived to recreate me more perfect than even the original. And already I was born in blessed perfection. I am an immaculate conceit – each limb lithe and long, shining eyed and glossy haired and so very hale, healthy, happy, and whole.

Almost whole.

But even in my perfection this flawlessness will not maintain itself of pure will. It has to be eked out of the hiding place where cosy softness dwells, the firm muscles rippling beneath my smoothed skin are tamed into compliance with daily undaunted exertion.

I say daily, I mean nightly.

At night she swims. It is three, four in the morning. The council-maintained pool is deserted, glancing moonlight and the infra-red eye of the burglar alarm shoot across the barely rippled water. She sails beneath the surface for five, six lengths at a time. Rising only to gasp swift silent oxygen pure into her lungs, smooth gliding through pools of scattered moonlight. The bloody red eye-beam does not penetrate to the depths of six feet below and she swims without thought in the silent night pool. There are no sounds to be heard but the small regular splash against the sides, no sight but milky lunar beams caught in tiny wet pools at the edge of her night vision. Her body is cold and naked and perfect.

In the peace of the cool pool my embryonic plans are hatched. There is a moment of detachment, the lengths of swimming work on the physiology and, at the peak of exertion, when I am flooded with the endorphin rush that is the only true reason, I receive knowledge. Where to touch next, how to move next, when to kiss, to smile, to scream, to fuck. Each moment of the seduction is strategic and analysed through thought via exercise and into reality. Jonathan would be proud to know I have spent so much energy in creating his future. And surprised, he thinks this is natural magic. I take deep breaths and firm, long strokes, the liquid sluices past my naked skin caressing it into longing more readily than his touch could ever do. I come and go far beneath the surface, deaf to even the empty pool echo. I am easily pleasured by the swift water flowing past my skin, flowing around my limbs, enveloped and flooded by the fluid, I come as part of it. This time is my one release and when I scream out my longing into the ten-foot-deep silence I am blessed with the knowledge of what to do next.

I think perhaps little Sally might like to watch.

Nine

What Sally saw ripped back the love cataracts that covered her baby-blue eyes and sent her blind with despair. The salt bath wash she fed her bloodied eyeballs threatened to drown her already mushy brain. Threatened but did not succeed. The slow beating tide of pain eventually receded and, just moments before her frenzied mind dived into a crashing wave of self-loathing and blame, the remaining sliver of sane girl placed a fierce carapace around her heart. And breathed a sigh of relief.

She watched Jonathan and Cushla from a safe, candlelit distance, having wandered by what magic she did not know into this new bar, a surprisingly quiet bar for this corner of Covent Garden. A long place, dark underground, running beneath the street where with her fiancé she had often held hands and they had whispered into each other's ears the seductive charms of lounge suites and sale bargains and quick fucks stolen in secret, hidden corners. Sally strayed into the bar from yet another wedding-list shopping trip. Tired feet and racked arms aching from carrying the plastic bags full of her future, she saw a hand-chalked sign for the wines and coffees and ciabatta sandwiches she enjoys as part of an 'in town' ritual, the foods that make her feel like a grown-up when she consumes them alone, the foods that make her feel like a child when Jonathan laughs at her pretensions. The foods she enjoys but no longer tells Jonathan of. After all, everyone needs their little secrets, even the about-to-be-weds.

Sally had placed her pretend-adult order at the bar and found an empty table, laid down the bags in a sea at her feet and was flicking past serious articles about Third-World poverty and three-a-night orgasms, turning to the horoscopes in her magazine, brie and streaky bacon and the light white and water to come wetting her mouth, when she heard his laugh. Jonathan's laugh. Straight through the dark and swift to her soul like a soft whispered kiss in the middle of the night. Sally's pretty head turned automatically, a delighted smile dancing a welcoming jig across her face.

They were six tables away. The woman had her hand high on his thigh, her head nodding in time to the rhythm of her drumming fingers, just brushing the edge of what Sally had sweetly called his 'privates' and what now, quite plainly, she knew to be Jonathan's very ordinary cock. He was touching the woman as he spoke. He couldn't keep his hands from her perfection as he talked, on and on and on. And while Sally could immediately see that the woman was very beautiful, long and lovely in the dim warm light, she could also see that Jonathan was not.

Candlelight and the woman's well placed hand had suddenly given her perfect vision. Her Jonathan, the one with the sparkling eyes, with the big strong hands, with the gentle way of following Sally through the life they planned together – that Jonathan was not sitting with the beautiful woman. That Jonathan was reeling back, lost in the mists of planned suburban time. Here instead was a man with boorish hands, hands too big to stroke that woman's fine soft skin, fingernails too rough to glide over her flesh without catching on a prominent bone, accidentally grazing her. This Jonathan was just a bloke, a letch. This Jonathan was falling and drooling and bumbling laughter and the sweat he surreptitiously wiped away with a dirty fat finger made Sally gag.

Jonathan was looking at the perfect woman as if he was the guy in that field they'd visited on holiday last year – the peasant Greek farmer who, ploughing one hot day a hundred years ago, had simply turfed up Venus from his dry dirt plot. Jonathan was regarding the woman before him in awe and fear and just a little stupid surprise. At a distance of six knee-high tables Sally understood that this was the look of love. She'd seen it often enough in the mirror. And surely she was Alice now, tumbled right through to the other side where the look was merely foolish and her heart just a solid lump of thick bloody flesh, beating away beneath her too small breasts. Arteries and veins, aorta and valves. A thing of merely plasma and tissue, all sentimentality rinsed out. Sally rose and walked, on legs that couldn't believe they were capable of moving, to the ladies toilets. She had some shards of broken mirror to remove from her back.

From the dim corner to the powder room, a place of pink and chintz and girl chatter and soft, skin enhancing light. Sally goes to the toilet and throws up. Disgorges all of Jonathan that she has so happily swallowed, the stories of his childhood, the loving mother, the distant father, the schooldays with Jim, university terms of beer and babes, the empty, pale, waiting days before Sally. Vomits it all into a limescale-free white porcelain bowl. Retches until there is none of

34

Jonathan left, only a thin and empty Sally. And when she comes out of the cubicle, face flushed, eyes swollen wet, stomach still heaving, the woman is there. That woman. Smooth and cool and elegant. Sally hesitates a moment then throws herself in the forward motion of an impossible step. The legs are completely independent now, Sally is a torso and limbs and neck and head, disjointed and jumbled. The pieces of her stack up in all the right places but Sally can't feel any of them. She stands beside the woman at the mirror, washes her spleen-spattered face while the woman reapplies her lipstick, a dark maroon with just the merest hint of pearl. Sally is falling apart, just waiting for her head to topple from her brittle neck, and the woman beside her is perfect.

The woman, a clear head taller than sweet little Sally, turns solicitously, looks down at the pale trembling thing beside her, kindly enquires, 'Are you okay? Can I get you anything?'

Sally barely shakes her head, scared it will slip down the sink and be washed away, terrified of what words might come out if she opens her mouth.

But the woman will not be rejected, persists, 'A glass of water perhaps? Or maybe I should order you a cup of tea? You look like you've had a shock.'

Sally's mouth opens by itself and a tiny 'No' emerges through sticky teeth, tight lips.

The woman, who knows exactly what she is doing, understands just where to turn the knife like the finest oyster opener, adds one solicitous sentence more.

'Maybe I should get my boyfriend to drive you home, he can't stand to see a woman unhappy – I'll call him shall I?'

And then Sally surprises herself, stuns herself, drags herself back out through the wobbly side of the looking glass to reach the full strength of her own tiny height, turns her pretty, pained face up to the persistent woman towering over her and she spits at her. It misses the face of course, and it is a small, pitiful drop of bile-tinged saliva that lands on the woman's beautifully combed red glow of hair. But it is a spit nonetheless. Sally pulls herself away from the sparkling sinks and gleaming mirror, leaves the room. The door slams and the ladies toilet inside remains hushed and flesh pink. Cushla turns to regard herself in the mirror, she smooths away the tiny trickle of saliva with one hand and with the other blows herself a congratulatory kiss. It has been a very good day's work.

When she turned her back on Cushla, Sally walked surprisingly steadily to the bar and while her new vision hardened her sinews, the three straight whiskies added to Jonathan's bill strengthened her resolve. Belgian chocolate soft-centred indifference transported itself into Dutch courage and she went home to change the locks.

Ten

Bitter rage and violent revenge was not an art Sally had a great deal of experience in. There's not a lot of call for brutal retaliation in the lives of most tiny blonde girls. Not in the life of this pretty wee thing anyway. True, there was the occasion when she'd pulled her little sister's hair. Pulled it hard enough to wrench three long hairs from their roots. Janey had taken Barbie for a walk in the rain, foolishly dressing her only in Barbie's Fun Beach Wear and forgetting to add the Barbie Rain 'n' Shine parasol/umbrella combination. Sally herself had never forgotten to take Barbie's umbrella when going out for the day. Long before she'd started school, Sally had learnt you never could be too careful. Janey came home bedraggled and Barbie's wet locks and the ruined Beach Barbie bikini were too much for little Sally to bear – at eight Sally already understood that Barbie wasn't wearing a bikini simply to get it wet – and she'd yanked a handful of Janey's six-year-old curls in frustration. Which had been seen by Mummy (making tea), who'd reported it to Daddy (on his return from the office), who

37

gave Sally such a stern (yet understanding) talking-to, that she immediately went and offered to surrender the still-damp Barbie to Janey as compensation. Daddy said she didn't have to, correctly judging that a little tenderheart like Sally would now forever know the difference between a deliberate wrong-doing and a small error in judgement. Such as taking Beach Barbie outside wearing incorrect attire. And she did. Mummy and Daddy were always right.

Sally grew up fair hearted and honest and always ready to forgive her friends for any little mishaps. Minor inconsiderations such as forgetting Sally's birthday or a slight indiscretion like suggesting perhaps Jonathan was putting on just a little too much weight after another of Sally's fabulous Sainsburys-created meals. As long as the nastiness wasn't a deliberate wounding, Sally was prepared to forgive anything. Sally was generous and open-hearted to the point of foolishness, but that was her experience. Because in pretty blonde Sally's lovely little world, who on earth was going to be intentionally nasty?

When Sally went back to the maisonette to change the locks, she had twenty-six years-worth of tiny blonde niceness to get bitter over. Twenty-six years-worth of pretty little thing ignoring unintentional slights to be furious about. Twenty-six years of patronising friends and ignorant comments about her little girl's intellect and the added build up of condescending Jonathan to be pissed off with. Rome however, wasn't built in a day and the pretty blonde isn't dyed away without a few copper rinse splashes on the bath mat. So Sally started where she could. The locks first. Then the clothes. Typical, classic, she'd seen it done on daytime telly, nothing new in the action of throwing out her boyfriend's attire, but it felt good anyway – all of Jonathan's elegant suits in black plastic bags and all the black plastic bags in a dirty, smelly rubbish bin, with all of Jonathan's fancy perfume bottles smashed and thrown dripping into the bin just in case the smell of dirt was too much for him. She couldn't bring herself to go as far as the posh woman she read about in the paper who'd actually cut up her husband's suits – and anyway, Sally knew that Jonathan would never wear something once it had been in the bin for a day, so why should she blister her thumb and blunt her sewing scissors? After the clothes, the obvious next move was the car, a rush for the superglue and Stanley knife and then, hand poised over the lock, a brief pause for thought. Sally stopped herself. Bitterness is a surprisingly quick teacher and the new clever Sally realised it wasn't a great idea to ruin the car Jonathan had sensibly made out to her so she could claim the tax allowance in her name and he could claim the greater allowances in his. Very sensible Jonathan.

Sally was proud of herself. She'd actually done revenge. And hadn't said sorry. Yet.

Two hours later Sally turned up on Susie's doorstep, tired, tearful and trembling. Clever Sally had been left out in the unlovely rain too long and she was now very much My-Boyfriend-Done-Me-Wrong-But-I-Still-Love-Him-Anyway Sally. Susie gave her valium, wine and a man-size box of tissues. Then she gave her Peking duck, egg-fried rice and a giant bar of hazelnut Galaxy. Then, after the fifth time she'd slammed the door in his face, she gave her Jonathan. Which gave Sally a good place to throw the last half of her fourth glass of wine. Not a great shot at the best of times, Jonathan had to acknowledge Sally's imperfect aim was a surprise direct hit as the warm wine-and-tear spritzer hit his groin. His groin still aching from the fuck of the night before.

'I'm sorry.'

'I didn't mean for this to happen.'

'You're too good for me.'

'I was as surprised by it all as you are.'

'It's not you, it's me.'

'I admit it, I'm a bastard.'

'I can't help myself.'

'I can't give you what you want.'

'I didn't mean to hurt you.'

'This is bigger than me.'

'Don't blame yourself, this has nothing to do with you.'

And eventually, predictably, finally – 'I love you, I need you, I want you . . . I'm just in love with someone else.'

For a man who swore he'd never said those lines before, never had anyone to say them to before, they sprang from his tongue like over-ripe peaches falling from a tornado-rocked tree. Perhaps they are the lines of the collective unconscious bastard. Or bitch. Just the same-old same-old lines of anyone doing the thing that must be done while hating themselves for every second of it. Sally's world was spinning around her and if she thought a contrite Jonathan was going to come begging forgiveness and pleading with her to come home, then she was looking for a heart in the wrong tin man. Tarnished man.

Jonathan, sadly, still hadn't got a clue, 'You see Sal, I do love you. Really I do. I've loved you for years. I wish I could have you both.' Sally heard the conditional and started to open her mouth, Jonathan sped on before she could interrupt his unrehearsed performance, 'But Cushla . . . well, she's . . . Sally, honey, I'm sorry, this is just different, it's like nothing I've ever felt before. I didn't expect . . . I don't know how . . . I can't explain . . . I'm sorry. I really am so sorry.'

New love forcing repetition and cliché from Jonathan's mouth.

Sally lied right back, 'I don't want to hear. I don't want to know anything about her.'

Relieved to be let off the inquisitor's hook, Jonathan gladly took the cue to shut up, 'Oh right. Okay. Whatever you say.'

The silence lasted all of three seconds. Sally's broken heart went careering through her brain, an out-of-control pinball, hitting all the lights and bells at once. Want to know, don't want to know. Want to hear, don't want to hear. Want to be told every little detail of your sordid sexual coupling . . . can't bear to think you even passed each other on a pedestrian crossing, let alone touched her. Touched her, kissed her, fucked her, reached her.

Reality won out.

'Where did you meet?'

Two hours later it was all over. Jonathan and Sally emerged from the closed door sitting room to tell the tea-soaked Susie and lager-headed Jim what the plans were. Jonathan and Sally were being very sensible. Jonathan was being sensible because that way he could get back to Cushla's soft spread breasts as soon as possible. Sally was being sensible because, three hours after the revenge euphoria, she'd had a hint of what alone might be like and was silently praying that maybe Jonathan would still come back to her if she was good. If she was very, very good. Sally would call her parents, Jonathan would speak to Jim, they'd let the grown-ups get on with sorting out the mess of a pre-wedding divorce. Sally would go back to the maisonette. Jonathan said he would stay with Jim. Jim knew Jonathan meant he would stay with Cushla. Susie knew Jonathan meant he would stay with Cushla. Jonathan knew he meant to stay with Cushla. Sally was happy to live with the lie as long as it meant she didn't have to picture Jonathan having sex. At least not tonight.

41

And that was that. More or less.

Except that when Jim dropped Sally off at the dark, cold maisonette and she invited him in for a cup of tea because she couldn't bear to be alone just yet, she also invited him upstairs for a quick fuck. In the car on the way home she'd realised that if she was going to spend the rest of her life being very, very good, then she'd better get the bad out of the way in a hurry. Not that Sally said those words of course, 'quick fuck' was far too guttural for her sob-swollen throat and tear-chapped lips. Sally's invitation was couched in the more traditional vein. Not a brothel phrase, but a brides-maid's phrase: 'I just need someone to hold me for a while.' Sadly, with Jim still waiting for the Only Perfect Girl, a quick fuck was all he could manage. Still, it lasted long enough to put Sally off to sleep, that and the valium Susie had slipped into her tea.

And the other little problem was when Jonathan turned up at Cushla's house. Cushla's place in Crouch End. Cushla's place that was a lie. He stood outside an address he'd been given but had not yet visited, a house he'd long imagined but never actually known. At the half-opened door Jonathan was greeted by a very nice Turkish lady with four screaming children around her feet and one at her half-exposed breast.

The little boy in blue hit the little girl in pink.

'No, I don't know no Cushla.'

The older girl in school uniform hit the little boy in blue.

'No, I never did. Not here. The family been here six years.'

The biggest boy hit all three smaller children and the little girl kicked her mother.

'And no, I didn't make mistake. Maybe you make mis-take?'

When the feeding baby turned its head from her breast,

Jonathan looked into the pure and innocent little face. When the baby-blue eyes became the deep dark brown of Cushla's and its three-month gurgle became her sexy giggle, a teeny, tiny light glimmered somewhere in the dim recesses of what had once been Jonathan's mind. He started to wonder if maybe he did make a mistake. And when the baby projectile-vomited all over his one remaining suit, Jonathan became just a little bit worried.

Eleven

I like this. No. The statement is too thin. Like this? This fucking well makes me come. This fucking makes me come. Without release. I am orgasmic with my own brilliance. Sadly I must sing my own praises, who else knows enough to honour me? Bless me as I would be blessed. They are done. All done. Undone. Jonathan and Sally split and sundered and rendered half. Two made one made two again and not now one plus one, but so very much less. She is tear-stained and bitter and yearning, he is bewildered and pained and strained and perfectly unsure. I could not have planned this better. Though I did plan it. I am meticulous. You never know, of course, cannot be certain of the outcome until the conclusion. Even in my homeland there are times when things go a little awry. Look at me. Her Majesty's daughter supposedly content to languish in unobserved obedience and power-free compliance. No. I will have my own kingdom come. And then some.

This consequence is truly marvellous. I am in awe of myself, to have done my job so well. I watched him outside the Turkish lady's house, nearly choking with the need to laugh silently as the baby vomit dripped milky acid down the front of his only clean, sharp, double-breasted suit. I could have kissed myself with pride. Longed to kiss myself with pride. I hurried back to Notting Hill.

Home again I climbed the many steps to the tower. I long ago let down my long golden hair. Shunning the lift with its dank smells and dirty corners I ascended the pristine never-trod steps, feeling each firm sculpted leg muscle hold me up, dancing to the beat of my no-heart drumming bliss rhythms in my chest cavity. This glorious heartspace with which I am truly blessed. Body that is pure muscle, veins and blood and tissue and no stench of pity. My perfect body that functions without a heart, survives beyond a heart. I consecrate this heartless form, praise it for its purity of action, for the fact that it is never befuddled by passion or desire. I adore the sobriety of my sacred heartspace and in this time of ceremonial completion, I honour the tube train that kept the Compassion Fairy from my naming day.

You thought I didn't know? But how could that be? I lay the body on the tracks that stopped the train.

I close the door behind me with deliberation and anticipation. The tower flat is quiet, stilled. Empty bridegroom awaiting its fill of me. From huge unguarded windows comes London light, orange and reflected white on the ceiling. I remove my wet clothes tenderly, gently uncovering the smooth frame of my present body. Coat then shoes then dress then tights then bra then knickers. The garments drop in a humid heap and my feet slip cool to the delicious bare wood. Outside the rain washes streets with still dirtier water and sweeps tired people into huddling corners. A few floors closer to the ground you can hear the swish of car tyres streaming home through the reflected night, pumping wet

45

roads dry for the expensive safety of their air-bag-cushioned drivers. But I am far above that and in my home it is silent. In my heartspace it is silent. The rain beats hushed against my window and gravity mutes even the sirens below.

The siren inside is not mute. I lay myself naked on the bare polished boards, their varnish reflecting my skin, my polish refracting the grain. We are two on one, the wood and I. It is as natural as I am. As unnaturally here as I am. It did not grow to be walked on by me. Nothing ever did, though much is. I watch myself reflected at close range. Adjust the lens of my eyes for clearer comparison. My immaculate smile, my flawless skin, my perfect hair. I am the combination of a lifetime of crass pop songs, recreated into virgin brilliance. I curve my shoulder to my lips, full soft mouth longing to touch the cool skin still damp from the world. I hold my lips apart not more than half a centimetre. The room is cold and my warm breath sends a rippling shiver across my back. I kiss the left shoulder, then the right. The left hand, then the right. I am always fair, treat both sides with the same sober desire. I hold a mouthful of fore-arm flesh in my hungry mouth. My tastebuds start up at the recognition that the meat is me. I taste sweet. Because I am. Sweet and fresh and so very well bred. My free hand runs through this red hair, lightly massages my long swan neck. I arch to meet myself and I am ready to begin.

Both hands run fast from my shoulders, across my breasts, full and swelling, to the tiny inlet that is my waist. There is the temptation to rest, but more tempting still is the rest of me. My hands do not stop there. This is a race, I am the event. I love this loving me, I am well trained. I reach for my left foot, nibble at the elegant manicured toenails. I scratch the smooth thin skin that covers my shin. I turn from gentle into an attack on the body, bite and lick and scratch and cut and caress and twist and bleed and bless. I take me. Take me there. There and then. I am so very good at this. If I had done this to Jonathan he would not be with us now. I gave him just enough to know what he could have had. If I had unleashed all that I am on Jonathan, he could not now withstand the loss of me. I am the lion that roars herself into readiness, the sacrificial lamb ripping past the tender flesh to reveal the free and empty whole. Just finished and ready again. I am so fucking good. I am fucking so good.

Eventually I exhaust even my own ample desire. It is hours later or days later. The sun has been and gone and the rain continues. This is London after all. I lift my hand-polished body from the hand-finished floor and heavy-limbed climb into my bed alone and sated. I may sleep for a week. And when I wake there will be another ready moth to feed my flame. I will be hungry again.

Twelve

Martin and Josh are the bee's knees, the cat's whiskers, the *crème de la crème*, the ultimate union in the eye of truth, whistled into grace by the blessing breath of the Universe. They are really it. A multi-ethnic, multi-religious, multimedia coupling of such overweening perfection that merely to gaze on them invites self-loathing and self-pity on both an intimate and a grand global scale. They belong in Sunday supplements and are found in Soho cafés. Martin and Josh are simply flawless. Josh and Martin are absolutely perfect. A publicist's dream, hugely photogenic, colossally talented and, above all, bloody good fun. Everybody loves Martin and Josh. Josh and Martin deserve every lick of love they receive. There is no gradient of 'more' to describe their perfection.

They are gay, they are out, they are desired, they are together. They are fêted and cherished, yearned for and dreamt about. Men and women alike adore them. Martin is black and young and clever and surprisingly, given the above, he is also known to be really, honestly, nice. At twenty-three he is a highly regarded, thrice-published, intellectual giant who can converse on the simplest of terms with the clearest of fools. He writes for the *Guardian*, the *Independent* and, when pushed, and purely to send home a political point, for the *Telegraph*. His natural habitat is the nine till ten a.m. slot on Radio 4 and he loves, he simply adores, to play Twister. Josh is a little older at twenty-five and has had twenty months more to make his mark on the world. He is Jewish and an atheist. He is a highly successful artist in several disciplines, he has exhibited at the ICA, the Photographers' Gallery and Tate Modern. The latter before his twenty-first birthday. He is a film-maker, a sculptor and a poet. He is a great cook, a wine buff and an ardent practical joker. He is devoted to Martin and to the post-Narnian works of C. S. Lewis.

Their families adore them. Josh and Martin live a whirl of traditional rites and post-modern rights. There is Hanukkah supper with Josh's mum and midnight mass with Martin's dad, Passover with Sarah the maternal grandmother and Easter with Aunt Mary – also known as Sister Teresa of the Mission Sisters, Cricklewood. The old nuns love 'the boys' and send cards of blessing at every holiday, Sister Zita sends a special handmade one for Diwali. With Martin's mother they plan family trips home to Ghana, with Josh's father they work through his memories and honour the grandparents who left him behind, waving goodbye from Polish trains. They babysit for the six family babies and are perfect godparents for the other ten non-blood children.

Their lives are so full. Each year is mapped out the November before, delineated by events that fall open in the clean thumbed calendar, whole pages of the diary devoted to joy. A playing which they work at intensely and are wholly committed to. There is EuroPride and Winter Pride and

Northern Pride and Manchester and Mardi Gras and Carnival and Mayfest and the London Film Festival and the Edinburgh Fringe and the Hay-on-Wye Book Fair. For Josh there is also an alternate marathon – London or New York, for Martin a twice-yearly retreat at a silent monastery in Bedford. There is the Booker and the Turner and their yearly party for the Eurovision Song Contest. There are the cosiest of Sunday evenings stretching long and slow, and then the wildest of Monday midnights trawling from Camden down to Clapham with sixteen bars and three clubs between.

They are gorgeous and happy and wealthy and healthy. They came of age in a time of sexual awareness and fear and both emerged through the terror with an educated enlightenment. They are HIV-negative and monogamous and safe. They have been lovers for three years, lived together for two and next year they will travel all the way to Peru where they intend to make silent vows to each other witnessed only by the circling winds. Every year there are two holidays – one for education, this year to St Petersburg, and one for rest – a small Greek island in the Cyclades where wealthy Athenian families go to play and gay boys are as rare as the arms of the Venus de Milo. They are quiet on the Greek holiday and dream and sleep and rest and eat and prepare again for the fifty other weeks of passion and debate and the agony of creation and the intimacy of desire and intellectual rigour and full and total abandonment to being the life and soul of the party. To being simply the best.

They have close new friends and good old friends, straight friends and gay friends, couple friends and single friends, aged friends and young. Martin and Josh entertain beyond Delia and shop after Conran. Josh makes his own pasta and Martin gives beautiful jars of homemade preserves as gifts at

50

Christmas. Their tins are stocked full of the cakes they feel no need to eat, succour for those knocking at the door of their famous hospitality. They have an open house with room for anyone and always a quiet corner where the two of them can be alone. Girls love them and men respect them. Old women praise them and new boys bless them. Straight couples with tiny and terrifying new babies find in Martin a solace and an understanding so lacking in their single, childless girlfriends. Gay couples with parent problems find both hope and elusive tranquillity at Josh's table. The despairing mothers and angry stepfathers of teenage daughters and sons are soothed by Martin and coddled by Josh and returned to the bosom of their resentful families refreshed and energised and so very much nicer.

They live in a self-designed, recently gutted, empty, white, stark, bright Victorian terrace in Islington. The planned and specified home is ever-shining chrome and cool clean lines. They respect their cleaner and pay her well over the going rate. They do their own ironing. The garden is a walled delight of heavy scented flowers year round with a damp corner of ferns and succulents. Inside there are open spaces for the sun to swim and smooth dimmed corners to ease the passage of brilliant thought as it comes to birth in Josh's attic studio and Martin's adjoining office where creation happens, joint but separate. Their house, at times crucible and at others dedicated cloister, is but a hop and a skip and a five a.m. stumble from Tony and Cherie's old family abode in one direction and a stumbling spit from the tired drunks on Islington Green in the other. They could not be more in the centre of it all. Martin and Josh are the centre of it all.

Josh and Martin rejoice in a fierce sex life that is still constant and passionate and enduring. Unlike their coupled friends, their sex has not sloped off with time or been disturbed by real or imagined jealousies. They have not lesbian bed death nor new babies to interrupt their desire nor gay boy's inability to remain faithful. None of the lying clichés that other couples use to explain away the falling off of sex. Their joy in each other's beauty and success has not been eroded by one's bitterness or the other's failure. They are each other's best lover and each other's best friend. They are mentor and teacher and disciple and damn good fuck. Josh loves Martin and Martin loves Josh forever and ever. So there.

All of which makes them more than ripe for the plucking the taking, the faking. The doing over, the doing in.

I'm going in.

Thirteen

Unlucky for some.

Something unprecedented is happening in the land remarkably close and equally far distant. There is a rumbling, a remembering, a rumination. The King is wolfing down bread and butter sandwiches and thinking on his life and his wife, the two are practically one he is so in love. The King is happy, but then, the King is always happy. Except on the rare occasion that there's a butter shortage. However Her Majesty the Queen, usually thinking in split-second synch with her husband, is disturbed when a disparate, uninvited thought suddenly occurs to her. She is working in another wing of the palace so distant that her husband sits in Spring as she ponders in Summer. While carefully placing a thimble on her index finger so as not to prick herself and drip royal red blood on the snow white handkerchief she is embroidering, it occurs to her that perhaps there is something missing. Or maybe it is someone. Like an irritation of the eye, the thought flies across her mind and then is gone, only to resurface a moment later. The Queen continues to feather stitch. She knows she need only apply her mighty mind to this concern and an answer will arrive. Perhaps in the second post. Safe in the knowledge that wisdom will come, she allows herself to smile, for now in the Palace there is a son. Quite naturally, he is a beautiful boy of charm and intelligence and, thanks to the revision of the underground timetables and a slightly updated pay structure for the transport workers, he is also a boy of charity and compassion. In fact, the Compassion Fairy, with her over-full basket of generosity and her big fat heart of guilt, gave the lad a double dose of perfect love as he lay gurgling in his crib. Gurgling and then practically drowning in his own grace.

The Queen lays down her tapestry, looks closely at the picture she is embroidering – a Madonna and child – and remembers. Of course. There was once another child. A daughter she believes. Perfect in every way. Except not quite. Too much ambition. The Queen has just remembered her first born. She will alert her husband to the matter. He will not know what to do, he never does, but perhaps in discussion with him, she will come up with a solution herself. The journey back to Spring takes some time and she kisses the buds of May as she travels. Where can the silly girl have got to? The Queen had not noticed her slip away, perhaps it was at breakfast that she silently left the table? The King wonders if maybe it was just before afternoon tea while the muffins toasted and the honey waited to ooze itself across the warm yeast-buttered base? Or perhaps she left last month, last year, last decade? The questions stand awkwardly and unusual in the Palace where normally all is certain and serene. Dash the blasted girl. She has upset perfection. This is too much for the King and his crown droops a little – he is not used to frowning, does not know how to hold himself aloft in a state of consternation. A nation state of concern. He falls asleep.

Her Majesty of course, has a plan. She will check the daughter's room. One of the servants must know where it is. For the Queen is a woman of great intellect and in a fat volume on a library shelf she remembers there is an equation for the measurement of dust, the number of unattended particles being in direct proportion to the hours undisturbed. When the result of that calculation is multiplied by the errant minutes wasted in contemplation of the missing child, the resulting sum can be taken to represent the fixed co-ordinates of where the girl is not. From which it is a simple matter of basic calculus – via the inversion theory – to determine, if not exactly where she is now, then at least how long she has been there. Opening one eye to check on the frantic mathematical proceedings, the King is delighted to remember how clever he was to marry a mathematical genius and runs happily to the Autumnal playroom, there to explain to his three-year-old son the hugely important properties of counting houses and money. Or was it honey?

It takes Her Imperial Majesty no longer than six weeks to complete the analysis and the entire fiefdom waits with bated breath for the announcement that their Princess has been missing for either six hours, or six days or perhaps, since she was sixteen years old. Time then, is immaterial, for the Queen has discovered what we knew all along. Her daughter is on the loose.

The rumblings and ruckusings continue. Soon there are envoys and messengers from the people to the Palace. There are decoys and derringers from the streets to the King. The monarchy is feeling a little insecure. Which is possible even in the best of royal houses. Something must be done. Or, as is more usual in these cases, something must be seen to be done. Then it happens. In a flurry of carriages and coaches, the Compassion Fairy arrives. With her sister Wisdom and their brother Beauty and the three of them stand in the old hall and face the new boy child. The Comedy Fairy was not needed at this juncture. She stayed at home to mend the gags, enforced silence might still be necessary in the end. And the three who are so old they have no need of years and so clever they have no need of fears announce what just had to have been coming all along. That the little bitch is out there and fucking things up in a big way. There is only one answer. The son must be sent to make it better.

The little Prince is grown up, tucked in and sent off. At least this time the King and Queen remember to wave good-bye and give him a very elegant travel alarm clock to take with him. Time warps and mellows with age and the distant realm comes so close there is a chance you could almost see it if you forgot to look. But you don't, and neither does the Princess.

The land goes back to work and the King and Queen go to the kitchen to make a pie for their children's return. Ravens possibly, blackbirds are always a little thin, and you have to use so many. It may be a very long time before the boy is back but he does not mind, for in his own land he would only ever be a Prince and in our world he walks head higher than the rest, every inch the King and every step a challenge.

Maybe there will be a duel at the end and maybe the duality will kill them both. For now though, the Prince has gone from little boy to grown man in the space of a single sunny afternoon.

Which is pretty much what usually happens.

Fourteen

Josh and Martin. I must get on. Something is happening, someone is stealing my seconds. I don't know who or what and how is far beyond my comprehension, but I sense urgency. I begin again.

The choice here is not so direct. A decision between any two men is never simply black and white. Though in this case, it is that too. If we must talk in absolutes. But while Martin, who is black, is plainly that, he is also burnt toffee black, warm coffee black – I mean bitter gritty Arabic beans rather than Colombian mellow. His is not an easy Peggy Lee ballad of black coffee, simple and stirred same through the cup. The dark brown of his face and arms and strong chest fade to soft chocolate melting in hot shop window – he is lighter and less rich at the edges. We're talking damn good chocolate here, seventy per cent cocoa at least. Expensive and specialist. Martin's shades of black are many and variegated. And yet in description we must be so London, very careful, our words precision-picked for safe political correction.

The white man too – what is this colour white? The

reflection of all colours, the absorption of none. White is an everything and a nothing. Tell that to those who have based their entire bibles on the colour of perfection. But Josh is no more only white than Martin is plain black. He is neither the pink white of the Celts nor the grey white of the tower-blocked poor, not the translucent blue white of the carefully preserved hothouse baby either. Josh's skin is the dark ivory of the Spanish pre-Inquisition Jew. A Sephardic blush of burnished copper yellow runs through his flesh, beneath the skin, thin above the lean muscle. In winter he is pale and interesting, in summer he is a fine and dark Mediterranean.

Josh and Martin know their physical beauty is a minefield of politically correct description. Luckily the relationship is old enough for them not to require pussyfoot ballet around the appropriate terms and phrases. They have kissed and fucked and fondled each other sufficient. There needs no delicacy in the awareness that they are different and same. Genetic ethics play but a tiny part in their partnership. For they have love. Love which merely scents the flesh and is blind as a bat.

Gets in your hair too.

Before I decide who I am to be, I must first choose which one I shall take. Shake. Re-make. Everywoman will simply not do here. I must be Everyman too. Everyperson. Truly a *Woman's Hour* of the created miraculous.

Could I be a man? I look inside and check out the ovaries, the uterus, the central cavity that is my gender definer. I breathe through the lunar contracted flow. My blood is thick and mineral-deposit rich, I am light-headed with the heaviness of it. No, I will not abandon woman. It doesn't appeal. I am far too fond of the void within, the empty womb room that holds an indeterminate future. I am heartless, but not soul-free. Besides that, I adore being a girl.

I weigh up their propensities and protestations. Martin has done it before, Josh has not. But then Martin already knows it didn't really work, he didn't want it, did it simply for the craic. Josh doesn't know that much yet. You might say Josh is in a don't know/don't know situation. And what he doesn't know can't hurt him. Much. Oh, and ignorance is such bliss . . . who am I to destroy that for him? And perhaps the she he tried wasn't the right she for Martin. For we shes are as many and varied as the hes, are we not? More varied perhaps, given the many choices of disguise available to us in every department store in the land. I am a master of disguise. I am a mistress of Masters and Johnson. And Johnson and Johnson.

I give it long and careful thought. Then, waking possibilities exhausted, I take their images to bed with me and dream of the two men through the extended darkness and the short light. I shun the starshine that might falsely illuminate my choice, I allow the dry vase flowers to die. My tower room is practically a polar icecap while I prepare, I permit few hours of daylight and in the dark I experiment and play and turn myself inside out to accomplish the transformation. Then I see the perfection that she is. Now I know how to do these two. I will play the female accompaniment to the male main dish. I will not try to usurp but simply to complement. To compliment.

I am black but comely, O ye daughters of Jerusalem.

I am black and comely, O ye mothers of North London.

And I come to take your sons.

Well, maybe just one or two in particular.

I am a nice North London Jewish girl. *Fooled you!* Yes, I have probably chosen the cliché, but there is something about those mothers' sons, a scent of forever about their conditioning. I had thought to play either the black girl to the Jewish boy or the exotic Jewess to the black man. But

59

then I remembered Josh's bar mitzvah, the last religious act of his young life, and it occurred to me that his grandmother probably left him more than just her pale green eyes in an unlined dark skinned face. She left him suffering under the heavy yoke of the élite. Of course, Josh has educated himself well in love and politics and gender awareness and past the mere acknowledgement of collective unconscious and genetic guilt. His is an educated knowledge, a sympathetic comprehension that stretches beyond a primal awareness of 'chosen'. A swelling of all knowledge in the one small glass of fresh rendered apple juice he drinks daily.

It's not that I don't want to fuck Martin. I would generally rather fuck a man who has done it at least once, than take my chances with a heterosexual virgin and in fact, I may even try to have both. As a release it will be worthwhile. But I don't have forever and Josh will undoubtedly be quicker. I have a triptych of lovers to complete and time hurries on.

When Josh looks at me, he sees the female version of himself. I have the light eyes and the dark skin, the thick and curling heavy black hair and the long fine hands. I am his sister and his mother and all his grandmothers and Freud's daughter loves me. I am a hundred matriarchs to Martin's sole offering of brother and friend. Our full lips are dark soft to soft dark matching. What man can deny for long the mirror image of his own beauty? I am his identical invert. Josh the Jew calls himself an atheist, but what will he call out when he comes inside me? And when his manchild pisses against the wall, won't he want his cock to look the same?

What? What? To accomplish my mission I will have to fuck, to fuck over, either a black man or a Jew. Which would the liberal conscience rather I cheated?

(*And what colour do you think I am anyway?*)

60

Fifteen

On the day Martin met Cushla he immediately thought of Josh. Not because of her looks, but because of herself. He was certain Josh would like her, want to know her, would welcome her into their charmed circle of friends and dinners and Sunday morning walks on the Heath. Martin was introduced to Cushla in the course of a work day. He was introduced to her by the magic of the Internet, by a teeny tiny innocuous flashing memo. Cushla wanted to talk to him. And Martin loved to talk.

She was researching her second novel, she'd heard him on the radio, read four of his latest columns, was halfway through his third book, she simply loved his work. Martin didn't question her enthusiasm, he was used to it. Almost expected it. And when he responded to her email, the number given by a friend of a publisher's assistant's girl-friend's friend (as usual), he said he would be delighted to help. He loved to assist other artists in creation. He agreed to meet for lunch. All in a day's work for Martin and Josh. The perfect media couple, too young to have been tainted by commercialism and greed, they did not see a two hour lunch as a waste of earning time. To them the lunch hour, the lunch afternoon was research, part of exploring the human condition. A good lunch would likely fully feed another chapter, another article, another painting, another frieze. Martin understood meeting for lunch to be the same as business. He approached the meal and meeting with the same considered care he would form an opening phrase. A single sentence might take half his morning. A thousand words could take half an hour. Martin's muse measures quality rather than quantity.

Lunch though, would take more than half his day. The preparation, the preoccupation, the dressing, the travelling into the West End. Lunch in Soho, dinner in Islington or Clerkenwell or maybe even Clapham, Battersea, but only ever Soho for lunch. The giving over of his insight, imparting of his secrets, the use of his generous brain for an hour and a half; all of those were well worth the price of lunch for two. At least they were according to Martin's accountant. Martin was happy to offer the scattered parmesan shavings of his brilliance and the lucky recipient would be fortunate to pick up the bill. Which tax office they sent it to was not Martin's concern. The meal was simply a transaction. Martin's love was given free to Josh, but his wealth of wisdom could be bought in mealtime chunks by anyone entertaining enough to capture his attention.

Martin paid the bill the day he dined with me.

Martin dressed in a sober black suit with a startling sky blue brushed cotton shirt. The double-breasted Armani emphasising his size, the pale silk boxer shorts encasing his thighs. Something for Josh to think about. Josh was thinking, about to be creating. When an idea was gestating in his artist's heart, Josh would grow it to fat health in the heat of

62

the kitchen. Only then could he transfer it upstairs to the cool studio. Only then would he force it through in the precision of the white light. For two weeks the house had smelt of baking bread and honeyed preserves and the garlic yearnings of the notion Josh was waiting to happen. Martin was growing full on Josh's creation. He loved this time. Soon, he knew, Josh would confine himself to the studio and they would become slender again feasting on the leftovers of art. The pattern of Josh's muse generously allowed them to remain lovely as well as loved. Martin smiled to himself as he walked, beautiful, down the stairs. He had chosen his artisan husband well. Josh was hand picked with pleasure and precision.

Martin kissed Josh goodbye when he left the house at midday. Kissed with both care and passion, the uncommon mix well rehearsed to prevent excessive dry cleaning costs. He kissed Josh in the kitchen where Josh was baking bread – soda bread with granary flour. Kissed first Josh's floury hands, the light dusting of ground grain milking the dark maroon of Martin's lips. Kissed next the strong forearms that gently captured the precious air, one oxygen bubble after the other, supple soldered into the sour dough. Kissed next the rolled sleeves of crisp white shirt, laundry fresh scent clinging to Martin's smooth cheek as he dredged his face across Josh's cotton covered chest and up past the fine night's stubble to the full lips breathing fast with exertion from the kneading, exertion from the needing.

They kissed each other without hands, without arms, without bodies. Kissed with lips that held sense memory enough to imagine the rest. Kissed with a certainty of many more licked lips, slow bitten tongues, just clipped teeth.

Martin walked to the tube with Josh's kiss rolling on his tastebuds, his lover's breath still warm in his mouth. Martin walked slowly the easy stroll to the tube and counted the hours until he would be home again.

He smiled at old ladies and remembered the bread would be risen and warm. He passed a beautiful African man and knew that this evening he would fall, hot bread mimic into Josh's waiting hands, open mouth, ready body. He bought his ticket, descended to the under-London and studied the map of his day. Lunch would take four hours from door to door. Two hundred and forty minutes of passing time. That was fine, he could allow those minutes, free those seconds from his real life. These lunches with strangers were never wasted, his appetite would be all the sharper by the time he returned. Martin and Josh would certainly have four hours again in their lives, each chunky quad a sixth of preciousness for each perfect day in their perfect future. This particular four hours would be a very small sacrifice.

Martin would bring home good wine to drink with the new bread. And pale pink lamb for dinner.

Lunch is a banal word for the event that followed. Lunch for Cushla and Martin was no meeting in a café over prawn mayonnaise or baked bean branded potato. Four hours stretched to five, reached into six. Martin was having a fine time. Martin was eating fresh pasta and wild basil and drinking frost-crisp sauvignon blanc with a touch of might be greengage summer about the nose and then there was strong sweet espresso and then a small glass of soft amber brandy. Martin was having a second espresso and just a tiny snifter more of that very fine brandy. Martin was having a bloody good time.

Cushla had done very well. She too had dressed with care. Honest and clear woman here. No hint of androgyne about her. She'd made her choice and gone for it. Small framed, wide hipped, full breasted, nothing testing. Long dark locks almost held back but just managing to tumble art-fully free and thereby frame a face of uncommon prettiness. Though not beauty. Cushla's approach needed more than mere beauty. Cushla wore warm olive skin and surprisingly pale green eyes and long thick lashes and fine narrow fingers and sweet gentle makeup and a soft laugh and she was simply very pretty. Pretty safe.

Wrong.

Cushla could have been Josh's sister but that she spoke of Foucault and Lacan instead of babies and bassinets. Cushla could have been Josh's mother but that she smelt of L'Air du Temps instead of lanolin-based toilet soap. Cushla could have been Josh but that she was woman. Cushla could have been any of their friends, their lovers, their close coterie of the adored and adoring and Martin threw himself into the meeting of minds and souls and adjusted his timepiece accordingly. Of course, he also called Josh twice during the lunch to inform him of the revised ETA. Quiet calls, gently rendered on a discreet mobile phone so as not to disturb the other diners. Martin's rightly famed brilliance is sometimes ostentatious, his manner is not.

Josh didn't mind the adjustment. Their relationship was not one of petty jealousies and traditional demands. Martin was working, Josh understood that. Martin's vast knowledge was being pumped, Martin's not undersized ego was being primed. Josh understood completely. And would his darling please pick up a bottle of something good when he eventually came home? Quite some time ago Josh had correctly reasoned that demanding and complaining created irritated resentment rather than guilt. And guilt brought home much nicer gifts. Today Josh would expect at least champagne. And not that cheap New Zealand version either.

The lunch was a great success. The waiters had sweetly

left them to talk in the corner, Cushla's lunch-long flirting with them all had paid off. Staff quietly reset the evening dining room, created the space for Cushla's attack without Martin even noticing that danger twisted her hair opposite him. Perhaps the late afternoon light was too dull. London night had returned and the plate glass windows were full of commuters, tired faces lined with the thought of frozen dinners to come. Their table glowed with completion. Cushla had taken notes. Martin had told her all he knew. About at least one subject. Cushla had plenty to think about. So much to be going on with. She was very grateful – for his time, for his enthusiasm. For the chance to meet him.

Yes, Martin is wonderfully clever, but Cushla does have both magic and royal blood on her side.

And then, how might she repay his kindness?

'You must let me pay for lunch.'

Martin shook his head, as if it were unheard of. As if it were a ludicrous suggestion. Ludicrous but lovely. Cushla's head fell a full two degrees to her shoulder, she smiled, the left side of her mouth rising half a centimetre more than the right. She spoke soft and low and Martin thought he heard Josh singing in her voice, 'You're very sweet Martin. Then perhaps I could take you to dinner? You and Josh, of course?'

Martin must have looked a little surprised, a betraying eyebrow perhaps. But of course Cushla knew about Martin's boyfriend. Everyone knew about Martin's boyfriend. How could she have missed the reflected glare of the golden couple? Put that way, what choice did he have?

Martin reluctantly relinquished his half-formed pictures of hours alone with Cushla, 'Oh, well yes, perhaps you should meet Josh. Yes, of course. Maybe he can help you with your piece too. You'd like him. He'd love you. Yes, that's it. We'll all go out together.'

Martin emphasised the brilliance of the idea until he felt sure it had been his own. Cushla allowed her face to light up a moment longer than was strictly good for her blood pressure. Bright eyes and happy face a sparkling reward for Martin's generosity.

'If you really don't mind. That would be wonderful.'

Cushla took his hand and with his eyes on her face, Martin felt the hands she touched him with were Josh's and he found himself inviting her into their beautiful home.

Home round, home safe, home alone.

Cushla would be delighted to come to them. She'd love to see their house, eat their food, drink their wine.

Break their hearts.

Thursday evening, seven thirty. It was a date.

Sixteen

It isn't always obvious from an answerphoned invitation that the potential perfect evening is to become the dinner party from hell, remembered for all time as the cheese straw that broke the ice-carved camel's back. One plans the ideal meal, selects the appropriate drinks to accompany the delicacies. One chooses the scented candles, the unscented flowers, the temperature – just cool enough to make company a pleasure. The guests are sorted. Hand picking each varied and interesting person, each lovely couple to complement and adorn the evening. The individual components are chosen with the sole intent of making the meal a delicious success and yet, by a chance crossing of mismatched chemistry, even the best laid tables of mice and men may simply not quite gel. She finds him a bore, he scrapes new-lad comedy across her post-feminist sensibilities. This he-and-she find that she-and-he too coupled. The gay boys in love are astounded by the gay girls' cool distance, twice divorced. The babysitter cancels unexpectedly and doesn't turn up. But the screaming baby riding colic hell does. Someone's widowed mother-in-law is staying from Yorkshire and at the last minute the unfortunate old lady is thrown into the extra chair melée where blasphemies shock and jokes fly over her thinning grey head and the innuendoes are too quiet for her fading hearing to catch.

Or worst of all, she smiles at him. Inclines her head to his. Just grazes his flesh when she passes the salt and, somewhere between the aubergine flan and the ostrich steaks, what used to be a stable relationship is shattered to an accompanying symphony of tinkling glasses and backs of knives whipped against still sharper tongues.

Martin and Josh have spent most of the day cooking. They love to cook together. Skate around each other in synchronised patterns through their white and chrome kitchen, with its clean wide surfaces and huge windows. The room is perfect and the plain glass that opens on to the autumn-ended garden at the back of the house has been too well designed for condensation to mar the view. Martin marinades and Josh juices. Josh steams and sweats and Martin dices, dribbles, drains. In the rest of the house Rosie is dusting and vacuuming and polishing. She is a part-time design student and merely cleaning away their dead hairs is an inspiration. Paid at two pounds an hour more than any of her other clients and never mentioned to the taxman. The three of them eat an early light lunch together before Rosie packs away the vacuum cleaner and Josh and Martin give up on their backdrop of Radio 4, turning it off at two – neither of them interested in BBC bad American accents – and run upstairs, stumbling over each other to fuck, fast and hotter than the Aga. Martin showers and returns to the kitchen perfectly attired now, his creation even more careful. It would not do to stain the silk. Josh walks two streets away, officially to scan wine shelves and bring home nectar, unofficially to admire the cut of his new soft leather jacket as it glides past darkened shop windows.

Back in the warm kitchen an aproned Martin creates the finalities of dinner – tiny parcels of homemade puff pastry; stilton and asparagus sweetly hidden inside the crisp folding layers. He warms little rounds of wild salmon interlaced with fresh herbs from their own sheltered herb garden. He meticulously presses individual baby spinach leaves, gluing them back to back with spice-tempered egg white and then barely sautés them to a thin and tender crisp. He takes three hours to do this and then arranges the offerings, tray-beautiful for the arriving guests to munch on with glasses in their hands and mouths full of words. They do not notice they are eating art. But Josh and Martin know, which is enough.

Cushla arrives. Via a taxi journey and street stalking of several others, any others. Just making sure she is as desirable as intended. She is. The man in the off-licence offers a hundred per cent discount on the Laurent Perrier, the taxi driver will not take her tip, kisses her hand instead. For a moment she almost runs away to play. Quick turned heads possibly offering an easier and more delicious evening than even the one she has planned for herself. That would be fun, this is work. But Cushla is on a mission. She has a hat trick to complete and now is not the time to break for tea. She enters the perfect hallway and, as intended in this company, does not really stand out at first. She stands, small stature ideally framed in the wide doorway, champagne in one hand and chocolates in the other, her handmade body simply attired in understated light grey linen and pale green silk.

Next to the cool American beauty of Melissa the art dealer, thin sheathed in bone wrapping silver, Cushla is small and maybe a little too female for Melissa's comfort, 'Why darling, where did Marty find you? You're positively sweet!'

Cushla smiles as Melissa publicly dismisses her, a tall woman's gesture to magnify her size and amplify her importance. Cushla knows Melissa must exaggerate herself because Melissa sleeps alone and fucks her other single friends for company. Melissa cannot keep a lover any more than she can keep her skeletal figure without disgorging the entire evening before she slaps on the night cream and falls into lonely dreams, waking in a quiet house that has no man to disturb her morning hangover. How Melissa yearns for a man to disturb her morning hangover.

Beside the fearful charms of Sunita, infamous Asian actress draped in red and purple velvet, this grey-point Cushla is positively lost.

'You're not an actress, are you? No, you couldn't be an actress. You don't walk into the room as if you're about to eat every man there!' Sunita laughs her famous reverberating laugh, catches Melissa's eye and adds, 'And half the women too, of course.'

Melissa turns away, back to the boys. Yes, she will fuck Sunita tonight. If she has to. Sunita will fuck her if she must. But they are basically straight and for them the girl sex falls just on the empty side of satisfying. These women would rather go home with a man. Any man. Then again, they would also rather have sex, any sex, than another night with no warm flesh to keep them company.

Among the male camaraderie of Josh and Martin and each of their respective ex-lovers, Cushla is simply, prettily, negatably, female. She is choosing not to turn it on. Cushla can do simply pleasant, easily nice if she has to. And tonight is the perfect time. She will turn the heat up slowly. She will start out almost plain and in the course of the evening will become amazing. They will not notice the transformation

71

that takes place in front of them. At least not until it is too late. Compared to the worldliness of Joan and Peter, old-school journalists, old-school couple, she is positively youthful. And innocent with it.

As the evening wears on and the wine wears down and the tempo winds up, Cushla's own charms begin to come into focus. Where Joan is bitter and crucifying of her media adversaries who have abandoned the left, Cushla is witty and self-deprecating. Joan's used-to-be feminist aggression simply welds more lines into her harsh face etched with years of passionate smoking, Cushla's giggle erases even the laugh lines at the corners of her eyes. Where Melissa attempts to stun all with her talk of Saatchi and Guggenheim and cross-Atlantic dollars and pounds, Cushla whispers to Josh how the much maligned pre-Raphaelite room at Tate Britain is her favourite. Those green and red dressed women, their long hair, their gentle hands. Josh silently nods his agreement and passes her a pomegranate. Where the men talk of magazines and cars and house prices and the women talk of time clocks and cars and house prices, Cushla moves chairs to join Josh and talks to him about himself. Not how he met Martin or how he loves Martin, but simply all about Josh. Cushla nods and smiles and whispers in low tones. She does not get drunk, does not mix her wines. She is the only guest who remains clear. She eats neither too much like Melissa nor too little like Sunita. Her easily proffered smile reveals a tiny overbite that Josh, to his own surprise, notes he finds sexy. This is not the kind of note he would leave in his diary. The diary he knows Martin reads. The diary he writes nightly for the express purpose of exciting Martin in the morning.

If Josh hears the warning bells at all, he must assume it is the burglar alarm in the solicitors' office down the road. He does not see the flashing lights and the signal does not pierce his ear. But Martin sees and hears it all and curses himself for bringing that woman to the house.

Martin and Josh wave their guests into after midnight minicabs and as they clear the plates and wipe the dishes, the brewing storm stews itself into a flash flood.

'You certainly seemed to be having a good time tonight.' Martin slams the plates one by one into their chrome rack.

'You have a problem with that?'

Josh passes him the wine glasses, stems so thin they almost bend in his fingers.

'You liked that woman?'

'I assume you mean Cushla? Yes, I thought she was charming.'

'That much was obvious.'

A glass snaps in Martin's hand. Josh takes it from him and drops it into the bin. Each one of them whisper an imprecation to the goddess of omens. They whisper too quietly for her to hear, the goddess is taking her makeup off and getting ready to go to bed. Playing very loud Carole King while she does it. The goddess has had a crap night out and is something of a drama queen. In Martin's head Josh's voice begins to whine.

'She's your friend Martin, you invited her. I was simply being nice to her. We got on. Would you rather I'd thought she was dull and boring and left her all to you?'

'I would rather you hadn't ignored our other guests to make her feel so special.'

'I hardly think Sunita would have noticed if I'd have turfed her bodily out of the door so I could talk to Cushla. She was pissed as a newt by nine o'clock.'

'That isn't exactly news.'

'And her insobriety is a reason for me to converse with

73

her? Come on Martin, she doesn't give a damn anyway, she couldn't wait to get off with Melissa.'

'Not so. She just couldn't wait to get off.'

'Whatever.'

'All I'm saying is, it looked a bit strange to me.'

'Strange?'

'Yes.'

'That's shit. You're jealous.'

Martin's irritation expresses itself in a sharp and too camp, 'I'm sorry?'

Josh shrugs away his lover's ire, dismissing him as a small child, 'You met the woman, thought she might be a special friend, someone all to yourself, now you're just pissed off because I got on well with her.'

'To the exclusion of everyone else.'

'Which you would rather have been doing yourself. Martin, you can't be angry with me just because I did what you wanted to do.'

Josh has made the wise decision to stick to sense and sobriety. He won't take the bait, doesn't want to play angry. He doesn't want to defend himself. This is just the beginning. He attempts to placate, 'Our other guests were perfectly happy.'

Martin scowls and will not be soothed, the dishes clatter still more furiously, Josh turns comfort into canker, 'It was you who spent the whole night sulking.'

'Good. So you did notice I wasn't happy?'

'I noticed. We all noticed. No doubt Peter is already writing you into his column – jealous Islington husband toys with his linguini, the knots reflecting his ulcerous rage.'

Martin sneers at Josh's impression. Peter is a well respected comic essayist. Martin knows it will hurt Josh to intimate that he does not match up to his ex-lover's style.

Josh is stung by the curl of Martin's lip and attacks further, 'It was obvious you were having a tantrum. I just didn't see the need to feed your ego by pandering to your ridiculously childish jealousy.'

The argument lasts as long as the washing up. When the plates are clean and dry and the remaining glasses shine soft-cloth-polished in their dark cupboard, the kitchen floor is swept and Martin holds Josh and kisses him. The room is warm with hot water and nastiness, stale smoke has filtered through from the dining room and Josh opens the doors to the garden. Outside the dinner-time rain has cleaned the sky and now frost tries to settle a month too soon, rime reflecting an empty moon. Martin walks on the cold grass in bare feet and Josh follows him. They kiss under the chilled stars and Josh tries his hardest to feel it. He really wants to feel it.

Upstairs they fuck in soft red cotton and it might almost seem to be an easy goodnight they wish each other. But the new moon hangs upside down, pouring out its luck and Josh turns in sleep. He and Martin dream, back to back apart, and the thin two-inch divide is a lunar sea.

Seventeen

Cushla flies home across London on perfect feet, slippered with magic mischief. Tonight she does not bother with the on-street flirt. She is in the middle of her mission, body and mind concentrated in the singular moment. The strand of long black hair she left behind her, apparently floated without care into the bathroom sink, slowly curls itself down the plug hole. The sheen of the daily polished chrome strainer belies the dark green mould that grows two centimetres down, all of Rosie's houseproud attention cannot hold back the forces of algae forever. The hair lodges in the bend, waiting there to grow into a blockage, a forced dam. Cushla damns Josh and Martin. Now she will not be wiped away, not by love nor by violence. The silver earring she left sitting unnoticed on the butcher's block of bleached beech listens intently to the snatches of shouted argument, catches hisses of spitting kisses, and sends reverberating sound waves of victory clean across the sleeping city to Cushla's ivory eyrie. The single mascara caked eyelash she plucked to let fall on Josh's clean pillowcase magnifies his open face in the moment of their post-fury fuck and then bows a lingering wink to his tight shuttered eyes. Josh and Martin are being spied on, but they are as aware of this as the aged stag who, with blind faith in the power of Bambi, leaps to an idiot assumption that the child hunter will not shoot. The stag dies slow, surprised and bloody. Love has set Martin and Josh free, it has papered the walls of their perfect home with sweetness and light, but it could not teach them caution.

From the sanctity of her cold virgin bed, Cushla watches the men making love, watches them making love from their anger. The alchemistry is truly impressive, but it cannot last forever. The art of turning life into gold requires constant effort and attention. She will show them the base metal of their ways. After the fuck there is peace of a sort and the two men slip sweating into sleep. Josh turns, slumbering in uncertainty and Cushla's freed eyelash catches in his own eye, the briefest of encounters is enough to irritate. To ingratiate. She watches still. Sleep continues, she does not rest. In the morning Josh is not his usual fresh self, his green eyes are red and sore as if from crying. Or sighing. Or both. Josh should be tired, he has dreamt a night of fucking Cushla, a night of fucking She. His solar plexus aches from the force of dream pounding. Josh has never dreamt like this before and wakes with a blush of teenage crimson on his cheeks. Martin mistakes his boyfriend's glow for heat and reminds himself to turn the thermostat down. Their house is too well heated perhaps. Love will surely be enough to keep them toasty warm through the pantomime season to come.

Oh, no it won't.

Martin has appointments back to back all day; an essay to write for publication next year, an article to research for the *Observer* magazine, a potential film to develop. He is full of the promise of his successful young life. Martin kisses Josh goodbye and sails easily from the quiet white house, safe in the knowledge that he is making their wonderful future meeting by meeting and that his loved one will spend the day in contemplative creation. Martin will come home in the dark of the late afternoon and Josh will emerge from the attic studio, both sated with their respective days of invention, respectfully hungry for the other.

Last night's tension and irritation will be forgotten and they will meet in the heart centre of their home, kiss, eat warm fresh bread and drink cool wine. Their kisses will taste of lust – past, future and very present. Martin knows this to be true, it has happened before. He is too young and has not yet suffered enough disappointments to know that a past pattern of alleviation does not mean every joy can necessarily be relied upon to happen again. But he will learn. The fighting is forgotten in the ease of a grey good morning. Martin does not recall his jealousy, or if he does, it is merely as an aberration of alcohol. Martin loves Josh and knows he is safe. He leaves the house in his dark blue Paul Smith suit and an overcoat of self-satisfaction.

Josh climbs the stairs to his studio. Nine-thirty is raining on the skylight. He does not know where to begin, something wants to come out of him but he is not sure what. He tries to paint at first, but the colour will not emerge from his box of tricks. The blue is too pale, his red an insipid aspirin-thinned blood. He leaves the two dimensional for another day. In the corner is a chunk of mutating limestone. The crumbling matter needs careful handling to remake into recognition. He had started it weeks ago, but the image of Martin would not be held tight in the slippery young carbon. Today however, a clearly defined head appears fast beneath his long fingers. After three hours Martin's potential lips have been cut away to form the perfect line of a girl's mouth. Of her mouth.

Four hours later Cushla grins at Josh from her skylit corner. London washes the windows outside and Josh licks his lips, Josh licks her lips. The limestone should be chalky dry but to his tongue's sharp surprise, it is moist and yielding, the carved Cushla mouth is warm. Darkness comes winter-fast and Josh sees himself reflected in the angled skylight above, sees himself kissing the dream girl. With the movement of streaming rain on the pane, her lips curl at the corners and the Cushla head laughs at him. Josh cannot see what is coming. Josh knows he is coming, covers the smirking head with his body. Josh is too caught in the moment to even be surprised at himself, the blank walls of his studio reflect back only a slight disdain at his lack of self-control. The room is for art after all. An hour later Josh is sane again and, more perplexed than embarrassed, he acknowledges his actions may have a taint of wrong-doing but could not be construed as actually bad. As the first-faith partner in this Judeo-Catholic marriage he rejects the more self-serving confession and takes instead ablution for absolution, scouring himself with oatmeal soap and the punishing chill of fast cold water. He is clean again for Martin's return, ready and waiting as expected. Though he is clear he will not exhibit the work he has made today.

Cushla allows most of a day to re-educate herself. A quick round of the V&A, the Sainsbury Wing, the Royal Academy. Allowing herself only a brief smile at the security guard. Who goes home, leaves his wife and catches the next train to Paris. A hurried rifle through thirty-nine books of twentieth century art and a long lunch-minute snatched between rainfalls as she watches the sluggish Thames flow beneath her feet on Waterloo Bridge. An old man and a lonely young woman walk past her on the bridge, the man contemplates throwing himself in and hurries on back to work rather than face the truth of his unfulfilled existence, the woman saves the moment for Battersea Bridge where her feeble attempt to end it all results in her committal to a BUPA paid hospital by her wealthy family and a bravery award for the young special constable who talked her down. Cushla continues her learning programme. She has had this knowledge before, back at the Palace. She knows this information, today's work is simply a matter of remembering. The Palace offered a very good education, excellent tutors full of their own creativity and dedicated to passing it on. Now she is up to speed, which is more than the Thames will ever be again. She is ready to launch herself on Josh.

There is something else Cushla should remember, but she is far too enchanted with her own plans to look behind.

Eighteen

While the whore city readily slammed open her thighs to Cushla, London is taking a little longer to allow the Prince to get close. He is no Dick Whittington come to seek his fortune. He doesn't like cats for a start. Anyway, Prince David already has his fortune, carries it with him in his heart, knows without help from Dorothy that there is no place like home and expects to bear with, rather than succumbing to, his sojourn in the fortress town. While his very nature forces each paving stone before him to turn to gold, he would still rather wander country lanes than red routes. The Prince has always preferred the pastoral, his wing in the Palace looked out on to fields and the river. His translucent left eye retina is more amenable to starlight than to light pollution, while his right eye, which might usually choose to see as it pleases, is now constantly trained on the movie that is his sister's life. He screens out her antics to watch the traffic and screens out the traffic to follow her walking and working and waiting for her next move. He could, if he wanted, follow her bedding and bathing, but with instinctive chivalry he closes both eyes against the perfect nakedness it would not do for a brother to see. And so the ideal modern David, thin and pale and aesthete-beautiful, finds himself walking the city streets at night, chain-smoking and humming strange music, blinking unthinking winks at passing minicabs and miniskirts.

He is learning London, the first semester – the vocabulary, the phrases, the tenses, the tension. Though he tried at first, gave it a good shot, marshalled all his resources and plunged on down, he has already given up on the tube. The constant unavoidable ignorance of the elements hurts his regal farmer's soul and he would rather wait stranded atop a Number 13 bus for hours of traffic to pass, than fry underground in the hot breath of a million commuters. He is a sensitive soul, this little Prince.

After language comes geography and he maps the new land with fresh blistered feet, takes long walks from Hackney to Stoke Newington, then Highbury, Islington, King's Cross, Euston and right on into town. As if what is not the West End could be considered country. He checks off the monopoly board as he makes his moves, always with his right eye trained on his sister's life and no need of top hat, boot or two hundred pounds.

When David observes Cushla through his long lashed right-eye lens, he does not watch her with reproach, rather with an anthropological interest. His sister is an alien species, let loose among a race that cannot see her distinguishing marks, a people that eagerly breathe in her foreign scent and yet deliberately choose to fool themselves into believing that she is one of them. Could be had by one of them. David is as entranced by their foolishness as he is by her audacity. He does not remember being brought up with his sister, has no recollection of whispered confidences in late night shared rooms, no memories of Christmas presents pried open and quickly stuck back with a paste of saliva and guilt. But he knows Cushla is his sister, can feel her from three miles and through the poorest air quality. Simply by being in the same city, she stirs a small genesis in his DNA.

David has never been among strangers before, it excites him and he sucks in their difference. In Highbury Fields he takes off his designer boots and walks on grey frosted grass to feel the footsteps left by those who have walked there before. He is surprised that his sensitive instep registers only DM's and trainers, Caterpillar and Nike. Where he grew up, grass was a welcoming beckon to the bare foot, not easily ignored or rejected. But then he did not grow up in the city of Londoners, doggedly walking the illegally unleashed through urban parks.

In Abney Park cemetery he pushes through the under-growth to recover an overgrowth of angels and cherubs, each one playing a broken lute air to quicken the decomposition of the long dead. He lays his head on the headstones and listens to the whispered confidences of Londoners past. They do not have much to tell him, neither the long dead nor the late dead are any more *au fait* with fate than the recently born or the nearly grown. Instinctual insight is a grace little prized in capital city circles where more often knowledge is measured by garden size and number of spare rooms and wisdom in the wit of the nanny. Not of course, in Hackney, where nanny still means grandmother. But in comparison and constraint and by listening and watching – real life and the reel of life his sister is spinning before him – he learns much about his new home, this clever little Prince.

This perfect Prince. Six foot and more of pure, modern matinée idol. The traditional matinée idol is a lesser known occurrence in Stoke Newington Church Street, but admired when spotted there all the same. The truly modern version though, is a delight. Angles anglicized through late Bowie out of early Bolan and rounded off via a fine wool suit into all-man gender certainty and a perfection that might just cross the boundaries if it felt, if it really felt, the desperate urge. Full girl appeal and not a few boys as well. Fop fringe an invitation to look behind and far into the eyes. David glides on limbs lightened by his beauty, slides through streets that usually taunt and tumble with litter, his overstated elegance flying right over the sniping of gutters and he lands feet-first in puddles that lay out their own cloaks for him.

This Prince is truly a prize. And while women smile knowing and girls giggle wanting and the occasional young man lays a gentle hand on his unaware arm, he shakes them all away with a knowing smile. He was dispatched to our land with reason and purpose. He is here to stop the carnage, to halt the murder of love. He is a missionary. And if it took his mother six years to remember her and his father six seconds to forget, no matter. David is a man of integrity. Not for him the dallying among mere mortals that Cushla has succumbed to, not for him the gobbled tasting of people-flesh. He is the pure monk of Hackney, the aesthete of E8. David is here for a purpose and will bide his time for her one mistake. He lingers over the view of her inventive charms, takes slow steps until she begins the third romance and he is permitted to make his move. He must wait for her third. In both lore and law the Palace is fair – a miscreant will always be brought to justice but they must be allowed a little fun first. The three strikes rule is not so very new. All magic runs in trinitarian rhythms and the Prince fully understands the need to accomplish his task in perfect waltz time. He walks and waits.

Of course, every now and then in the geography field

trips that are his first days, David passes a video shop, newsagent's, bookstore, television rentals, ice cream parlour, sex shop, church, synagogue, mosque or temple and has a glimpse of what they're all selling. And he has cause to wonder, very quickly, so the thought doesn't have time to take hold, just what is all this fuss these people make about fucking? Why is it such a big deal for them, the carnal act, the animal instinct just to do it? Why all the music and literature about it? What is their problem, why don't they just fuck and have done with it? However he quickly turns his mind from that minor occupation and back to the matter in hand. Someone has to stay calm and cool and take on the role of family virgin – in attitude if not in reality. God knows, it's not a job for the slut sister of Notting Hill.

Nineteen

A meeting engineered is no less random for the pre-creation that has taken place. Cushla knew the time and the location, but even she could not have hoped for so auspicious a start.

Bumping into Josh on the tube was not her idea of the perfect coincidence, it would however serve to test how great an impression she had made on him. In the city of crowded people, Cushla had quickly learnt how easy it is to lose oneself on the underground. She had noted the ease with which one can ignore a tedious acquaintance, a now fattened and aged old school friend, even the ex-lover who sits, engrossed in their *Evening Standard*, just four seats away. Of course, it is easier if both parties partake of the intentional ignorance. No deliberate eye contact, no corners of mouths lifting in passing strangers' mirth, and the ready path of escape swishes open every two minutes when the train shudders to a brake-stinking halt. It is as easy to turn from contact on the tube as it is for a politician to turn from giving coins to street-dwelling beggars. Camels' humps notwithstanding.

Cushla knows now, sitting five crowded seats from Josh,

he could easily get up and leave. There is no finite demand on his attention. The wall of flesh between them would be a ready excuse for not seeing her, not scenting her, not hearing the soft shush of her hair as her hands lift it free of her low collar and naked neck. Yes, she is cold dressed like this, undressed like this, and the wind snaps against her small girl's collarbones in the street, but sensibly muffled against the elements she could not present such a pretty picture. The country house charms of sensible clothing aside, bare flesh will always win out against even the softest of downy cashmere. Besides that, Josh is allergic to cashmere and, if nothing else, Cushla's research is always accurate.

From the corner of his eye he sees her. Immediately the tube carriage is too hot, too small, the people too many, it is stuffy, he can't breathe. Josh doesn't want to breathe unless he is close enough to breathe her scent. His own perfume mingles deliciously with hers and he can taste the smell of her on his mouth. The train comes into Leicester Square, he cranes his neck around the fat American, the thin Croat, the tired commuters, the young lads edgy for a beer, a curry, a fight. He cannot see her properly, two *Guardians*, a dripping umbrella and an old thumbed Penguin Classic mar his view of her face. He sees her left leg, her left arm and the fold of her unbuttoned suede jacket where it catches against her left breast. He strains his eyes for signs of movement. Nothing. He is safe, she is still sitting.

At the next station three people get off, two get up for the next stop, one more comes on, four sit down and, the chess move taken, the seat beside her is now empty. Josh stands, not giving himself time to plan. As he is about to sit beside her, a woman runs on to the train, inching herself between stubborn doors, she scoops around Josh's already bending back and silently triumphant steals his planned place.

87

Victory, but no eye contact. The train pulls away and caught off balance, half-caught between sitting beside and not understanding his reasons, Josh is thrown. Toppled from the pedestal of his own feet, he lands crumpled on both of hers.

Cushla does not wince in pain or cry out. She does not snarl or sneer or even turn her head resignedly to her neighbour's newspaper. Instead she looks up, smiles at Josh as if this new bruising is the nicest thing that has happened to her all day and, after the briefest of pauses, allows her eyes to light up when she mock-registers who it is that has attempted to cripple her and is now easing himself backwards into the crowd, red faced and stuttering.

'Josh, how lovely! I have a card in my bag for you!'

She has a card for him. Why? Why is she writing to him? Does she know? Does she know what Josh can't even acknowledge himself? Won't even whisper to himself?

'A card? Um . . . good.' Blind lust stupidity wins out, 'Why?'

'For you and Martin I mean. What a wonderful evening we had. Well, I did anyway. I can't thank you enough. I've spent most of today smiling about last night.'

Smiling. She's been smiling. Because of him, them, him. Does she mean it? Does she mean she has been smiling at him? Laughing at him? What does she know?

Josh has been through enough therapy to recognise what is going on. He fully understands the nature of his paranoias, his guarded fears. He recognises that he would not care if he did not care. He assesses the danger. Yes, he is attracted to Cushla. Yes, this is the first time he has felt this way. But what can that mean? He is gay, he has a partner, he is happy, Martin is happy, they are successful, they are respected, they have a home, the blessing of their families and community. And after all, he does love Martin. And he's gay, Josh is a gay

88

man. She's a woman, but she's like him, very like him. And so in her face he has his answer. Cushla resembles him, in which case it is a purely narcissistic desire, understandable as such, probably he needs a few more women in his life anyway, after all he never meant to live in a ghetto . . . and so it goes. More to the point, this is not any woman he is attracted to, this is a particular woman. He is not behaving in a generalised heterosexual manner, but a specific individual to individual manner. Josh reasons his lust out of sight and himself into a very tricky situation. Thus in a five second bungee jump of self-deluded rationalisation he plunges head-long into the probability of plunging headlong into her.

'Look, are you busy? I mean, Martin won't be home for a while . . . and I hate going home to an empty house. It's my stop soon, there's a nice café sort of bar thing . . . near our place . . .'

Josh is losing control fast. His words stammer from him in a sixteen-year-old parody of could-be infatuation. He takes a breath and tries for cool.

'I mean . . . if you don't have any plans . . . though of course, Friday night . . .' Cool doesn't work. He means Friday as a weekend night, the start of sixty-three hours of escape-from-the-office for the working girl, but as soon as the phrase falls from his lips he remembers he is talking to a Jewish girl. She is probably going home for supper, to her North London parents in their North London semi with their bottle of North London Palwin No 4 in its place. And then again perhaps she doesn't ever do that traditional thing and now he has categorised himself as one of those Jewish boys in her eyes. He is in a Woody Allen nightmare and he loathes Woody Allen. He always wants to slap the irritating little man and tell him to grow up and pull himself together. She appears not to have noticed. She is still smiling at him.

'No. I don't have any plans either. I was just wandering really. I've been in town all day. After last night I was inspired. I've spent the whole day in galleries, soaking it all up. London is very full of beauty and we ignore it so often. Don't you find?'

She lifts her head to him and he cannot ignore the full beauty she places before him. The praising phrases sparking through his cerebral cortex are feminized versions of the accolades Martin offered as blessing in their first year together.

'God, your lips are so soft.'

'I want to kiss you.'

'I love the fierce coil of your hair.'

'I want to touch you.'

'Your eyes are the green that twists the edge of paper-whites, I could lick the tint from them.'

'I want to feel you.'

'How can your hands be so long and so strong and so smooth?'

'I want to hold you.'

'Your breastbone is perfect.'

'I want to fuck you.'

'You are gorgeous.'

'I want to fuck you.'

'I want to fuck you.'

She is still looking at him, the tube moves on, the people grow more sparse, 'London? The galleries?'

He nods, agreeing with her and with Martin and with himself. Yes he wants to fuck her and yes the galleries are just great. 'Yes. Yes. We do forget don't we?'

The seat-stealer leaves, Josh moves to his place beside Cushla. All of him is just a little bigger than her. His head a little larger, his neck a little longer, his body a little wider. She is very like him, they turn heads to face and he sees that just below her bottom lip on the left hand side she has a tiny cut, his hand comes up to his own face and feels the identical cut below his own lip. Josh is confused but he is not lost.

The next stop is his and they exit together, he leads the way up the escalator without looking behind and they do not speak again until they have passed through the narrow ticket gates and stand in the station foyer. The warm café is on the other side of the road, noise and lights and sweet cigarette smoke waiting to suck them in. The road that bars the way between the two of them and ease is full of speeding wet-night traffic, motorbike riders ludicrously jousting with taxis and street lights reflected in refracting puddles. For a moment the impossibility of crossing the street hits him and Josh is almost able to turn back, to relinquish the excitement and danger and allow himself just the one quick espresso and a brisk, relieved walk home.

Then Cushla takes his arm, her skin touches his, she is beside him and close, breathing fast and she walks right out into the busy road. The speeding traffic separates before them, the dirty pools dry up and she leads him across the road and into the promised land.

Twenty

In the run to the café there is a second where it might just be all right. Where Josh could leap across the road into his unknown and still choose to drink the single espresso and leave. They stand together on the left side of the road and even in the moment of running, as the traffic parts before him, Josh is still deciding. They reach the centre together and are not killed. Josh has seen the effects of her magic, feels the hot fingers on his arm, he is astounded. Yet it could be different, Josh is not a Calvinist, free will is his and in this moment he could live forever on the traffic island. Then he crosses the line, the white line laid out four years ago by Les Holloway on the second day of his new job. It is all over.

Cushla and Josh cross the white line laid down on a muggy summer afternoon. A new line clean and fresh, and on that day Les almost felt his new job might be worth doing. In his first week after two years on the dole, he actually enjoyed himself. Outdoors, fresh air – of a sort. Four years ago the new job and the new flat and the new wife all seemed an idyllic reality. Les knows better now, which is why he is alone and halfway through his ninth pint in a dirty pub in Bounds Green. Les will drink until the weekend is over and he can wake to curse Monday again. Les hates his job, the monotony, the weather, the arsehole drivers who fuck him around every day, the stench of road paint. But back then, the job was new and the line was new and the loving sun shone on Les and his new life. Shone so that Les praised his new job and as he painted this thin white line he told himself that what he did actually mattered. His job made a difference. And because Les said so, it did. The line Les painted is a hard one to cross, but once over, there's no going back.

The espresso turned to wine and water, the quick drink to two hours' intensity, the handshake to a finger-twining handhold. Then Josh was not scared anymore.

'Do you want to come back to my place?'

He asked my, not our.

'Is Martin there?'

'No. Martin's out tonight. There is no one else at home.' When Josh said home it sounded like a single man's house. It sounded like an invitation. Cushla didn't need to be asked twice.

Twenty-one

He lies facing her. The fresh bedsheet just rippled beneath their weight. It is clean right now. They are both clean and sweet smelling. She slightly sweeter than him. She is a girl after all. Created from the sugary end of the home baking shelves in your friendly local supermarket. Their faces parallel, her breasts are in line with his pec-managed chest, her chin just tipping under his. In the passionate kiss her nose finds its way easily around his, her top teeth make the fast enamel clash a casually balanced note, sharp surprise mutates into perfect C. Her eyes open and through a strobe of fluttering eyelashes smile into matching Josh eyes. Features in unison. Ears, eyes, nose, lips, teeth, tongue, their two faces are looking into a melting mirror pool.

Josh is not thinking about this, he cannot afford to think about what he is doing. He is just going with it. Going the way of all flesh. Collective unconscious and twenty-five years in the real world dragging him along the classic boy meets girl path even when his own road has been clearly signposted boy meets boy. Unlike the gay boy virgin trying men for the first time, Josh does not have to ask what to do. Josh grew up here. He has seen the movies, read the books, slept through the TV mini-series and analysed the data. He knows where it goes, what it does and how to do it. Like the elephant riding the bike, he has no need to remember what he was never allowed to forget in the first place.

Josh reaches out and touches her, takes his mark from her long index finger which matches his. Up her arm, over shallow flesh skin, palest blue veins almost exposed beneath the ivory shaded skin tone they share. Upper arms and shoulders, swimming pool definition. So far, so same. Now his left ring finger, with its direct connection to the heart, continues the exploration. She is silent, watching. One, two of his fingers touch her lips, they part, breathe a kiss and close, a tiny fingertip bite then he is released. The line from lips to chin to breast is direct. Three fingers now and a tentative caress. Josh remembers that homo sapiens developed opposing thumbs not for holding hammers but for holding hands, breasts, cock. She is holding him. She has long hands for a girl but they are still smaller than Martin's. Smaller and softer. Martin may be a mannequin of elegance, but Cushla has the hands of an XY chromosome perfected match. Josh allows himself a brief moment of rationalisation masquerading as thought: this woman in front of him is the other-same. Looks the same in colour and in tone. But she is not. She is like him but female. Martin too, is an opposite match. Not like him but also male. And she is like him but also female. Same-other, other-same. Well thank God for that, if you look at it that way, then he's practically fucking Martin, isn't he?

He's not fucking anyone yet.

To continue. Her breasts are the just lush side of medium, firm and natural. They fall to her left side as she lies. Smooth

95

over her no-heart. Josh remembers evolution and takes her breasts in his hands. There is enough mellow flesh for him to almost cup, her right breast slightly fuller than the left. Josh is surprised, he had not expected asymmetry. Martin's left testicle is just bigger than his right. Other same again. It is not especially warm in the bedroom but there is more heat beneath her breasts, heat held in the fold of the skin. He watches her lungs rise and fall. Notes her close patterned breathing and listens for a moment to his own body. But it is silent. His heart is not talking to him today.

Cushla is kissing him and he rolls on his back to make the kissing process more full. Cat woman prowling over his body, lithe limbed and cruel pointed teeth nibbling at his torso, biting at his chest, his arms, his hands, shoulders, nipples, stomach, toes, feet, calves, thighs, cock. She is biting his cock. Tiny bites, girl teeth, just painful enough to register, still soft enough to enjoy. Josh acknowledges the biting and then it stops, she is not biting now but drinking, eating him all up. If Josh closes his eyes he is safe, she could be anyone, she could be anyman.

If Josh closes his eyes, he is in big trouble. I learnt all my Italian from the natives.

Josh keeps his eyes open, he wants to know what is going on. And anyway, this isn't it really, this particular action he could do with anyone, has done with anyone. It is not as if he is risking his marriage for a ten-quid blow job. Josh is ready, he can do this now. More, he wants to do this now. She appears beside him and now over him and like magic, like a glove, he is the more perfect metaphor, and he finds he just fits. Josh and Cushla fit together as if Mr and Mrs had been made for them.

It doesn't. The man is gay for fuck's sake.

But oh, I am malleable!

96

Josh has spent years seeking out the hidden gay literature, gay TV, gay movies. Like all his kind, like any group, minority, clique, élite, he has searched out that which represents him. Hunted for the recognised spark that allows him the occasional chance to see himself, his life, his very breath reflected back at him from the creative screen. He has been to Jewish films and gay films and sometimes films that are both and once or twice he has even seen a gay black/Jewish couple presented as if it really happened. As if it really happened somewhere that wasn't his own home. An avid film buff, Josh has seen one movie out of every hundred that represents what the rest of the world take so for granted they don't even know it's happening – the presentation of his very own sexual life slap bang up there and painted in lurid technicolour celluloid.

And now, now he's doing that. Doing the thing he has seen so many times, sung so many times, read so many times. Yes she is soft, yes she smells fantastic, yes she is smaller than him and her smallness makes him feel so strong, yes she is sexy and God yes, she is good at it. All of that, but really, now that he's there in the pulsating, fucking act of it and viewing the instant replay movie of the moment, the fact of her being Cushla is almost redundant. Josh looks at what is going on and sees just boy fucks girl and for a moment he is inside it all and it is so fucking easy. He is inside her and it is so fucking easy. Their bodies joined at beating cock and cunt, Josh is at one with the myth and falls head over heels over arse over tit into the trap. Josh isn't straight, will never be straight, but the classic nature versus nurture debate rarely acknowledges how very much easier it is to sing the nursery rhymes when you already know the tune. Josh grew up among the rest of us, in here, in the flesh world. He knows the tune all right. And as he sings along in

97

panting, fuck-syncopated time, it is so simple and safe and there is no conflict and no drama and all he has to do to stay in that easy safe place is to fuck her. Which he does.

Josh discovers Norman Rockwell in his second-floor bedroom in Islington on a cold winter evening and fucks him senseless.

Not bad for an amateur.

Twenty-two

Cushla knows the development of the new campaign must be something really special. This incursion into the realm of twinned devotion will need more than just a white heat of passion for Josh's old relationship simply to buckle and fall. A quick fuck will not break apart this loving couple. Now her strategy is one of the slow burn. She embarks on the seed of a relationship with Josh, a drawn out development in which the carcinoma of distrust may not appear until some time after the hot day in the burning sun of their sin. She is prepared to wait it out. The rewards will be even greater for her effort. And meanwhile, she's actually rather enjoying herself. For all her desire to break up couples, any couples, Cushla would rather mix with a better breed of adulterer if possible and Josh and Martin do have great taste in bed linen. She is the Princess, after all.

Josh's heterosexual virginity was admittedly a good score for Cushla, a shiny, chest-enhancing, breast-enhancing medal. But the real prize is Josh himself. Josh is well known to be articulate and engaging. He has publicly aired his views on the state of Europe and holds opinions about a classical education. Cushla will discover that he also likes slow walks and fast runs, likes fast sex in bed and slow fucking in the bath, and he loves Maria Callas and successful Chelsea football games. Ideally at the same time.

But while stolen hours and brief afternoons are moving Cushla pleasantly enough along her planned route, they are also getting the job done. Her elegant plans are an ergono-maniac's wet dream. The good times are beginning to erode the edifice that is Martin and Josh. And Martin is not Sally or Jonathan, he is neither stupid nor gullible. Nor is he prepared to give in without a fight. He doesn't know exactly what is going on, but he is intuitive enough to know that Josh's exhaustion is not your usual winter sunlight-starved deple-tion. The distance he notices in Josh will not be remedied with a simple week for two in Florida. Martin is clever enough to sense a problem, and he is in love enough to be scared. Whatever is happening, he intends to find the source and root it out of his life completely.

On Wednesday Josh folds away two easy hours in a soft hotel close to Broadcasting House, before going to fetch Martin from another stint on Radio 4. Martin's views on the integrity of architecture in the wasteland, with a witty addenda on post-millennial construction combinations, are broadcast to a willing nation just about the same time as Cushla moves her perfectly constructed lips from Josh's breast-bone to his willing cock. For the second time that afternoon. Even after almost two weeks of stolen afternoons and thieved hours, in Josh's mind the girl sex act is still perverse enough to be exciting and strange enough to be new. The repeat fuck over, Josh dresses, orders afternoon tea and leaves Cushla naked in the trashed bed, sating what remains of her hunger, warm scones and warmer Cushla dripping butter and rasp-

100

berry jam on to the hot sheets. Josh sips a tepid mouthful of her weak lapsang souchong, kisses her crumbed lips and leaves in time to reach the swing doors of Broadcasting House just as Martin is thanked for his afternoon's contribution.

Martin makes his assured way down in the lift, emerges into the foyer and briefly loses his gracious poise while watching Josh smooth his hair, pushing back from his guilty face the thick dark curls that will one day recede that way naturally. Martin plans to be around for the recession. He clambers across a messenger crowd to Josh and, ignoring his lover's worried glance and the smoke taste of tea on his breath, kisses him and holds him into the street and a taxi and home and their own bed. And as Josh lies, double spent and sleeping in his arms, Martin schemes his assault. It will be fast, effective and carefully hidden. First, he will need to remove the cloak of the pretender.

On Thursday morning Martin makes his move. He follows Josh into town. But not until he has woken him three times in the night, and once again very early that morning for sex. If today's strategy doesn't work, he can at least hope to exhaust Josh so much that he won't have enough energy left over for the cheating. Martin follows Josh to a business meeting in Soho, then to their shared hairdresser in Old Compton Street where Josh's curls are trained just a little more casually unkempt than nature would have them while Martin huddles against a shop window diagonally opposite, polystyrene cappuccino for warmth if not flavour. Martin trails Josh on a succession of irritatingly ordinary errands within the confines of gay central London. Finally Josh crosses the boundaries back into straightland somewhere north of Oxford Street. Martin is ready to give up and just go home when Josh walks into a café, spreads his arms wide and Cushla jumps into them.

Cushla is about to kiss Josh, to soothe his cold lips with hers, lipstick protected and hot tea warmed, when a wave of infrequency in the periphery of her vision draws her attention to a man in the street. A man in a heavy coat and a dark hat. A man in pain. A man who is watching this scene far too soon for Cushla's plans. Cushla re-angles her head and brushes Josh's cheek with her kiss.

'Smile, be glad to see me and sit down.'

Josh doesn't understand, has almost grown used to meeting, greeting with girl kisses in public, 'But why . . .?'

'Martin. He's over the road. He's watching you. Watching us.'

Josh is terrified, neither fight nor flight are available so he descends into the more traditional human route. Immediate panic.

'What? Fuck. Oh fuck! Fuck!'

Josh loses his thesaurus mind as the adrenaline rush takes hold. He wants fun and passion and lust. What he doesn't want is a scene. At least not unless he has choreographed it himself. His terror babble continues. 'Does he know you've seen him?'

'I doubt it. Maybe.'

Cushla knows he hasn't, feels he hasn't, but chooses not to tell Josh. Decides to allow Josh a moment of the frisson of sexual tension rubbing hard against guilt.

Cushla persuades him into calm. Josh sits unwillingly, quads and gluteal muscles protesting as he forces himself down to the seat. They order more tea and cakes. When the waitress comes with their plates, Cushla stands to help her, turns swiftly toward the window, registers a look and then waves, friendly and excited.

'Oh look Josh, it's Martin. In the street. How lucky!'

Josh turns in wooden performance and Martin is waved in

102

to join them. He enters no happier than Josh remains but Cushla smooths the moment with a carefully spilt teacup and in the fuss to clean the mess the awkwardness is brushed away. Eventually more tea is brought and then there is an explanation about Cushla's interest in helping Josh perhaps publicize a new exhibition. It is offered languidly enough to be just possible and a triangle is formed, isosceles, no equal angles. Josh slowly resurfaces from his fear.

Coffee is ordered for Martin, another cream cake for Cushla and Welsh rarebit for Josh. Martin does not have much of an appetite. Josh finds he has gone off cheese. But time passes and the teacups empty and soon the triangle is squared and their laughter can be heard in the basement kitchen. Cushla is playing fag hag and the men are afternoon tea queens as the sun sets beyond Oxford Circus. Martin plays with Josh's curls, Josh eats half of Cushla's cake and Cushla picks up the bill for all three. They leave with 'must have dinner' forcefully said. And meant.

Josh goes home to feel guilt and unrequited passion in equal measure. He also feels relief but is not sure if that is because he got away with it this time, was saved from being found out, or if he is merely relieved that today he has not had to lie. Not sexually anyway.

Martin is soothed and ready to assure himself his suspicions were unfounded, for tonight. Martin will take any opportunity to put away his suspicions. He is a naturally trusting soul and would not batter his instinctual faith any more than necessary. Besides, even if Josh is secretly seeing someone, it's certainly not going to be this woman. Martin has had his moment of bitterness about Josh stealing Cushla for a special friend, he is over it now. As a couple they can do this jealousy, it is about selecting friendship and can be annoying, sometimes even painful, but ultimately it won't really matter. It is about she's my friend not your friend, being the leader of my own gang, not being part of yours. To Martin and Josh, playing special friends is about being a fourteen-year-old in love – it is not about sex. The special friend relationship is secret confidences and hidden hand-holding, not secret kisses and well hidden fucks. Today at least, Martin knows Josh has been truly faithful.

Cushla has thoroughly enjoyed being with the two of them, playing close chum in their happy couple fantasy even while she has continued to plan their downfall. She intends to take cream cakes for her next liaison with Josh. And, in their pleasant company, she has laughed enough through the long grey afternoon to almost lose the nagging sense that someone is watching her. And now too, she knows that someone was watching her. Her sense of other awareness was right. Martin was watching both of them. And so was the Prince.

Twenty-three

With his voyeur's eye Prince David is enjoying this sex. It is different to what he expected. What he's used to. Different to the Palace sex. He is starting to think that maybe he understands some of why these people care about it so much. Back home the coming together is pleasantly routine. It is occasionally forceful or even passionate. But it is never new. The unhoped for but inevitable outcome of a liberal attitude to modern sexuality, in the land of his birth the sex act is now so natural that it is ordinary. What David the pale and beautiful sees between his sister and Josh is far from ordinary. His Imperial Highness is on the No 43 bus going home but has missed his stop by miles. It is impossible for him to watch out of his left eye for the greasy spoon that signals his stop, while his right eye is so full of Cushla's sex show.

Sex education at the Palace follows a well defined pattern. Even for boys who grow up in the space of an afternoon. In his land, time is a moveable feast, the menu though, is strictly defined. The instruction starts at the age of five. A late-Spring trip to the far meadow with the afternoon tutor. A day of bare feet and shorts, little boy body free to the sunshine. Young David lies flat on soft cool grass and looks out across the meadow, it is an unswept carpet of tiny daisies, each yellow eye standing level with his forehead, clustered petals still while the whole head quivers in partial breeze. The tutor lies beside him, Royal Botanist and Apiarist. At a word from the tutor, David's attention is drawn to a distant hum, growing louder, coming closer. The hum arrives in a small black cloud and then breaks itself into hundreds of separate tones. The little boy is surrounded by a swarm of royal honey bees and, unconcerned, allows them to ruffle the downy hairs on his arms and legs as they climb down him to alight on the willing daisies. The greedy bees pull pollen from the open flowers, then depart as one, slower than their coming, fat bumble bodies swollen with pollen. The Prince has learnt the bees.

Then the birds. Now David is six and he is egg-stealing with the Palace Ornithologist. They climb tall pines together and peer into rooks' nests and owl holes. The tutor carefully pockets an egg and hurries back down the trunk before the parent birds can return and begin an attack. His Highness climbs trees slower but it is nonetheless fine exercise – two lessons in one. With his tutor supervising, David carefully cracks the unready egg, revealing a half formed chick. The tutor explains the body parts, the life stages and the young Prince nods seriously, his growing knowledge weighing down the young head. They leave the cracked and finished egg at the bottom of the tree, healthy nutrients for passing foxes or squirrels. But not cats. David hates cats. Back at the Palace, his Highness draws pictures of hives and chicks and honeycomb and eggs. He learns Latin and modern Greek and begins to read Anaïs Nin. Now he knows the birds.

Following his seventh birthday and the killing of age festivities, David receives his library key and is set loose among the millions of tomes, some of which he understands now, others he will never comprehend. He is a voracious reader and by the time he has attained his sexual majority young David is more than ready for the challenge. First and second sex are with Palace staff, third with his mother's best friend, fourth with the Passion Fairy and fifth with a passing salesman. His Highness is no longer a stranger to desire and now he is grown and now he knows what to do.

Thus the hero Prince has played and practised and learnt all the ways of lust. And they have all been easy and fun. But of all the ways he has learnt, none of them has ever been even remotely dangerous. Which is why, try as he might, David just can't get his watching eye to turn away from his sister and Josh and concentrate on the walk home. At the Palace there is no danger in swarming bees or climbing trees. David lights another cigarette, looks on and knows what he's been missing.

Twenty-four

He lies on me, his body covering mine, head arched to lean, succour-seeker on my shoulder. Where his curls are longest, at the narrow nape of his neck, they tangle themselves into mine. Our locks lock arms. The hair I have chosen for this endeavour is perfect, it melds so eagerly with his. I could brush out the knots in mine and his conditioner would clear the way. Breast to chest our skin tones are identical, where the shimmering pale olive turns to dark pink at my nipples, his does too. The smaller man aureole is nonetheless identical for the masculinity. We are so close to one. Slightly wider, a little taller than I am, he just fits over my body. Boy cover closest of mis-matches to the girl gene pool. He overlaps my edges. For now. Soon I will make this me a little bigger and, almost without noticing, he will slip in, fall in, dive in, drown.

Fucking in the afternoon has a raft of tea-time pleasures. The anonymous, expensive hotel rooms are clean and warm and white-cotton sweet. Beyond the gilded doormen, London is edging itself into impatient late November,

Christmas decorations hung too soon are no match for the lazy sun setting early, rising late. Windswept and rain dirty, the narrow streets fold from outside cold to overhot shop interiors, cafés with cappuccino steam, milky condensed windows. There is an effort involved in crossing the city to reach him. I don't mind the exertion, I am at work here. I take my job very seriously. It is well paid, it deserves all my attention. I travel by tube, or in the worst weather, there is a taxi journey from my virgin tower. The perils of the underground are well documented, the almost-touching men, the angry women, on all I turn my charming smile. And surprised at their own gesture, they fall back, offer me seats, make room for my delicate feet. I save most of my power for Josh, but it is appropriate to use a little to smooth the way. The taxi journey is somewhat harder to enjoy, in the black hole of the cab there is no one to distract me. I must endure the one to one. There are the pitfalls of rancid conversations from the back seat, shouting over the diesel engine to be heard and ignored, leaning back on grubby seats, sitting on the sense memories of unhappy souls, metaphysical stains left for me to wallow in. I would avoid the angst of others if at all possible. I do not wish to share their pain any more than I desire their love. I am on my mission and need clarity for the plan. But I ensure all my efforts are rewarded. We are being a little more clever now, my Joshua twin and I. Plotting our escapes with perfect attention to ingenious detail. We are being safe.

We meet mid-afternoon, the sun just arrived for the half-hour entrance it makes on these early closing days, thirty minutes squeezed between rainy day and mean sunset as dictated by Greenwich greed. We greet in the street and I follow him, four paces behind in non-subservient obedience to the strictures of married-couple protocol. Another grand hotel, doorman, porter, receptionist, all well trained in upper crust discretion, for he and I are a good looking couple, a rich-looking pair, they know we can afford to pay for our pleasures. Joshua books us in as another Mister and Missus and the Dickensian tones are not lost on the desk clerk. Then the elevator extended journey to the room, flowers that will last only an hour out of their cellophane cell and curtains too bland to bother closing. The Do Not Disturb sign is hung, the door double-locked behind it. The sign faces the corridor, not me. I do not need to heed its bidding.

I am incapable of heeding its bidding.

Joshua had not done this before, not ever, the ritual of deceit is new to him. But quickly he has learnt the form and function of the afternoon minibar, that my taste is to slow sip both half bottles of champagne, perhaps some sex-shared chocolate, and then the kiss and then the fuck and the bed and the bath and the shower and the TV and the radio and, if we have another hour to spare, then I will order room service. A silver tray and linen napkin gift of white bread and salted butter and several thick slices of good fresh ham. Some sweet fruit jam perhaps, pips to pick later from my teeth. A fine hotel has many facilities and I will use each one to corrupt him.

Swiftly the new becomes routine, a pattern is set. I am under his skin, Josh cannot get enough of me, but even his passion must be meted out in metered hours. And of course there is his guilt. I have insisted that I will not be disturbed by his shame. He may neither mention Martin to me, nor address aloud his fear that we will be discovered. This way I am still more powerful. In absenting myself from the collusion, these activities must be owned totally by Josh himself. He books the room, he arranges the meeting place, he names the time. My presence is my acquiescence. I am simply going along with all this, bowing to his greater need, accommodating him as easily as the rooms hold us. I am a loose leaf flowing in the river of Josh's desire.

I am a loose canon waiting for the perfect time to explode.

And timing is all. Timing in the kiss, timing in the fuck. Timing in the offered fingernailful of cocaine, well cut and loose dropped into the hollow between my collarbones. Timing in the transferral of champagne from my mouth to his, from free poured between my breasts to the tiny tip of his eager tongue. Timing in the swift muscle contraction that forces my orgasm to a perfect union with his. We are no more naturally rhythm compatible than any other new couple, but I am creating this fusion immediately. Not for us the months and years until we are two equalling one. I divide myself at will, surrendering each fresh thought in his company until my every imagining originates in him. We are in symbiosis and Josh is astounded. Locked in guilt and desire and shame and wonder, he ecstatically despairs over our couple-finished sentences, our cloned yearning. He sees that already we behave as two fine-tuned to each other. The coupling it took him and Martin years to achieve, we have already in the space of the stolen fuck selection. He is amazed. He thinks it is magic. He believes it means something.

It means I'm fucking exhausted by the time I get home.

There is a persistent voice hammering at the back of his heart, it grows slowly louder. The voice is starting to suggest that maybe he should confess, make amends, make right. The wandering Jew in confession to the apostate Catholic is not what I had in mind. Not yet anyway. Reconciliation is hardly the most appropriate sacrament on offer, I have always preferred last rites. And there is a time to go before

111

inquisition and expulsion are necessary, I must have more of him. Furthermore, confession requires absolution to be complete.

Absolution is the fulfilment of forgiveness. Which would not be appropriate. I did not embark on this venture, put so much effort, such self-sublimation into the scheme to be robbed of my prize by a couple strengthened through painful infidelity into a deeper, more permanent bond. There is no point if my bounty is not the complete destruction of their union. I am nothing if not thorough.

I am nothing if not heartbreaking.

We fuck again. I'm getting there.

Twenty-five

David is waiting. Assembling data, collating evidence. Waiting for the third part will take as long as it takes. He cannot hurry his sister nor, now that he has discovered London, would he. He will take all the right measures to watch her ways and while he waits, he will enjoy himself too. So the Prince sleeps until noon and, as even a thin aesthete has to eat occasionally, he graces a different restaurant for lunch every day and finds that in the winter city there are warm corners to hide in and smoke and simply watch the world until the light dies, bleeding dark red behind boarded up shop fronts. David is having such a good time watching. Back there at the City of Palace there's nothing to look at, not really. The sun shines constantly, the moon is always blue, the birds sing, all's right with the world. It is certainly beautiful. But David has discovered that perfection doesn't necessarily provide a fun afternoon's entertainment.

He leaves his flat for another day's walking. It sounds like working but he knows it isn't. He roams London and, when his feet are cobbled over with battered streets, he climbs on to buses, looking out for the old Routemasters, wishing to sway round sharpened corners, afternoon mist dampening his perfectly flicked fringe. He eats falafel in St Martin's Lane and Chinese coconut rolls in Little Newport Street and then travels all the way home for Jamaican patties and strong beer. He breathes in the mismatched entertainers and side-street shufflers, swimming swift through a day of fast edit movie in his head. David is happy. He is pretending he is on holiday. He is lying to himself. While the Princess of a matriarchal lineage can make her own rules occasionally, the Prince will always have to follow the house rules. Mostly. Eventually.

When he gets home his mood is broken by the answer-phone, blinding red with timed accusation. Messages from the Palace. The King wants to know why his only son wasn't in the Counting House this morning. The King has always been a little absent-minded, but since they invented the new monetary system, things have really got out of hand. Not even the saltiest of butter for his bread can soothe him at the moment. He frets and whimpers and hangs up in irritation.

Her Majesty is just a little more in control.

'Darling, it's Mummy. Me. The Queen. Look dear, the thing is we were rather wondering how you were getting on. Only the reports you've sent tend to suggest a somewhat limited amount of movement. On your part, I mean. Obviously the female genetic combination has been on the job with alacrity. As it were. Now I know she's more or less in charge of her own order of events but couldn't you speed things up a little? Look into it will you, there's a dear. And it's not that I'm complaining Davey, but time passes and none of us are getting any younger. Well, strictly speaking, that's not quite true, not since the age-inversion dynamics were worked out – but, la la, you know what I mean. And I do so want you to be here in time for the ball, both of you, of course, you and ah . . . your sister, yes, that's the one. If that's at all possible . . . but if it isn't . . . well, actually we've come up with another route you might want to look into . . .'

The machine beeps, Her Majesty has used up her allotted two minutes, technology has no respect for divine right. It beeps twice more. The Queen again.

'Mmm, yes, la la, where was I? Oh, that's right. Now, as I was saying, I do want you both here for the ball if possible, but, um . . . how shall I put this? If you come home alone, that's fine too. You see, I'm having another one. Another little Princess we assume. Isn't that nice? I had thought of going for the full twelve, but Daddy said we couldn't afford all those dancing shoes and there's something of a dearth of eligible Princes nowadays, and anyway as we only need one of each . . . well, if she can't be brought back, then that's okay with us. Wouldn't really do to have two Princesses wandering round now, would it? We'd never get the paparazzi off the front lawn. And to tell the truth, I rather think she might be starting to have designs on my job, and that would never do, would it? So look Davey, just do what you can to press on with the thing and then finish it. Before she starts on the next three. You will remember to bring her heart, won't you? Archaic I know dear, but we have to obey the rules and the public do like their proof. Then again, there's only room for one Queen of Hearts in this palace, isn't that right? Must go baby, big kisses.'

David rewinds and wipes the messages. He is confused. He has always assumed his sister has no heart. That was the story he'd heard from childhood, the one everyone knew. He puts in a quick call to the Palace. Protocol demands he asks after the health of the graves of all four grandparents, his mother's sex life and his father's bank account – and completely ignore his mother's pregnancy. With positive answers to all the questions, he is then able to ask about the heart.

Her Majesty laughs, 'No dear. You're quite right. There isn't one yet. But I expect there will be.'

'It's been foretold?'

'Not exactly. I saw it in the entrails yesterday. We had a young man executed.'

'What for?'

'Kicked a football through one of the Palace windows. Shattered glass everywhere. Very messy.'

'Oh Mummy, that's not fair.'

'We gave him his life back afterwards darling, don't be such a softie. But Daddy and I absolutely had to know if it would be good weather this afternoon. We're having a picnic and since His Majesty's given up on caffeine there were no tea leaves to look at.'

'And is it sunny?'

'No. Pissing down. I must have got the lower colon mixed with the upper. Anyway the lad's appendix was dreadfully swollen. We whipped it out so it didn't give him any trouble in the future. It's a sign, believe me. The Health Fairy assures me. Your sister will be growing a heart. Before the year's over I shouldn't wonder. Don't worry, it won't be too big, you could probably whip it out with a pair of nail scissors if you wanted. Must go now darling, Daddy's just made lunch.'

'What are you having?'

'Honey dear. Bread and honey. No change here, we do like our little routines. Now you won't forget the heart, will you? Bye baby!'

David replaces the handset and stands up slowly, he looks around his small home. The warm sunshine has gone. His room is dark but for the orange light from the street. His woodsman's knife lies on the table, sharp reflecting the cold ochre. He sighs and gently fingers the blade. Time to get on with the job.

On the other side of town, further to the West, the mid afternoon sun has a few extra moments to leave dark red streaks across Josh's shoulders, in three minutes it fades to deep pink and then makes its Southern Hemisphere debut, handing over the night to streetlight pollution. Cushla holds him, the soft sheets heated by their sex and Josh's sleeping body. In five minutes she must rise and begin again, but for now she lies quiet, gathering her resources, allowing the billowing dark to replenish her sexual energy. Outside messenger bikes career around screech-halted taxis, unexpectedly disgorging their occupants, clogging the streets at the descent to Selfridges Food Hall. From the top end of Oxford Street Cushla can hear London closing into the early night, the hum of the outside traffic just muted by double glazing and thick blue velour. From her position in the bed, Cushla thinks she catches the sound of something beginning to open.

She lies with Josh in her arms, circling his sleeping body with a warmth strange to her. Comfortable and yet dangerous at the same time. Her chest lifts and falls in the darkening room and she cradles Josh with an uncertainty new and difficult to look at. Josh lies on her right and beneath her left breast is a tiny stirring, and again at the pit of her stomach, a gentle fibrillation, easily missed against the rise and fall of his sleeping breath. She holds him closer.

In the dull light Cushla senses a translation waiting, a paused comprehension she knows could happen before her very eyes if she would just turn to look.

I am surprised, I had not thought it possible for it to grow of its own accord. The taste of it is gentle in my mouth. The taste of him is tender on my tongue. Perhaps this is what they cry for. I hold him smiling and there are tears behind the touch. It is a bittersweet cliché, the want and must not have and for a moment of bite the edge of his little fingernail I think perhaps this is possible. The warmth is so very comforting, I almost contemplate being like them.

On the edge of believing, Cushla snatches an aftertaste of fear and closes her eyes against the possible. Instead she wakes Josh, blindly kissing him, fucks him and forces him into her. Drives him into her until there is no room for the unexpected, no place for the unwanted organic – for that which she cannot control. Cushla might not notice sentiment when she feels it, but she damn well knows fear on the tip of her tongue and she knows how to deal with it.

The time passes, I am come to myself again. I am the proud Princess who will one day rule, simply because I choose to and I know better. I will not have it. I will return to my tower and cut it out. By hand if necessary. It shouldn't be too hard, anaesthesia is for those with feeling.

Two siblings, just the one job. The outcome will depend on who gets there first. But then, it's always something of a lottery in matters of the heart.

Twenty-six

Josh takes the next step. He is tired of lying but does not remember how to tell the truth. He does not talk much to Cushla, their time filled with appetites, he does not know what she thinks about their future.

Nor would I tell him the truth if he asked.

When he is away from Cushla, he wonders what she thinks about all this, what they are doing, to themselves, to each other, to Martin. When he is with her he has neither the time nor the inclination to ask. And yet he cannot keep up the pretence, something has to happen, change will come. All Josh knows is that he must make some move. He does not want to give up Martin. He has no intention of giving up Cushla. Josh wants cake, cream and no diet. And no exercise either. But the stasis of constant uncertainty is beating him down. He wants someone to make it all better, but Martin is his best friend and now there is no one to tell. Josh is finding half-truths far more painful than he could ever have imagined. He is welling over with the unsaid. He tries to tell Martin that maybe they need a break.

To Josh's surprise, Martin jumps at the idea, 'Yes my darling of course, you're right. That's a brilliant idea.'

Martin is so insecure at the moment, he would call a day trip to the Elephant and Castle Shopping Centre a brilliant idea if the suggestion fell from Josh's cheating lips.

Martin adds to Josh's weight of guilt, piling on the haste and fear, 'London in November is hideous. Grey, ghastly. God yes, you're right. We do need a break. Where shall we go? I'll take you to warmth, to the sea. I've got it – Thailand. Would you like Thailand? Yeah, brilliant, Phuket, long days in the sun, you sleeping in a hammock. I can work anywhere, I'll take the laptop. Shall I book it? Would you like that? Will I make it happen?'

Martin's whole body pleads with Josh to agree, his stomach tensed for the kickback. Josh fumbles with his knife and fork, spills his wine as he reaches for the glass. The waiter is quick to wipe up the mess, even quicker to pour more fumé blanc. He camps it up for a greater tip. The gay community believe in helping out their own with discarded five and ten pound notes. Or so the waiter hopes. The crisp twenties are understandably reserved for the altogether more rewarding process of throwing cocaine at delicate nerve endings and never-to-be-replaced brain cells. The waiter departs. Josh doesn't actually look at Martin. He studies his plate, he stabs the unyielding mange tout.

He tries again, 'Well actually, I didn't mean together. You and me. I meant a break. I mean, I need a break. From us.'

Martin freezes. Lower colon clenching in sure knowledge that even Martin's brain cannot hear yet, that Martin's heart would be deaf to. Martin has spent the past week or so suffocating his concerns in willing ignorance. Stifled the small voice which whispered rebelliously that all was not well. Yesterday morning, in a moment of clarity after two hours sweating out the truth in the gym, he had consciously put away his worries and planned to ask Josh for honesty in a year, in five years. To claim a future integrity when truth would have become history and lost its power to hurt. But now Josh is throwing reality in his face. In a restaurant. In the safety of a public place.

Still Martin does not fight back, the wild fox cornered first plays sweet, 'What do you mean?'

Martin knows enough to act easy, he has been here before. He has failed here before. Take the slap in the face as a gentle nudge, don't attack, don't pressure, give the untrained puppy dog a longer leash on which to run so he'll come back loving you all the more. Give the lover more rope with which to hang himself. Or you.

Josh is surprised at the lack of challenge. Too caught up in his own churning deceit, he does not notice Martin's fear, cannot recognise his lover pussy-footing around his own pain in order to keep Josh close. He shovels rare lamb into his mouth, chews the soft pink flesh, gives it a moment to melt untasted on his tongue and answers, 'It's nothing Marty, really. Only a small break. I just want . . . I feel – smothered.' Josh attempts a search for the word as if he hasn't been rehearsing this speech all afternoon, as if he hadn't booked the dinner table in anticipation of this moment. Martin can't eat, can't look, can't hear. Josh stutters on in studied nonchalance, 'It isn't anything really. I'm tired. Just a few days. I just need some time to myself. Just a few days.'

Josh says 'just' like it is perfectly fair. As if he's not perpe-trating an injustice. Like it doesn't matter at all. Josh says it enough times to convince Martin that he's lying. The rule of three. Once is truth. Twice is either potential for hidden agenda or simply an irritating habit of self-confirmation.

But the third repetition is verification of certain falsehood. I love you, I love you, I love you, is one love too many for most couples.

Martin now has three options. He can make a fuss here in the restaurant, draw attention not only to themselves but also to his terror of loss, thereby rubber-stamping their disintegration with the covert public gaze. He can wait until they get home and deal with the matter in private, knowing that whatever may happen behind their closed doors, without witnesses it can always be turned into another variation of the truth sometime in the future. At a later date they can always pretend the trauma to come never happened. Or he can take Josh's words at face value. Martin is not stupid, he considers matters carefully and takes the third option first. Smiles, agrees, chats about where Josh might go and what Josh might do, finishes his dinner, allows a mango sorbet enough time to melt in discussion about weekend breaks, even lingers over a second coffee to complete the impression of placid disinterest. Josh pays the bill, over-tips the expectant waiter who mistakes it for recognition of his skill, not Josh's gratitude at the lack of a scene. They walk home quickly, air too damp to bother much with conversation, lock the door behind them, enter their centrally heated safe paradise. Then Martin takes option number two.

Martin throws his coat, his wallet, his keys to the floor. He would throw Josh to the floor but he's been too well brought up. He rounds on Josh the minute they walk in the door, slamming him against the artfully bare plastered wall with the force of his words, 'What the fuck was all that about?'

Josh is surprised. He shouldn't be surprised but he is. He should have seen this coming, would usually have known better, but that now all his thought processes are fogged up, blocked with images of Cushla, plans of escape.

Surprise renders Josh inarticulate. 'What? What was what? What?'

'That crap about going away. By yourself. How dare you drop that on me when we're out? What the fuck did you think you were doing?'

Josh has had a moment to regain his composure, synapses snap back into action, he is standing in the perfect entrance to the perfect home. He will not lose this. He will not lose Cushla either. Attack urge overcomes defence impulse and he too begins to shout.

'I'm not allowed a few days away? Is that what you're saying? I can't have a few days to myself?'

'I don't believe you.'

'You don't believe what?'

'I don't believe you want to go away by yourself.'

Round One to Josh. Martin has made a serious tactical error here. Lost the first foray in his eagerness to push for truth. He has given Josh the opportunity to change his plans. True, Josh was hoping to go away with Cushla, but what if he does go away by himself? Time to get perspective on both relationships. Not only can he now continue his lie, both to himself and Martin, but he can run with it all the way to the moral high ground. In half a second Josh has convinced himself that he planned all along to go away by himself. Every man deserves a few days alone. Not only is Martin behaving unreasonably but, a far worse sin to those who live in the contained world of commitment, he has admitted to not trusting his partner. Josh reasons this all out in the minute and a half it takes him to remove his coat and Martin, waiting in fear and fury for an answer, actually confirms Josh's position of high ground integrity with his next demand.

'I don't know where this has come from Josh. We've never been apart intentionally. I just don't trust this.'

Josh leaps gratefully on the sacrilege, 'You mean you don't trust me.'

'I didn't say that.'

Too late. Down again in Round Two. Martin has intimated a lack of trust. He's actually said it out loud. Now Josh has an open field. He launches into a litany he has no need to rehearse. It is an inventory that is born along with first love and first kiss, it is inbred and genetically programmed. Every coupled individual knows the manipulative credo by heart:

If you don't trust me what kind of a relationship can we have anyway?

How can you not trust me after all this time?

If you don't believe in me, then what are you doing with me?

Without your trust this whole relationship is worthless.

Followed by Catches 22 through to 98: I may have given you reasons not to trust me, but if you don't trust me, then you are in the wrong, not me.

Josh is not intentionally manipulative. It just comes out that way. Josh is human. Far better to position Martin in the place of sinner than acknowledge it belongs to him. Far better to turn the table, than sit condemned at the other end. Josh is mortal, his animal instincts flare up in times of strife. Fight or flight. He chooses both. In that order. First he floors his lover with the twist of mistrust, then he takes his ready-packed bag and leaves. He does not know where he's going. He will not take his mobile. He will call Martin in a few days. There is no kiss goodbye.

Martin sleeps alone and cold. And wakes bloody angry.

Twenty-seven

Cushla prepares her room. Sprinkles sweet rose water and orange blossom in corners, immerses herself in a bath heavy with sea salt. She knows what to do, has watched it happen once before. Once was enough to print the pattern indelibly in her mind. She had not been meant to see, but she had.

Aged seven and tired of the constant mellow beauty of the Palace, she had kissed her nurse, cancelled her afternoon's lessons in ancient Greek and modern Cantonese and taken a walk into the town. She was safe, the people were happy, the land easy, any child could walk for ten miles round without a parent wondering where they were or if they were safe. A little Princess could walk further than most. At least that was how the myth went.

Cushla wandered on, nibbling at her packed lunch as she went. Quails' eggs and olive bread and fresh caviar and mature brie. A small vial of chilled champagne and a little box of raisins to finish. She went through the Palace gates, a backwards tourist in her own land. The guards nodded to her in barely perceptible gestures of their ramrod trained backs, and she continued down the new cobbled steps into the city streets. She walked through the nice part of town and the nicer part of town and the nicest part of town. She walked until she did not know where she was walking anymore. Until her lunch was finished and it was time to go on or go back.

At the point of decision there was a river to cross or a different path home or a forest. Cushla chose to walk into the trees. She wanted to walk in dark green. She entered the forest and much too soon there were bluebells and forget-me-nots and a clearing. A small house with curling chimney smoke and creeping honeysuckle and sunflowers three heads taller than the child Cushla. But despite the sun filtering bright through the trees, the cottage was encased in dark green shade. She crept up to a window, her bare feet squeaking against damp grass, small insects running for cover. She pulled herself to tiptoe height and looked directly into the workroom of the Compassion Fairy. Where the Compassion Fairy created love and wonder and passion and joy. The workroom where the Compassion Fairy created heartsease from the discarded hearts of others.

The Compassion Fairy was leaning over an old man. Even with her tender years of inexperience, the Princess could see he was tired, age had worked on him for years and now his eyes were rheumy, his joints arthritic, his back stooped. Even in Palace land, age eventually brought its distractions. But his heart was still pumping blood and love, he still kissed his wife of fifty years every morning and every night. Still held tight to her hand in his sleep. Still asked her opinion and love before he made any decision. And she'd been dead fifteen years. The Compassion Fairy knew this and the time had come for the old man to pay his dues. She smiled sweetly and leant over him, tightening the bonds on his ankles and wrists, 'You've had fifty years of her love, you don't need it any more.'

'But I don't know how to live without her.'

'You'll learn old man. Come on now, I gave you an extra fifteen years. I could have made you stop this loving lark when she was cold and dead in the ground.'

'But she isn't. She's alive in my heart.'

The Compassion Fairy nodded sagely, 'My point exactly.'

The old man was crying, Cushla's feet were sore from standing on tiptoe, the Compassion Fairy was impatient.

'Time's up, old guy. Give it away.'

The Compassion Fairy leant forward and with a sharpened fingernail ripped open the man's cotton shirt. His old man's chest was concave thin, the sparse thatch of grey hair no match for the cold of the air in the workroom – a constant ten degrees to keep the love fresh – or the heat of the Compassion Fairy's blade. Cushla watched transfixed. Under his liver-blotched skin she could see his heart beat fast against his ribs, a caged bird readying itself for flight. The Compassion Fairy twisted the old man's tied hands above his head, pushed him back against the wooden table, arching his back up and closer to the knife. With one hand she held his hands and with the other she carefully sliced through his flesh. The man's scream was drowned out by the gentle lullaby the Compassion Fairy sang. Dropping the knife on the table, she reached into the body cavity, up and under the ribcage until she held his heart tight. The lullaby and the soft stroke of her hand on his heart soothed the man, she let go of his hands and his arms fell limply behind his head. She kissed his eyes as she severed the veins linking him to life. The heart did not know that its man was dead, in the Compassion Fairy's hand it pumped itself in time to her crooning lullaby. Cushla's little girl feet were aching, her calves screaming out with overstretched cramp, her fingers numb from clawing the windowsill, but still she watched.

The Compassion Fairy took the heart to her workbench, deftly sliced it into four. 'One for kisses, one for wishes, one for passion and one for love.' She talked to herself and sang snatches of the lullaby at the same time. She measured and analysed each section before placing the heart quarters in four separate jars. She added rose water and orange blossom to each one and then sealed them up. She kept singing. Behind her the door opened and an old lady walked into the room. The old man rose from the table, the bonds on his arms and legs untying themselves. The man smiled at the woman. He walked free to her, held her in his arms and kissed her. Then the old lady lifted up the man and carried him out over the threshold. The two of them went out the front door and away from the house. Cushla tried to follow their progress but once they had passed the shade of the house and walked into the sunlight she couldn't see them any more. The Compassion Fairy didn't turn from her work. She heard her front door open and close, sang out 'Goodnight' and 'Thank you' over the sixteenth verse of her lullaby.

Cushla watched the Compassion Fairy at work until night fell. Watched her make love potions for heartsick boys and bravery mixes for underwhelmed girls. Listened as she fashioned baby kisses from the continual lullaby. When the last ray of sun left the forest, the Compassion Fairy came to her front door and offered Cushla a lantern.

'This will help you light your way home. I hope you've paid attention. Though I would not wish it to happen, you may need the lesson one day. However, should you actually do the deed yourself, remember to cut fine and clear, but whatever you do, don't listen to the heart when it pleads.'

She handed Cushla the light and with a pale and gentle hand she ruffled the little seven-year-old head. Then she smack-slapped Cushla's face hard and added, 'And don't you dare bloody well come snooping around here again, nosey spoilt little brat!'

Cushla stands in her ivory tower, windows open to the old buffet of London spread before her. She waits in silence and listens for pleading. There is none. Good, she must be early. She turns on every light in the flat, her rooms a welcoming beacon to the cold night. She lays a clean white sheet over the wooden floor, removes her black silk robe and steps naked to the centre of the white. She holds the blade in her right hand, lifts her breast away with the left. The first incision is easy, a straight cut under the breast. The pain is minor, Cushla is used to the cut of many knives. She completed her own ritual scarification when she was nine, two years earlier than her maternal grandmother – the previous holder of the Palace record. She then slices down and across the first cut, peeling open her heartspace like a fig. She looks in. It is there. Tiny, pitiful, but definitely there. Cushla hears the singing and then the small pleading, hears but does not listen. Cancels her aural senses and swiftly cuts out the baby heart. The whole process takes approximately two minutes, Cushla loses no more than three fluid ounces of blood. She leaves the square of white cotton, walks to her open window and throws the small piece of her own meat down to the street where it is seized on by a passing Pekinese and swallowed whole. The Pekinese immediately loses its habitual nastiness and irritating yappy bark and surprises its owners by playing sweetly with their child the next day. It also loses its inbred sneer and therefore its title at Crufts the following year.

Cushla is very learned. She knows more than most. But

she has no experience in the ways of the heart. She does not understand that love grows like a cancer. It is not always possible to remove it whole. There are always creeping malignancies of lust and desire that can mutate into love in the blink of a beautiful eye.

In Stoke Newington High Street the Prince is sleeping. But lying on the table locked into its gazelle skin sheath, his hunting blade twitches and groans. There is a job still to do.

Twenty-eight

The restlessness is everywhere at this time. None of the players sleeps easy.

Josh's main problem was that after storming from the home of perfection he shared with Martin, he didn't actually have anywhere to go. Of course there were plenty of friends. Hundreds of acquaintances. But going to friends would involve telling the truth. Or at least a Josh-enhancing version of the truth. And Josh didn't know anyone he would dare to tell even a doctored truth. It is one thing to have an affair and possibly damage one's relationship and even admit to an actual infidelity. It is quite another to do so when, according to one's friends, that relationship you are in the process of endangering is a rare and beautiful institution. Josh was as likely to receive a good response from his friends if he told them what he'd done to Martin, as he would if he'd admitted to purchasing a fur coat. Worse actually, the fur coat could always be passed off as an accidental lapse into congenitally programmed comedy kitsch. Breaking up the perfect coupling of Josh and Martin didn't quite fit into a camp code of what might be considered just permissible, with enough post-modern drugs and alcohol inside you. And anyway, Cushla was a girl. Gay men who leave their long term boyfriends for younger women aren't usually accorded a great deal of understanding and sympathy. Straight men who finally get around to coming out, on the other hand, are given a hero's welcome. The inverted world is a gaudy villa of contradictions.

Worse still, Josh didn't think he did want to leave Martin. Josh still believed himself to be gay. Josh is still gay. But when Josh thinks of Cushla the lower pit of his stomach contracts in an unconscious ripple of lust. Josh remembers kissing Cushla's full lips and the mere memory of her stroke stirs him. Josh holds his breath until he greets Cushla and when he has said the first hello of the day, he holds in every molecule the fear that she will not reciprocate. And when she does smile, laugh, seem pleased to be near him, the relief is overwhelming. Josh is in love and delirious sexual tension crams out every would-be sane thought. He remembers when Martin made him feel like this, when the first glimpse of Martin at someone else's dinner party held a night of sweet potential passion for him. When he spent the evening listening to the half-noticed conversations that swam past him while trying to catch the scent of the intended. An evening when he followed his host from room to room, fulsomely admiring each new purchased piece of Heals and Habitat, in the hope that maybe Martin would be in the next room, in the next room. Josh remembers what it felt like to feel this way about Martin, the exquisite torture of sexual tension, the constant pressure where the before of a new relationship is all-consuming, all-devouring. Josh knows this has been replaced, as it is with all the long-termers, by abiding love, a fortunately still-strong desire, their planned future and the fact that they know each other. There is nothing else to uncover. Martin has done nothing wrong, he has just loved Josh for a long time. There is nothing to beat the shock of the new skin.

Josh goes from sexual tension to thinking about the sex itself. He does not understand it, how he came to be fucking a woman, looking forward to fucking a woman. Josh had never expected to want to fuck a woman. He has talked to Martin about it. Martin who has tested and tasted just the one, but that's enough to know a little something, and was honestly concerned that perhaps Josh might feel he was missing out. Martin had been very generous in his concern, leaning across a private dinner table in the early months of their coupling, holding Josh with one hand and offering him freedom with the other.

'I mean, I'd understand if you wanted to. You know, to try.'

'I don't want to try.'

'I know you know you're gay . . .'

Josh smiled, kissed his lover's hand, 'I've convinced you then?'

'Yes, it's just that well, what if . . .'

The question tried to hang in the air but Josh didn't give it time, he batted it straight back to Martin, 'What if I meet a nice girl? What if I want to fuck around? What if you're not enough for me?'

'Yes. All of that.'

'Then,' Josh declared with the confidence of the ignorant, 'I would tell you the truth. But I hardly think that I ought to go out and shag some poor girl just so that you can stop worrying about what I might do years in the future. That's hardly the action of a modern, post-feminist, gay man now, is it?'

Martin had to agree. He had no choice. Contradiction would place him in the camp of sexist pig and Martin was neither unreconstructed straight man, nor woman-loathing old queen. At least that was how he and Josh intended to live their lives, in left-leaning, wide awake awareness of every minority and majority group on the little patch of earth they called home. That corner of Islington that is forever liberal.

Josh replayed the picture of Martin offering him a chance to explore, replayed it for at least two minutes until the guilt became too much and he returned to his favoured fantasy – himself and Cushla. Josh and Cushla loving, Josh and Cushla fucking, everywhere Josh and Cushla. And everywhere Josh returning home to Martin. Josh wants it all. Does not picture future life without Martin nor present life without Cushla. For one renowned for his cleverness, Josh is suddenly startlingly lacking in imagination.

Josh leaving home without Martin. Holding tight to his pre-packed bag and his self-righteousness, he flings himself from the front door to the main road to a cab. The night is even damper now and the cab takes him to a B&B in Victoria. Not a country cottage to get away from it all, not even a couple of nights in Paris, the incongruously space-sharing dead souls of Père Lachaise to comfort him, Josh contents himself with three nights and two days on the third floor of a two star B&B. Part pause, part penance, he sleeps through the day and cannot eat the grease-cooked breakfast and his waking dreams are peopled by his lover. His lovers.

On Thursday morning Josh arrives at Sunita's house. He rings the nine o'clock doorbell and she stumbles downstairs in tartan satin pyjamas and hangover, hoping for a pretty postman-delivered parcel to placate her early morning fury. She is just about to launch into an attack on Josh when she sees his suitcase. The unexpected sight of Josh all alone wipes the crusted sleep from her eyes and gives her wild hope.

'Trouble in paradise? Then come in my darling, come in.'

Josh follows downstairs to Sunita's kitchen. Spanish slate and British beech and Swedish birch bought with one of her three years in a soap opera. Sunita played a drug addict and emotional cripple. The soap opera earned vital brownie points for using an Asian actress, Sunita got her kitchen, an amazing bathroom, paid off a large chuck of the mortgage and developed a coke habit that occasional appearances on quiz shows and Radio 4 can't quite keep up with. She was already an emotional cripple.

Josh drinks two glasses of cranberry juice, eats a third of an almond croissant and picks at a thin strip of smoked salmon. He tells Sunita a version of the truth. Sunita drinks a glass of cranberry juice, four black coffees, eats two croissants and a fat fistful of smoked salmon. Then she finishes up with a bowl of dry crunchy nut cornflakes when she discovers the milk is off. She tells Josh a version of her opinion. What Sunita would love to be able to say is – 'Brilliant! Another one bites the dust! Yay for couples falling apart! Now you get to know what it's like for the rest of us, in the real world outside your smug little couple cocoon! Ha ha, fuck you, absolutely bloody brilliant!'

What she does say is, 'Shit!' and 'Bloody hell!' and 'Christ!'

When Josh has told as much as he intends to of how it started and how long it's been going, Sunita opens a bottle of whisky to disguise the lack of milk in Josh's coffee and asks the relevant questions.

'So what are you going to do?'

'I don't know.'

'Have you told her you've left him?'

'I haven't left him. I haven't told her.'

'What are you thinking?'

'I'm not thinking at all. I'm feeling.'

'Do you love her?'

'Yes.'

'And Martin?'

'Oh yes.'

'But God, I mean, he introduced you to her!'

What Sunita fails to acknowledge is that she was also introduced to Josh by Martin. That as someone who came to the couple in Martin's friendship dowry, she might have been expected to have a little more loyalty to him than to be enjoying this scene quite so much.

Expectations however, are wont to wilt when the glories of good gossip rain down upon them.

Sunita is entranced by the story. She wants to ring their mutual friends, tell her scoop to the wide eyed world. Josh has a girlfriend. Josh shakes his head, he does not have a girlfriend, he has a lover and he has a partner. One of them matters much more than the other. But Josh is having a hard time prioritizing right now and he's just not sure which is which. They move upstairs to the sitting room, taking the whisky with them. The sun swings into the room, Sunita lowers the calico blinds and in alcohol warmth they continue to chew it over. Where and what and how and, Sunita gets the information at last, how often. And how good. How very fucking good. Eventually the whisky makes its presence known and Josh finally tells Sunita what he knows of the truth. He is not certain of the whole truth, has not really made the effort to question himself too closely on what he thinks, just in case the answer scares him too much. He loves Cushla and he wants Cushla and he knows he loves and wants Martin too, but one of them does seem to matter a lot more than the other right now and the one the light of lust is falling on is Cushla. Sunita too speaks her truth. She didn't trust Cushla from the moment she met her. She knew Cushla was bad news. But, that said (she really has to be honest here, she's just slipped upstairs for a couple of lines) she's glad Josh is going through this. Glad Martin is too. Not only her, but all their single friends feel the same. Didn't they know?

'Sure everybody loves you guys, but Christ, all this happy beautiful couple shit? You're just too bloody smug for your own good. Perhaps this will wake you up a bit.'

Josh nods as if her bitterness is fair and just. They are both safe, even while drunk, they know the alcohol-induced honesty will be obliterated by midday hangovers when they wake.

Josh and Sunita fall asleep on the couch, a miserly fifth of whisky left in the bottle beside them. Three hours later they are roused by the ring of the doorbell. Two rings. Sunita staggers into the hall, opens the front door and turns back almost immediately, hand clasped over her dry mouth, running to throw up in the downstairs toilet. Smoked salmon and crunchy nut cornflakes are not the perfect accompaniment to a good single malt. Josh hears her stumbling footsteps, the voices in the hall and raises himself on one numb arm in time to see two figures poke their heads round the door. He blinks rapidly hoping to bring his cross-eyes into focus, dispel the double vision. He looks up again. The double vision is still there. Martin smiles at him in love and concern. As does Cushla.

Twenty-nine

Martin smiles at Josh, 'This is your idea of a break?'

Josh doesn't have words, not yet. His tongue is glued to the roof of his mouth, his stomach churning, he looks from Martin to Cushla, bleary eyes taking in his two lovers standing over him in interest and concern.

Cushla stands a little back from Martin. She doesn't speak. Martin can't shut up. 'I've been worried sick Josh. I tried all the usual places. Couple of the hotels we've been to together – that place in Suffolk you always said you wanted to go back to. I rang all our friends, no one had heard from you. Then I waited in all day yesterday. All day. Cancelled my meetings, the lot. Nothing. By seven o'clock last night, I was starting to get seriously worried. Finally I figured if the mountain wasn't coming home to Mohammed, then I'd better try climbing to the base camp myself.'

Josh's head is cracking open, his fat and terrified heart pounding his ribs to dust, 'What?'

'Well, I knew you'd been spending a bit of time with Cushla—'

Josh thinks he must surely faint now, or die, but his inconsiderately healthy constitution bears him up and through the shock wave into the next round of fear.

Martin appears not to notice, he prattles on, 'I went up to your studio – brilliant head by the way,' he adds, turning to smile at Cushla, to compliment her on her fine cheekbones, her perfectly proportioned jaw.

'And I guessed that maybe you were with her.'

At the possibility of a confrontation with the truth, Josh miraculously regains the power of speech, 'No, here. B&B and here. With Sunita. You know, drinking. Here. Not with her.'

Martin sits beside him, 'So I see. Actually, it was Cushla who suggested we try Sunita's place.' He lowers his voice to a conspiratorial whisper and leans in closer, 'Frankly darling, Sunita's the last person I'd come to for tea and sympathy.'

Cushla sits on Josh's left side, lays a cool hand on his clenched sweaty paw, 'I called you at home but you weren't there. I told Martin I hadn't seen you for three days either. Did you forget we were supposed to meet yesterday afternoon?'

Josh had forgotten. Paranoid mind skipping appointments, he'd missed a liaison planned four days in advance. Josh turns his head, hoping to see understanding in Cushla's eyes, expecting sympathy and an eye-widening glance of silent conspiracy. What he gets is harsh, cold and someone else. Blank shutters down and welded into place. This is not his Cushla. One quick look and Josh knows this woman does not love him. Now Josh is very scared indeed. Martin has his arm around Josh, is holding him tight from the other side, wittering on with I'm sorry and it's all my fault and of course you need time out, you've been working so hard. Followed by a loving *maxima culpa* of triple I understand.

Josh cannot hear Martin clearly because the pressure of blood beating against his eardrums is deafening him, because the pressure of Cushla's cold presence beside him is freezing his senses. Josh thinks this might be a perfect moment for his life to end. It doesn't.

Sunita bounces back into the room, bottle of champagne in one hand, four glasses precariously bunched in the other. She smiles at Martin, glares at Cushla and grins at Josh, 'Fancy a drink anyone? The sun's well over the yard arm now. As they say in old Islamabad.'

Josh extricates himself from Martin's grasp, stands, stumbles forward and throws up all over Sunita's coffee table collection – twenty-three pristine 1960's editions of *Vogue*.

Perhaps the smoked salmon was off.

It is all cleaned up, tidied away. The headache removed with the cleaned away vomit and the tension dissipates. The two men and two women sit in the winter sunlight room, pale light enhanced by the golden yellow of the walls and they chat. Sunita and Cushla prattle about shopping and men, music and good bars – girl talk, the kind of frippery Josh could never have imagined his very own Cushla could enjoy, and yet here she sits, gushing over Sunita's new Nicole Farhi as if a caramel-toned trouser suit was the most important thing in the room. As if Josh's soul wasn't free floating above them, waiting to soar or dive at a single word from her perfect lips. But she does not look at Josh and she does not talk to Josh and Josh could die from waiting. The men share more of the champagne. Martin keeps up his bright façade, they will stay for an hour and then go home. Josh would leave now but his legs have forgotten how to move. Forgotten how to move him away from Cushla. Martin would leave now but he is too polite to just arrive, pick up his baby and leave. Sunita is not a child minder after all. Sunita would leave, but it's her house. She desperately wants to crawl into bed and sleep off her hangover, wake up out of the fuzziness into a clarity that will allow her to order her thoughts properly before she makes the first of her tell-all phone calls. However, even with her alcohol blunted senses, Sunita guesses there's more to come. And Cushla would leave, will leave soon, but not just yet. Right now things are just getting good.

Afterwards Josh is not sure how he came to speak. Sunita maintains Cushla prompted it, by a look or a smile or a gesture. Neither Josh nor Martin can remember, want to remember – like the details of a road accident or childhood trauma, their brains block the reality rush from their present-minded recollection, substituting numbness where pure remembrance would force agony. Cushla however, carries the conversation with her, tattooed verbatim around the scar lines that criss cross her heart space. Cushla has never been one to forget the punchline of a good joke.

First she looked at Josh. Took in his matching glance, understood the terror in his heart. Josh caught her look, the first full look she had allowed him all afternoon and in the light of their gaze the room finally went silent. Sunita let the fêted trouser suit flutter to the floor, Martin's fragile hope of peace fell with it. Cushla's eyes smiled, then her mouth laughed, then her whole body doubled over with glee at the prospect of the inevitable. Almost her whole body – a tiny moan from the heart cavity did not join in the joy. For a semi-second Cushla wondered if maybe she should just get up and leave. In the middle of a heave of laughter she caught herself questioning her actions, the beginnings of an intimation of pity for Josh. A fine silver thread of compassion which almost stilled her. Until she ripped it away with her bared teeth.

Her laughter set Josh free, he opened his mouth and the truth just fell from his lips, 'Martin, I've been seeing Cushla. I'm in love with Cushla. I'm sorry.'

Sunita winced as her coffee table was hit again. This time with the force of Martin's right leg, pushing himself up and off the sofa, as far away from Josh as possible, to the window at the other end of the room. Martin stared out into the garden as if it might hold an answer, watched as a blackbird wrenched two worms from the grass and then flew back to its nest, one eaten whole, one impaled on his beak. Martin waited. He did not know what he was going to do. Uncertain of the impact of his words, Josh tried again. He'd got out the 'I'm' section of the excessively inept 'I'm sorry' when Martin sprang back at him, bitter boy instinct direct-ing his anger, the coffee table cringing in his wake. In the time it took Sunita to remove the trouser suit to relative safety behind her chair, Martin had picked Josh up by the scruff of the neck and was holding him with his left hand while pummelling him with his right. Sunita turned in time to see Josh hold up a barely protective hand as Martin smacked a right hook into his lower left chest. Cracking a rib just below his heart.

Sunita screamed, 'No! Jesus! Martin! Fuck!'

Shock and dismay reducing her sentences to standard single word exclamations of horror. Then she turned to Cushla, 'Fuck! Do something! Make him stop! Do some-thing!'

Cushla sat still, watching the two men in fascination. Martin beating up on the man he loved and Josh taking it. Taking it because he believed it was Martin's right, taking it because he knew he had done wrong, taking it because he didn't know how else to atone. Or even if he wanted to. The lack of retaliation however, worried Cushla. She knew there was a chance, if Josh was lifeless enough, that Martin's outburst would bring them back to an even keel – wicked betrayal and physical violence weighing each other out on the delicate balance of who'd done what and who was most to blame. She decided it was time to intervene. Pushing Sunita aside, whose ineffectual 'Stop it' and tugging on Martin's jacket had done nothing other than infuriate him more, Cushla calmly rose from her chair and, in a movement that was spontaneous and yet looked as if it had been practised for years, neatly placed herself directly in front of Josh. Cushla's early prediction had been right. Now Josh's body was smaller than hers, in his disorientation he had shrunk to fit her. She placed herself over him, hid him from Martin and offered herself as protector and victim.

In a crystal clear whisper she cut through Martin's sweat and rage, 'Try me. I'm stronger. I can take it.'

And she did, Martin took a step back, all his good boy nature railing against his wounded pride as his hand flew clear of his convictions and he smacked his fist into her face. Cushla smiled. She wasn't even bruised. But Josh was. The physical blows were painful but, while he'd felt he was receiving just punishment, he could handle it. But the pain that came to him when Martin hit Cushla was magnified. She acted as a Newton's Cradle for the punch, soaking up the physical blow, but letting the anger and hurt and betrayal charge straight through her own body and smack into Josh. Then she blew a kiss to Martin as he stormed out of the house and another to Josh when he left to go home and pack. This time for good. She didn't need to tell Josh he wouldn't see her again, the last pummelling had ripped Josh apart from his past. He knew he was moored to no one now.

When Josh leaves his home late that night, he takes three suitcases and a plastic bag full of stone chips and dust, what is left of Cushla's carved head after Martin has finished with it. The two men do not kiss goodbye.

Cushla and Sunita drink two more bottles of champagne and Cushla stays the night in Sunita's bed. The sex isn't great, despite all her girl practice Sunita is mostly straight, but it does give Cushla a warm bed for a few hours. Despite her best intentions she feels a whisper of regret for Josh and Martin, a night alone in the cold tower is not as appealing as it had once seemed. The women drink, they fuck, they drink more, Sunita smokes a thin joint and night falls.

Cushla's eyes fly open, forced suddenly awake at three in the morning. She does not know what has happened to rouse her and she lays still in the dark, Sunita's sleeping form curled beside her, scent of whisky and tired sex surrounding them both. She waits. Nothing. The house is silent. When she closes her eyes and turns her head into the pillow, Cushla's cheek falls against something cool and wet. She has been woken by her own tears. And the re-grown baby heart sings her back to sleep.

Thirty

The heart is a waltz. It skips and climbs. It dances alone though no one sees. It does not need light or air or fire, just water from tears or drunk desire. The heart finds its home, bidden or not.

Cushla doesn't understand the pattern that is beginning to gel around her, in the daze of her new state, intellectual translation becomes impossible. She leaves Sunita with a quick kiss, no exchange of interest, no desire on the part of either party to repeat the ordinary experience of a drunken shag, and then spends her afternoon in desultory hatching and planning. Finally giving up on reason as a means to comprehension, she turns to physical exercise for clarity, or at least new hope. Cushla is suffering the breakup of a potential relationship. She just doesn't know that this is what she's doing.

She makes the pilgrimage to swim her usual night swim but even the occasional moonlight on the pool is not a comfort, bouncing silent echoes from empty walls. She ought to be feeling good now, proud of her efforts, of the accomplished work that was the dissolution of Martin and Josh.

Now is the time to enjoy the remaking of her body into her own self, the recovery of her firm natural flesh. Now is the moment of celebration. Joy however, appears to have escaped Cushla's swim.

She pictures Josh's face as he left Sunita's house, but revising the teary physiognomy she finds nothing to please her. Cushla turns tail down, into the fifty-third length, arms stretching forward into the dark silvered water, cupped hands reaching for an answer. Empty liquid filters through her fingers, she receives no reply but a chlorinated band aid and the leftover hairs of Mrs Johnson who, at eighty-seven and counting, still swims every morning in the early bird session. Even swerving and beating the infra-red light rays gives Cushla no satisfaction and she stops fast on her return to the deep end. At length the ripples retreat and she is left, a silent point in a still pool. There is a thin layer of mist rising from the warmed water against the night-cooled air. The caretaker leaves the water heating on, to re-heat daily would be just too expensive, but the actual building heating is turned off at night. Perfect pneumatic, Cushla floats on top of the water, the back of her body cradled in comparative warmth, the exposed skin on her front puckering with chill.

She slowly exhales the air she holds and begins to fall beneath the water. Sinking steadily down, head heavier than the rest of her body, her light feet waver a metre above her. When her shoulders reach the bottom of the pool she forces her legs to unwilling parallel. She lies on the concrete floor, relaxes her muscles into the harsh surface and looks up through the water. The pool is illuminated with only green exit signs and red burglar alarms, the night is overcast and now there is a just clouded moon to glow through the windows. Ten feet under water Cushla's perfect eyes give her a round lens of vision into the murky twilight above. Here she is content. Here she is calm. She would stay on the bottom of the pool forever if she could. If she didn't know that forever ends at midnight, just before tomorrow is postponed for another day. She could stay here and float into morning and be at peace. She would forget her plan, will leave behind the mission of three she has mapped out for herself.

She would do all this, might do all this, but suddenly, two and a half minutes under, there is an urgent beating, a rapping, a knocking. The sound is deadened by the weight of water and Cushla does not hear it at first. Eventually though, the noise becomes so insistent unrelenting, that she sits up and takes notice. Sits up, swims up, breaks the surface of the pool in a suffocating crash for air. Cushla is gasping for breath. This is new. As is the heart thumping in her breast, the heart clamouring for freshly oxygenated blood. The heart that won't let her be. Cushla is not a happy little Princess.

She hauls herself from the water, drags stubborn clothes on to her wet flesh, slams her betraying body out into the street and walks home to her tower, a cold and bedraggled urchin. She runs up to the fourteenth floor, heart again pounding by the time she reaches the tenth level, she damns it, not listening and presses on, losing no time until near collapse at her door. This time there is no desire for ceremony. Cushla runs into the flat, ripping wet clothes off as she goes, grabs her knife, slices clean through the nearly healed stitches, rips back the folds of fresh knitted flesh and stares into the bathroom mirror at her heart space. She should not have looked. The heart beating in her breast is tiny but so very perfectly formed. It dances in three time, a minuscule translucent drum, beating for its life. It hasn't got a chance, Cushla has no choice, she has already staked out the next couple. The plan will be followed.

Cushla takes her knife to the heart and this time the severing of the tensile veins is hot, searing pain. She listens to the pleading and her eardrums beat in time with the heart, shattering tiny blood vessels in an attempt to be heard. She slices through the tissue securing the little organ in place, her shaking hand stabbing at her own flesh, each incision a paper cut deep and Pacific Ocean wide. Cushla wants to scream, fumbling hand in her own blood, she wants to laugh as right hand encompasses her flesh and she tosses the still beating heart out into the night. A passing screech owl opens his beak mid-flight and catches the heart, takes it home to the family, nurtures it among his screaming chicks. The cuckoo heart grows strong and fat, but when the time comes for it to leave the nest the mother owl throws it to the ground with her other babies. The chicks fly safe into the dark but the heart's last beat is dead fat splat on a concrete path. In the morning it is swept up by the park cleaners, someone else's under-cooked kebab gone to waste again.

The heart gone, Cushla reworks the catgut stitches, the seam a little less perfect this time, each stab of the needle into already ripped flesh pointed memory of her own failure. She cleans herself up, washes the polished wood floor and lays out the clothes she will need in the morning. She will take her new form soon and needs sleep to prepare. Cushla tries the bed, but dreams will not come easy and she wakes herself several times, screaming loud cries to no one in particular. Morning dawns cold with sleet turning to rain and even the TV weather girl looks depressed. Cushla is exhausted.

On the other side of the city, her baby brother sharpens his knife.

Thirty-one

At the age of seven His Imperial Highness, the Little Prince of
the Land ever so distant and actually sort of just round the
corner from here, went hunting for the very first time in his
life. The morning of his seventh birthday dawned fine and
cold and clear. Ideal weather for a ceremonial killing. He rode
out through the Palace gates on his happy birthday present, a
massive Arab stallion, many times his own size and perfect for
the boy who would be Prince. He was followed, as directed
by tradition, at a little distance by his mother, herself a fine
horsewoman who had killed four stags on her own seventh
birthday. Little David sang the song of blood and the merry
coupling of regal mother and son was greeted with garlands of
twined thyme and crocus as they made their way through the
city, past the areas of poverty and wealth where the rich threw
handfuls of coins to the poor and the poor were eternally
deserving and intermittently grateful, over the river of constant return and out to the dark forest beyond. Back home at
the Palace, the King was stockpiling ready-spread loaves of
bread and honey and the Princess was packing her bag.

They made camp at lunchtime and David, fine and thin even then, ate the egg and cress sandwiches provided by his father and shared a bottle of deep red burgundy with his mother. Then, while she sang lullabies and hunting songs, Prince David slept, his head on the Queen's lap, his young boy's body covered over with a shawl of hand-dyed Persian silk and a plaited fringe of finest man-made rayon. The boy slept sound without dreams and when the moment had come, his mother woke him. There was one hour until sundown, time enough to spot the prey, mark the plan and then begin the long wait until last star. Leaving their bags behind them, David followed his mother through dense undergrowth, his small form passing with ease through close trees and tall grasses. After a thirty minute walk, culminating in another ten minutes slithering through damp bracken on their bellies, the mother pulled her son up close beside her. They lay low to the ground and listened. The sound of deer was close. David lifted his nose to the wind and sniffed the scent of easy meat. The smell was strong in his head, his tastebuds leapt to the challenge. He was ready.

The Queen waited until her son had spied the animals' clearing himself, then kissed him and handed him the knife that was to become his own. Its blade was sharp and well turned, the bone handle carved in his final hour from the living thighbone of her own father, the late King. David took the knife with reverence and fierce excitement. His mother admonished him one last time to take care to wait until the last star, then kissed his boyish locks and left, as silent as she came. She returned to their little campsite, cleared the debris of her son's lunch, left him a flask of hot chocolate and two gingernut biscuits for a dawn snack and returned home. She and her husband feasted that night on brown rice and lentils, in preparation for the venison that

150

would be theirs for many nights to come. Though His Majesty did add a dessert of rye bread and heather honey. Neither noticed initially that their daughter was missing from the table and when the Princess' absence was noted, it was simply put down to a girlish fad.

As the Queen remarked to the King, 'It's her diet, I expect my dear. You know how teenage girls are, it takes an adult palate to fully appreciate the joy of pulses.'

His Majesty nodded gravely, his mind clearly turned to more weighty matters such as the fine stock of clover honey he had collected that afternoon.

David's thin young neck was aching. He had spent the past seven hours turning his head back and forth. From a close study of the quiet deer to a look at the far sky. Confirming the position of the animals he would kill, then checking that another star had arrived, and another. Well schooled in both astronomy and astrology, he knew not only to wait for the last star – and exactly where it would appear – but also in which astrological house it was appearing and what it meant to him. Tonight was an auspicious night for new beginnings. The Princess knew this too and she squeezed her makeup bag into the side of her suitcase. Eventually the last star came, as the Prince had known it would, as the star itself knew it would, perfect arrival, perfectly three minutes late.

Just as David could smell the deer, so too could they scent his presence, but after so many hours beside them, they had decided he was no longer a threat and passed their night in quiet contemplation of the rich wet grasses at their feet. He began to move closer, inching himself forward in painfully slow travel. David held the knife in his left hand, leaning on his right hand and his left forearm to pull himself on, conscious only of keeping the blade pristine sharp and of staying silent himself. He was ten feet from the oldest stag. In the brilliant light of the last star, just forty minutes before dawn, the stag's antlers loomed high above both boy and the animal, they stretched up past the tree tops and out into the night, each point of the antlers more finely honed and keener than anything the child had to offer. Two feet closer, three, four. The stag lifted its head, disturbing a doe to its left. The Prince held his breath and willed his molecules to stasis. There was silence and still the smell of the wine-breath child. Nothing had changed. The doe returned to her dreams and the stag ripped another mouthful of grass from the ground. It was time.

David threw himself off the ground and up to his full height. His full height being the heart level of the stag. The human and animal eyes met just once, then the knife plunged deep through fur and hide, tissue and sinew, and found its target immediately. The stag let out a surprised hiss of last breath and fell crashing down, coming to rest at the Prince's feet and impaling two kids on his own antlers as he did so. The boy then twisted in mid backwards jump, the bloodied knife leading his way, pulling him along behind it. Before he had a chance to do any more than register his next action, the knife was slicing the throat of the first doe, puncturing both lungs of the young stag and carving clean through the neck of another hind. A doe, a young buck and their two babies fled into the darker forest and imminent morning. In the silence the Prince stood, six dead at his feet, four by his own hand.

The sun began to trickle from the shadows around the eastern trees, and with cold light bathing him, he carefully removed the heart from each carcass. The two kids impaled by their own sire were not strictly his kill, but as they happened in the action of the hunt, he could name them part spoil. The child would not lie. There was no point. Each carcass would be dragged back through the querent city and up to the feasting hall, where groundswomen and poachers alike would gather to analyse the slaughter and write the song of the boy's prowess.

David put aside the hallowed knife, and he held each of the six hearts, cradling them to his own and whispering the prayer of sacred forgiveness. His seven-year-old body now held a man's conscience. He would do his duty and demand blessing for the task. He lay the hearts in a wooden box of proof and began his return journey. The box was heavy for his young arms and by the time he had reached the Palace gates there were hundreds of spectators, all following every tired step, willing the manchild to continue in safety, to arrive in the Great Hall with the hearts intact. He did, collapsing at his mother's feet with just enough grace to allow her to take the box from him.

A physician was called, the hearts were examined and found sound. Twelve virgins were sent into the forest to retrieve the carcasses which were then dragged up to the Palace and into the cutting yard. The hearts were matched with the victims. The child was stripped of his filthy clothes, his father rinsed away the animal blood with running river water and his mother gave him the hearts one by one. Each heart was replaced by the Prince's own hand into the cavity from which it had been cut. Each fit perfectly. When the six hearts were in place and the poachers and groundswomen had already begun composing the song of praise, the Chief Physician called for silence. When quiet came he held the knife low above the dead animal heads. He spoke the word of rebirth, whispered again by all present and finally, shouted by the child. At the same moment all six hearts began to beat again, the wounds healed, the old stag rose first, dazed and uncertain until he understood the gravity of his surroundings, then he woke his kin and they walked to David. All six knelt before the boy and the Prince was deemed truly to have come of age.

Then there was singing and dancing and fireworks and celebration. The two kids killed by the stag's antlers were returned to the forest and the four killed directly by the young Prince were led away to the kitchen courtyard where they were thankful to be butchered and honoured to provide the royal repast.

There followed the traditional eight days of feasting and laughter and venison steaks and venison pie and cold roast venison sandwiches and finally, when the townspeople had almost had enough, venison rissoles to finish.

The Princess was glad she hadn't stayed, she had been contemplating becoming a vegetarian for some time. And though the little Prince felt that something or someone was missing from the festivities, with his new hunting knife to keep him company, he didn't really have time to give it much thought.

Thirty-two

I rise long after first sun and still take more than an hour to wake. When I finally come to my senses from a hot bed of cold dreams, the morning light has left the city and a virulent rain hurls itself against the windows seeking cracks and crevices to crawl through and damage me. I am particularly tender. But now is not the time to be careful. I have slept badly, am not really rested enough for this next onslaught. Time passes without my noticing it, I am almost late.

The next move. In the mirror I examine the state I am in. I am stateless, I am a long time from home. My messy scar blooms against the puckered skin around it, dried blood covers the pointless stitches. I prowl my tower, occasionally remembering to eat, to drink. The old bread is stale and the water brackish. The rations here are poor, I should let down my long brunette locks and pull in a basket of fresh provisions from the street below. I should feast on pigs' feet and mead and fresh figs. I should live in the real world. Eventually I notice I am freezing and remember to pull on a thick towelling gown, the fabric-conditioner-softened material rips against my over-sensitive epidermis. I am thinner than raw. The heating is on full, I have closed the curtains against the elements, but a chill crept into my spine during the night, invading my central nervous system and sending shivers along my tired limbs. I had not planned on this, could not have planned for this. The new growth is not of my doing but it is of me. It is of him.

I think of him, wonder what he is doing now. I miss him. Part of me misses him. It won't last long.

I wash in the mirror-tiled bathroom, my back reflected into endless dim light corridors, hands scrubbing away dead skin cells, scouring myself in an attempt to exfoliate the left-over print of his touch on my skin. I stay under the burning water for forty-nine minutes. I am trying for a mysticism of cleanliness. I scrub with soapstone. Eventually my efforts break through and sticky scabs begin to fall from my fast healing skin. My slow healing heartspace. Dead cells and old hair clog the plughole. I wash the dead me away, cold rinse that man from out of my flesh. When I am finally cleansed, I change my sweated sheets and tidy the crucible tower, scour the floor again for any drops of blood I may have missed last night. The tower is ready now. I am as ready as can be expected. The work can be done.

I light the candles – safe night lights for my ancestors, for the past, for the future, a last flickering memorial light for the present me. When this has burnt out, I will be new. I remove the towelling gown and lie naked on the floor. I am cold. I miss his other-body warmth. I miss his lips. I have studied and made my decision on the new fashion, the next me. I am giving up on this one, it has not been as successful as I might have hoped. I was to have played the teenage temptress, instead this tiny beating part of me has become foolish woman. I am more like this world than could have been expected.

I lie on my wooden floor and close my eyes. I lay myself against the grain and begin to sink down into it. This is a conscious choice. I am making this happen. My muscles leap on the permission to relax and, giving themselves over to the time, they lose sense memory of both distant and, more importantly, recent past, musculature becomes one with the flesh swimming against the wood. I uncurl each taut limb and drip mellow slow down to the hard floor half inches and fathoms below. At a single point it will be ready, the body will know. Corporeal self has full knowledge of the mission that was ingrained in the genetics that made me. I am intended to be Queen. I will follow the path. I am following, falling, giving this up, giving him up, there is no choice and all choice. I am there now, it begins. From the cross grain, working in their own unmetered rhythm, splinters of wood reach out and stretch themselves, barbed splinters twisting into me. Like thick darning needles a tight seam of living matter weaves itself through my skin. Each plank of floorboard remembers when it was living tree, recalls roots stretching deep into soft earth, branches extending far into wet sky. This floor thinks I am real world made again just so it can live in me. My scalp is gripped by a thousand tiny needles, pulling and kneading. The length and breadth of my form, every single pressure point is activated in shock and torment. I succumb. This body yields its outer layer.

I hope this works.

I have never hurt this much before. In the past the revision has been a blissful surrender. Now I am crying out in agony. Screaming with a wide open mouth and no sound – I am a good neighbour. This is new and painful. However, it is as I expected, probably a fitting punishment. I have been stupid but I am not ignorant. I knew to expect distress. This flesh has been loved, warmed by desire, an original sensation. It does not want to let that feeling go. And I am learning another lesson, today was obviously intended for my personal development. I now know that expectation is not the same as experience. Pain is too short a word.

I continue. I am in charge, not this body. It will know that.

With pure force of wanting I lengthen the legs. The shin and thigh bones elongate to meet each other. New length shatters the patella and jams bone splinters through already stretched knee cartilage. Ripped cartilage springs back and twists into threadbare sinews. The expanding ankle bone smacks into myriad tiny foot bones reaching back to jump me from a size four and a half to six. I hold my twisted hands in front of my face to see the fingers pushed apart as their bones grow, knuckles crack of their own accord, skin stretches and splits to reach over the growing bones. Yellow grease seeps through the cracked epidermis, though that she was sweetly rounded and not overweight, the new me will be tall and very thin, I have no need of any body fat. The old hair has been wrenched away, pulled strand by pin prick strand from all of my body. New needle marks begin to appear from inside my skin, minuscule pore points all over the flesh spit out first blood and then a sharp shaft of hair, long straight blonde hair. Only slightly bloodied, I will wash later. My mouth is moving. Tongue swells, fills the gap between breath and delirium, passing through bloat to rip away the roof of my mouth. It sinks into new shape a short second before I asphyxiate. Teeth tear themselves from my gums, spitting away into corners of the room and are replaced by a new set, regular, perfect, large – I have the teeth and gums of a new Californian – and knowing why does not lessen the pain. Tell that to your seven month old. The new molars are ripped out in a last bloody rush, Gloria Swanson mouth, Joan Crawford cheekbones. Finally the spine. Each vertebrae separates at least an inch, I am racked by my own intent, now the screams are real and I cannot hold them in, not even for the peace of Mrs Mulligan's Tower Residents' Association. The tight knots of twisted spine are far spread, wide eyed, then snap back into perfect new alignment and almost ready for use. Central nervous system over-reaches itself to equate the long limbs, the stronger organs, thin skin covered. I am bloody and finished. The tight fastened wood pins retract, I am released.

An hour later I have the strength to stagger to my bed. The clean and cold sheets sweet welcome this new body, skin cracked all over, new limbs begging to rest, blood and juices still seeping. I wind the thin silk sheet into a cocoon, cover torso, arms, legs, feet and finally head. I close my new blue eyes and sleep.

Ten days later I wake. Even from my cocoon I know I am done. I rise and stare at this me in the mirror. I smile back at the woman before me. Good work. Ten days' sleep have left me thinner even than anticipated, the long arms and legs are spiderwoman slim. I appear fragile but find that I bend with huge strength. I am coated all over in thin pale gold down, this will wash off leaving me pure natural blonde – Viking warrior chick. My mouth is wide and full, cheekbones razor sharp, eyes piercing desert-sky blue. It has snowed in my sleep and London is pure and blessed. It pours back reflected white energy at me. I am calm, full and eager. I bathe again, a last baptism for the new flesh. The skin I ladle water over is naturally tanning, double cream turning to glossed amber and polished smooth with ten days and nights worming in silk. I am delighted at the touch of myself. There are no scars. The candles have burnt out days ago. The room is silent and cold. This body is silent and ready. I study myself in the long mirror.

I am fucking gorgeous. And I'm up for it.

Thirty-three

I've had my fill of men for the moment. I think I'll have a girl for a change.

The thin new Cushla lies in the sunshine, a warm cat smiling, glossy coat central heated. The bed beneath her is firm, almost hard. She lies full length, arms at her sides, stretched out in the sweet light that pours through the double-glazed, solar-enhanced, energy-conserving windows. A wind chime swings quietly in the distance. The room is thick white emulsion, buttermilk gloss and warm old oak. Pulled back from the window is a single, full length, cotton drape. She waits. Her eyes are closed.

A woman comes back into the room. She looks at Cushla, her glance is purely professional. So far. She does not speak. There is no need, they have completed the verbal part of today's transaction. The woman covers Cushla's naked torso and legs with thick, dark green towels and begins. Her practised hands pull the skein of blonde hair back from Cushla's neck, revealing a fine, thin collar, narrow shoulders with bony protrusions lifting through the tanned skin. Having

161

cleared the area, she slips scented oil on to her palms and begins to touch. For an hour and a half she moulds Cushla's new body, twisting and turning muscles against and into themselves, reworking the newly formed. She deep-tissue massages body parts that only last week were knitting themselves together, she smooths over already perfect skin. The woman is pleasantly surprised. She is astonished. She has never worked on a body like this before. Not an adult body. She is a mother and massaged her young son every night for the first eighteen months of his life. Then his body was as free as this. But at eight years old he already has the small injuries and early damage that mark him alive. She would work on his body nightly now if he would let her, but at this age his mother's touch is an intrusion, her gentle fingers an unwelcome incursion into the only land an eight year old can call his own, his body.

The woman lying in the winter sun beneath her hands does not speak or sleep, does not cry out in deep tissue massage pain nor groan in relief and release. She simply lies there, moving when requested, lifting this limb or that, turning to her left or right. Her back is as perfect as her front, each side in flawless mirrored alignment. Her pelvic tilt is a soft and easy swing, her spine a miracle of regulation twenty-four strong yet flexible vertebrae. Through skull, thorax, spine, pelvis and limbs each individual function is not only correct but textbook ideal. And she is beautiful too.

Frances Hunt fell in love with the only adult body she had ever seen with perfect structural integrity. And though she tried, and though she fought it and though all her sanity warned her not to, some time later she fell in love with Cushla.

Frances is a healer. Her hands are drawn to life as other people's eyes covet rich chocolate or jewels. This afternoon the woman gently yielding beneath her touch has presented her with the usual tale – backache, headache, stiffness, tender joints. Frances took the details, listened to the traditional list and shut off. She was busy this week, she would expect several old clients over the next two days, people who really had need of her, people for whom a healing massage was not merely pleasant but honestly therapeutic. People who were actually suffering and to whom she could give relief. Frances valued these customers enough to give them a good discount on continued treatment and make up the bulk of her money in the frequent one-off jobs. So she took the tall blonde woman's history and noted the trivial complaints and then asked her to undress.

As usual Frances busied herself with paperwork and folding towels until the client was semi-naked and stretched out on the hard massage bed. Not for her own needs, her paperwork was always perfectly in order, her towels returned fluffed and ready-folded three times a week from the laundry. The pretence of busyness is to reassure the client in the transition step from dressed to vulnerable. Make nothing of it, carry on, do not hide behind a screen or a desk, then the client can also relax into professional mode and will not have to fumble with shoes or shirt, stutter over outer and undergarments. The client can relax in the safe knowledge that Frances Hunt BSc, Dip. Op. Thal., BTC is asking them to remove their clothes purely for the purpose of professional practice. Which she is. She does. She did until today.

But the moment her hands touch Cushla's body they register immediate surprise. The woman had not looked so very special dressed. Tall, thin to the point of matchstick model emaciation, casually dressed with no makeup and her long straight hair falling free. Frances looks at between twenty and thirty different bodies a week, clothed they usually present some definition of what they might look like naked. They are stooped or fat or skinny or bald or tired or round, each one adjusting their dress to compensate for the supposed fault of imperfect musculo-skelature. Most people are far less attractive naked. Not this woman.

Frances runs her hands lightly either side of the spinal column. Her eyes are closed. Frances does not look with her eyes. The heat from her own hands increases. Usually she gives her energy over to the client, uses methods ancient and new to transform them if only for an hour or a day, becoming colder herself as the client warms and begins to heal under her touch. Sometimes it is traditional osteopathy, sometimes acupressure, sometimes it is psychic healing masquerading as massage. Whatever the method, every body she touches soaks up her own energy. Every fresh tired lump of flesh beneath her fingers drains her anew, sucking from her own vitality to replace its dwindling health stocks. Not this woman. This woman has vast energy. Huge reserves of it waiting to be touched and opened and poured. This woman has more power than Frances herself. She opens her eyes and looks down. Her fingers are red, her palms glowing. The woman beneath her throbs with passion. And now Frances sees that she is beautiful.

She should move away. Offer another therapist, find a non-touch method of treatment. She should break the bond. But Frances' hands are hungry for this, they have so rarely been fed themselves, they sweep up and down the woman's spinal column almost touching the vertebrae, almost not. Frances' own body is singing with joy at what it is discovering, at the meeting of perfect molecules, the co-joining of forceful energies. Frances gives Cushla a full body massage for an hour and a half. When she is finished she has the energy of a Christmas-morning four year old and no possibility of tears before bedtime. Her face is glowing, her limbs tingling, her heart flying. She knows her heart should not fly like this, she has willingly given her heart over to another. But unlike Frances' wedding-ring finger, her heart is free.

And high above the building soars Prince David the Hunter, he swoops, looks down at the small cottage below and pinpoints those particular eighteenth-century bricks and mortar as the spot for the radiant energy that has woken his knife from its half-daze.

Perhaps Cushla feels the vibrations of her brother's flying body or perhaps she knows Frances will never be more ready to begin. She decides it is time. She turns, opens her eyes, quick focuses on the joyous face above her and smiles deep into Frances' pale blue eyes,

'That was fantastic. You're wonderful. Can I book my next appointment now?'

Frances cancels two hip joints, a late pregnancy and a recurrent sciatica to fit her in. One appointment a day for the whole of the next week.

There. That ought to do it.

Thirty-four

Prince David has been talking to Jonathan. This is tedious but necessary, and while he may take time to complete his mission, the royal blood lineage and blood imperative would never allow his Imperial Highness to completely shirk his filial duty. His mother's word will be complied with, if not totally obeyed. Armed with foreknowledge and genetic compliance, he possesses his own flesh felt picture of the shapeshifting sister, what he needs now is a fuller picture of her method. He understands the reasons and he understands the outcome. He wants to know how. He wants to be able to get in.

Jonathan has plenty to say about method. The two men sit in an early evening pub, Jonathan now spurns dark West End bars, they hold memory for him and he would rather not contemplate his past. Of course, he does not expect a seering inquisition from another drunk bloke at six thirty p.m. This pub is an ordinary West End pub, with regulation tourist-tempting Dickensian prints and a daring divergence from the norm in the dark green wallpaper. As opposed to dark red. The landlady has some taste. Or would if she weren't a conglomerate – as it is, the decor is decided by palate samples in boardrooms somewhere close to the other side of the M25, each group-owned pub picked out in distinctively identical colours and furnishings. This particular non-specific free house is frequented by ageing Antipodean tourists, regular lads on their way somewhere better and ordinary older men popping in for a few halves before catching the suburban train back home. Or not. These days, Jonathan is one of the older men.

David watches Jonathan through a solitary round, then the two men are united by an easy talk that stretches from Middlesbrough, through traditional ales and Robbo from the radio, all the way back to Everton. The Prince may not choose to use his sister's guile but he has plenty of her natural charm and within minutes or maybe hours the rather more drunken Jonathan is spewing up the story of his past passing.

'Bitch. Fucking bitch fucking took my life and screwed it all fucking up. Fuck. Bitch.'

Two pints and three whiskies down, Jonathan's lack of coherence is as much to do with the fury that fills his mouth as the alcohol swimming in his empty belly.

David probes a little less delicately now, 'Your wife?'

'Nah. Secretary.'

When Jonathan utters the four syllables, he gives it all the vehemence of an Anglo-Saxon word much shorter and coats it with the thick corrosive bile of a man scorned. David is getting into his task now, orders another round for the two of them, slow drinking his own warming lager, and idly flicks a passing fingernail across the scab over Jonathan's heart. Where his pride used to live.

'She dumped you in it? At work?'

'She dumped me. Left me high and dry. Full stop. I had it – the lot, all planned and ready to go. In love with the girl I'd been with since school, gorgeous girl, lovely. Really. A bloody nice girl. Great little maisonette, climbing the ladder pretty happily at work, wedding plans all sorted and no problems with . . . well . . . you know . . . other stuff.'

Even in his drunken state the usually polite Jonathan is too gentlemanly to opt for 'bit on the side'.

'She wasn't your first mistress then?'

'Mistress? That's a bit much isn't it? No, not a mistress. I mean I've never had mistresses, sometimes, you know . . . after a pint too many . . . maybe a fumble, or something. But nothing really. Nothing that would matter. You see Sally, that's my girlfriend, I mean was . . . well, she and I were . . .' Jonathan searches for the right word, finds it, smiles congratulations at his intellectual prowess and utters the exact comparison – 'Fucking brilliant.'

David nods, thin and beautiful and understanding, lights another cigarette and sips still slower.

Jonathan is enjoying his theme now, 'We were fantastic, me and Sal. And you know, if I ever, well . . . you know . . .'

'Strayed?'

'That's right, strayed. Well, I mean, I wouldn't hurt her for the world. I loved her. Love her. Sally was never going to know and what she didn't know wouldn't hurt her, right?'

The Prince uses the occasion of lifting his pint glass to his lips to avoid having to lie. Hunting and the quick removal of unnecessary hearts comes easy in the royal family, lying does not. Even Cushla doesn't fib happily. She is always honest to the moment, telling the truth of the new she that she is.

Taking silence for acquiescence, Jonathan continued, 'And it's not like I planned it. You know, I just thought right, God! Here she is, gorgeous girl – the secretary I mean, amazing and, well, we could have a bit of fun, be all over by the wedding, then I can settle down and live happily ever after, right? No harm done.'

'So you would have ended the affair before your wedding?'

'Look, look – affair, mistress – these are big words. I was just out for something easy. Not to upset Sal. Nothing major. I never meant to fuck things up. I just wanted . . . I don't know. I suppose I was flattered, to tell the truth. She was amazing. Really. It was just a bit of fun.'

'But you didn't plan on having that kind of fun after the wedding?'

'No. Course not.' Jonathan downed his double whisky and cooled his startled throat with a long draught of ale, 'I mean. That wasn't the plan anyway. I loved Sal. I wouldn't want to cheat on her after the wedding. That's not right, is it? I loved my Sal.'

Jonathan struggled from the new-covered and already-cigarette-burned bench seat, heading for the gents. He'd started undoing his flies before he got to the door, addressing the back of the urinal as he finished his tearful sentence, 'I love my Sally.'

By chucking-out time David knew all he cared to know about Jonathan's failed plans to get Sally back. About the pleading and the begging and the flowers and chocolates and champagne. How Jonathan's best friend had shagged Sally but that was okay, Jonathan forgave them both. Well, he forgave Jim first.

'I mean, she asked him. She needed someone. It's all my fault, I know that. I do. And Jim told me she was crying. Well, you know what that's like.'

Eventually he even forgave Sally too. Understood why she'd done what she felt she needed to do. Susie forgave Sally and Jim too. After Jim took her to Florida for two weeks. And a weekend at a health spa thrown in for good measure. All was forgiven but nothing was fixed. The four of them even had dinner together a couple of times, trying to pretend they could still be friends, that perhaps all their co-mingled past really did mean something after all. But the co-mingled body fluids cancelled out the past and Jonathan found he had lost his lover, the ability to trust completely his best friend and his small but perfectly formed social life. Work was all he had left and he didn't even really care about that any more. It was all going down the pan. All because of her.

After they'd weaved two streets away to a late-opening Chinese place, David thought for a moment about re-education. He had it in his power to make Jonathan sit up and listen. To clear him of the fuddled alcohol and point out exactly whose fault it all was. Or rather point out the only truth Jonathan would believe. David knew he could not tell the whole truth to Jonathan, though a degree of joint cul-pability would do for a start. But just as he was about to embark on the lecture the prawn crackers arrived and in the moment of crunching through their fat glistening whiteness, David corrected himself. Much as the classic story would love Jonathan to be damned and to take heed from his mis-takes, the fact was that though he had been stupid, Jonathan wasn't exactly wicked. And only willing ignorance is a sin. The Prince decided to shut up and listen. His job was not to teach and the judgement had already been passed. While Jonathan had sinned, Cushla was guilty. All he needed to do now was to discover exactly what she was guilty of.

Jonathan told him, 'I don't know how she did it. She walked into the room and, you know, we could all see she was gorgeous, all the guys in the office knew that, but there was something else. Something special. Like only I could see it.' He clattered the unhelpful chopsticks on to the table and continued with his fork, shovelling prawn laden egg rice into his mouth, 'I mean, it's not as if I haven't been with a few girls in my time. I'm no saint, right? And I was really in love with Sally. We were happy. But this was, it was . . . oh, I don't know . . .'

A prawn fell from Jonathan's open, concentrating mouth and straight into his cold tea. He fished it out with clumsy fingers and left it sitting pale and wet on the tablecloth, oil and weak water soaking into a dry pond frame.

David tried a prompt, 'This felt like love?'

Jonathan spat out another prawn in negation, 'No. Oh no. This definitely wasn't love. I've had that. This was more than just love. It was all that other bollocks – you know, like in a foreign – desire and passion and . . . like I just couldn't help it. I honestly couldn't help myself. And not just the sex, though that was amazing too. It was just being with her. Being around her.'

'Her presence?'

Jonathan stopped and shook his head, put down his laden fork, 'Yes. No. Maybe. You know what? I could feel her in the next room. Feel her energy. I didn't have to see her. I knew whenever she was near. I just knew. It was weird. And I know it sounds pathetic mate, but I loved it. I really fucking loved it.'

David nods his elegant head to encourage more from his dinner companion. But his dinner companion cannot speak. Jonathan is crying. Big fat salt tears falling on to the tablecloth, mingling with jasmine tea and grease and prawn cracker crumbs. Jonathan has not cried like this for years, did not know he still could. Finally the words dredge themselves from his tired mouth, 'I loved her. You know? I still do. And I don't know where she is and I don't know how to

171

find her and I'm still going to try to get Sally back, because I don't know what else to do. But I'll never love Sal like I love her.' Jonathan shrugged and stood up, levering himself back to reality with a sad laugh, 'I'll never feel anything that big again. I know I won't. Not ever.'

Jonathan paid the bill and staggered home alone and the Prince nodded sagely. Because now he was wise.

Thirty-five

The centre is closed for the evening. The side street is dark, has been dark for hours but now there is the added dark of closed curtains, heavy bodies eased into sofas for a night of *Coronation Street* and egg and chips for tea, then *Newsnight* later with the kettle on and milk chocolate hobnobs at the ready, blow a quick kiss to Jeremy Paxman and it's up the stairs to beddie-byes. Cushla of course, knows nothing of the joys of domestic bliss. Her joy is other. There were no cosy nights in with Mum and Dad at the Palace. The dark was for masque balls and dancing and extravagances and climbing the glass mountain over and over again. What it lacked in waking up bright and early with the lark, it more than made up for in Cushla's well honed calf muscles. It also meant she wasn't likely to look at an eight p.m., rain-deserted street and wish she was at home with a nice cup of low-fat drinking chocolate.

Frances has spent the day with a ruptured disc, a displaced elbow, a displaced patella and three other clients with no problems at all, just too much money and the fear of an empty diary. There's not a lot of tennis gets played in the month before Christmas. Cushla is Frances' last client for the day, the other therapists have packed up their oils and lotions and tubes and towels and left, returning through season-candled streets to loved ones or empty homes, but leaving anyway. Frances' husband will care for their son tonight. He will cook chicken nuggets and oven chips for himself and homemade vegetarian lasagne for their son. He will satisfy both of his prime desires in the same oven – to care lovingly for his offspring and to ignore the chance to care for himself. He will however, run five compensatory miles in the morning.

Frances would have booked a babysitter, offered her husband a night out with the lads, but he rejected her conscience-assuaging offer and has sacrificed himself on the altar of good fatherhood for the night. It is not a great martyrdom, Philip loves an evening at home, alone but for the soft breathing of his son upstairs. He is delighted to sit in and read the paper, watch trash TV, think about nothing. His days are full of thinking about everything, he has become an important man and so is happy to have occasion to switch off. And nights out with the boys are not what they used to be either. All important men, conversation which used to centre on football teams and ales, now reverts quickly back to the economy and the government and planned fatherhood. Philip spends long days in taking care of the world and could do with a night off. After ten years of marriage though, he would not readily admit this to Frances. Their life together is a well ordered series of bargains and persuasions and regulated passions.

They did not intend to become this couple, the same couple as all the other couples. But they have. Their life is routine and planned and sane. They have a child. They love

174

their child, he is the product of their coming together, their lust. He is the physical memory of their hunger. And he is also their coming apart. They do not have money worries anymore, Frances and Philip. Those arguments were for the first years of their love. The fraught nights poring over joint budgets, the running to the bank in the hope the cheque had cleared, the re-heated lentil and veggy soup when it had not. But, while the money worries were constant in the first few years, there were also the compensations of the occasional weeks or days when Philip's consultancy work paid off, when Frances had a new client with a better notion of tipping. Nights of the miracle fifty quid, rushing home to the other, bottle of cheap champagne in one hand and vast desire in the flesh. The poverty paid off in sporadic perfect release. The worry worth the waiting. And now they are no longer poor. They work hard and are justly rewarded and while that should be plenty to smile about, their money worries have been replaced.

They are parents instead. And they love their child, adore him, all that he is and all that he could be. They could not ask for more. But the inevitable truth is that there is more passion in poverty than parenthood. Their energy goes into the boy and the house they have slowly made home and their work. They do not begrudge a moment of it, could never begrudge him, tumbling crying into their bed late at night, will not begrudge him waking them laughing at six in the morning. They love him. And he really is a very valid excuse. All parents use the same excuse. It isn't a lie, it just curbs the lay. And Frances and Philip still love each other and their life is well ordered and well run and happy. And if one of them lies awake through a cold night, night wondering 'Is this all there is?', they will not whisper the treason to the other in the morning. They will get up and get on with it.

175

There is breakfast to be eaten and a school run to be made. There is a small life to take care of. That is their truth.

So Philip is staying home tonight. He will earn extra points for the gesture. He will not allow Frances to get away with it easily. He will work on the guilt he believes she feels about working an extra evening, covering for a colleague, make much of it. He would feel that guilt himself. Theirs is an equal opportunity household. With opportunities for all to smile and all to suffer. Philip is right about the guilt, and doubly right about the earning of Brownie points. His ration will be so many that he could fly all the way up to Guides tonight. But he is very wrong about the cause.

Before Cushla's arrival, Frances had been completely and happily monogamous, with no unexpected desires outside her family and employment circles, her only needs festering unfulfilled being those of everywoman, everyman – the need to have it all, to be it all, to do and be everything in one short lifetime. She has easily maintained a pure and efficient coupledom with the hard working Philip. They have both wanted so much more and both known that what they had was more than most. Frances has been the perfect partner – apart from a brief snog and fumble with her best friend Janet, the night before Janet's wedding. Purely as a matter of Janet's pre-nuptial education. Now however, Cushla has unleashed the remembered bitch in her, and Frances likes it. Likes it lots.

Frances is about to give up on trying not to. Trying not to feel, not to want, trying not to breathe the same air as Cushla because the pain of desire is so great. The joy of desire is so great. Trying not to count anticipatory hours until the next appointment, trying to ignore herself. Frances could live on sexual tension alone she is so hungry for this woman. And she has thought about it and denied herself and fought the

176

desire and rationalised the passion and she understands all the reasons. The ten years with the same man. The stuck that comes with the ideal life. She has talked herself out of it and then found that her body has again talked her into it. She has argued with herself at three in the morning while Philip sleeps sound beside her and persuaded herself to do nothing and then imagined allowing herself and loved the imagining. And finally she has realised all the truths – that this fling could be a nothing or a something, but either way the outcome would be the same, and she would tell or she would not tell, but Philip would know and where would it get her in the end? And in any relationship passion waxes and wanes and that this woman Cushla has come into her life in a waning period is just chance but it is also magic and danger and then again maybe it's just right. Maybe this is what was really meant and how can she possibly know? Frances should stop denying and take the chance. Or Frances should take no chances and follow the already-future. Or Frances should be bad because what else is there in life but the moment and the passion and what if she were to die tomorrow? Or Frances should be good. Or then again, and thankfully and praise be all the prophets who have invoked fate time and time again, perhaps Frances really does have no choice. Perhaps this really is what must be. And in the time-honoured tradition of the ancient cop-out, Frances decides she has no choice. She has fought it and fought it again now she has yielded. This is love, it is desire, it is right and it is bigger than her. Frances' relief at giving in is immense. She simply has no choice. Seven generations of feminist foremothers spin in their crumbling graves. The girl can't help it.

The float room is dim and quiet. Frances takes Cushla's thin, narrow hand and leads her there. Down stairs, past the now silent wind chime, around the post of passionately receptive reception. The receptionist attended a Goddess workshop last weekend. This week she has given her entire being to every moment. It has been exhausting for all concerned. Cushla follows readily, allows Frances to take control, it gives her more time to think. They push the door open together and their faces are assailed by moist salt air. Frances has turned the central lights off in the room; on the sides of the pool, under the thick saline float solution, are two small covered bulbs, illuminating the room from under the water, liquid-shifted shadows catching against the tiled walls, elongating the starfish points to octopus tentacles. Cushla's shallow breasts rise to the warmth, Frances is more full, she carries a ready heat within her. Their naked bodies have been clean rinsed by a cool shower, feet leaving half prints on the floor, fast drying in the damp heat. Even as she guides Cushla, Frances notes the perfection of her footprint. She has longed to kiss this long, angular foot in daylight, held it in wondering hands. There is nothing about Cushla's body that does not provoke illumination in Frances. The women fumble with earplugs, move mute into the float water. Frances has arranged music, whale sound with distant pipes. Cushla would sneer at the New Age simplicity if it didn't make her so happy. If her water-refined body didn't soar with joy at this return to its element.

There is a promise already made. Even lost in adoration, Frances remembers her vocation. Eyes will be closed, ears blocked, mouths shut. This time will be of flesh touching only. The concentrated saline solution is merciless and Frances would be lover not mother nurse tonight. Cushla reaches her long body across the surface of the small pool, lays herself out and rests on the surface, liquid warmth encircling her back, small ripples curving over her torso. The near-healed heart scar prickles and then bursts into sharp pain as corrosive salt licks around the memory of ripped flesh. Cushla smiles, thankful for the healing hurt. She would be reminded of the pain she has caused herself before she sinks again.

I do not intend to sink again.

In another moment the pain has passed, Cushla floats and listens to the gurgling of her stomach, the sound intensified through the earplugs. She hears the twists as soft wisps of water curl around her neck, follows the more distant whalesong. Briefly she is cognisant of the whole, then ease takes over and she is gliding gently, in and out of awareness. Frances floats beside her, the women touching extremities, arms, legs. Senses shut off but for the smell of the air and the feel of heavy salt liquid. The touch of their skin, electric in water, current intensified by warmth and spatial blindness. Frances is holding her hand, Cushla can't tell which hand, testing each finger for pliability, for tension, for strength. Frances is touching her feet. Holding the reformed feet against her stomach, Cushla's feet kicking in where nine years ago the nearly baby kicked out. Frances is tracing the line of her sharp jaw, her pale hairline, careful that no drop of liquid rolls toward the precious, perfect-blue eyes. With mouth closed and eyes shut, Frances kisses and views every part of this long, thin Cushla. The angular bones are cushioned against Frances' wide, round flesh, caressed smooth by the soft water.

Their sex is the dance of uterine twins, coloured by flesh-filtered blood. Their sex is silent and deliberate. It is touch and tension and very slow release, each movement thought out and acted upon in the same instant, with neither cause nor effect, both occurring at the apex of instinctual knowledge.

Cushla is astonished. She did not expect to be taken care

179

of so well. The woman is gentle and calm and soft. This particular girl sex is easy and warm, touch without sound, invention without consequence. Cushla knows she will grow to enjoy this. She promises herself a little time of pleasure before the third break, maybe some chatting, some shared shopping, the girl things she has not enjoyed since she was twelve and first blood separated Queen-Mother and Princess-Daughter. That and her own fervent ambition. She will have a little ease after the difficult time she has put herself through recently. She will be more guarded with this one, keeping an eye on the heart and an ear out for its potential beat. She knows better now. While she will enjoy this woman's company for a while, she will also take more care of her own heartspace. Keep it clean. And empty. Meanwhile though, this is nice. Very nice indeed.

In the shower later, Frances takes her by surprise, slams her against the wet tiled wall and fucks Cushla senseless. After all that sweet stuff in the float room, she wouldn't want her new lover to think that she didn't know what to do with a girl.

Thirty-six

David's meeting with Josh was a much calmer affair than the long evening with Jonathan. Josh had sworn off alcohol for the time being. It seemed a good enough start in his attempt to purify his defiled soul. The Prince walked first to the house in Islington but found it locked and silent. He followed the scent of guilt and remorse to Josh's new flat in Camden. Martin had left the country, taken up a long-standing offer from an old friend to do a little work and a lot more play in New York and intended to be gone for three months. Josh could have stayed in the Islington house alone, but the cavernous echoes of his past with Martin sent him screaming from the house after the first single night. He rented a ready furnished one-bedroom loft apartment. It was still beautiful, Josh would not be reduced to ugliness even in his worst depression, but it was cold. Josh the puritan penitent would rather deny himself central heating than be without beauty. Martin left a long letter, waiting on the kitchen table. The letter promised a chance to try again after Martin had spent enough time away getting the pain out of his system and

Josh had spent enough time at home, reconciling himself to the truth of his actions. Martin believed himself to be generous and worthy in this gesture. And needy, he wanted to have his old life back. So did Josh. He just wanted Cushla to come with it too. He couldn't help himself.

When David turned up at Josh's front door there was a hesitant moment, a possibility of denial and then he was welcomed in. After all he had been through, a complete stranger asking to talk about Cushla did not seem that odd to Josh who had already bored anyone he could about the whole affair and was happy to take in a new pair of ears if he could tell the story just one more time. A tall stranger, thin, pale and beautiful with a scent of ambiguous sexuality seemed practically ideal. He invited David in for coffee and actually turned the heating on, albeit leaving the radiators at their lowest levels. Josh took little prompting to let it all spill out. He accepted David's story that he'd come to hear more about Cushla, that a mutual friend had told him Josh knew Cushla – Sunita's gossip fest in the week following Josh's departure meant that rather more of his friends knew what had happened than he would have preferred. It didn't surprise him in the slightest that this complete stranger knew something about it too. Sunita's power to gossip is legendary.

They drank bitter Algerian coffee with no tempering milk and, chain smoking, David listened to Josh's tale. Josh did not ask him to smoke near an open window. He reasoned the discomfort of passive smoking was yet another act of contrition he could well afford. He spoke about her beauty and her charm and her many talents. How Cushla could light up a room, fire a conversation, quicken the dullest of minds. David listened to a litany of Cushla clichés and then carefully introduced the only subject in which he really needed educating.

Swirling the dregs of the coffee in his cup, a knowing future forming in the spin, he simply asked, 'Ah Josh, forgive me if this is too personal, but aren't you gay?'

Josh readily affirmed the proposition. 'Yes. I was. I am. But with Cushla it actually goes beyond gender sexuality anyway.'

'How can it?'

The Prince's mission was blessed with Josh's intelligence. The man had obviously been struggling to find a pathway through this particular dilemma ever since the whole thing had blown up.

Josh launched into a careful explanation, 'My sexuality was not a matter of choice. It rarely is. I am not gay as a lifestyle thing. It's not like choosing between a Mercedes or a BMW. And I'm not gay either because I don't like women. I'm gay because of what I am, not what I'm not. I'm Jewish, I'm gay, I don't like olives – those are the givens.'

David nodded and smiled and listened hard. Somewhere in how Josh loved Cushla was the second key which would take him straight to her heart.

Josh ran his fingers through his hair as he spoke, 'And I'm not stupid. I can see that, as she is so physically similar to me, there was a degree of narcissistic attraction. But it was far more than that. Anyway, I'm a gay man, I understand all the arguments about finding the same attractive. But just as I don't love all men simply because I am male, I certainly didn't love Cushla simply because she looked like a female version of me.'

'You loved her?'

Josh closed his eyes, ran the word over his mind, inhaled the taste of her across his tongue. He opened his eyes and nodded, 'Yes. I loved her. Not by accident and not by chance but . . .'

183

And here even Josh's intellect faltered, David prompted him on, 'Yes?'

'I loved her because . . . she . . . I . . . look, this sounds pathetic but . . . I think she made me love her. I'm not saying I don't accept responsibility for my actions and I'm not saying I don't absolutely know that I am to blame for fucking things up between me and Martin. I am. I do. But Cushla made me love her. That's not an excuse, it's the truth.'

'Do you know how she did it?'

Josh walked to the sink, emptied the coffee grounds from the filter, added fresh ones and water, placed the pot back on the stove. Took more time to empty David's full ashtray, replaced it with a clean one. 'I think she willed me to love her.'

The words came slowly now, each carefully placed, thought about as if Josh believed that what he was saying could be dangerous, as if he believed he could invoke her destructive power by examining it. 'I think Cushla intended me to love her from the first time we met. Or before. I knew something was going to happen that night even while Martin and I were cooking dinner. It was as if she designed herself specifically for me. I know that's ludicrous, but that's why it was all so fast, so important. I honestly felt – I still feel – that Cushla was it. The One. And I don't believe in the concept of one true love. Never have. I don't believe in the idea of The Dream Partner. And yet that's what I think she did. Made herself the one for me, even though that's not what I wanted and not what I believe in. I think she made herself the one for me so that I could only have her. I had no choice but to have her.'

The coffee started to splutter on the stove and Josh reached around to turn it off, leaving the fresh caffeine to turn bitter in its pot. 'And the sex was made for me too. True, I have no comparison, maybe all boy/girl sex is like that, but I honestly doubt it. The statistics don't hold up. She made our sex so that everything I did to her, every time I touched her, everywhere I touched her, she adored it – and I don't believe she was faking. In return everything she did to me felt good and right and was amazing. We quite simply were perfect together. We worked together. I can't give you superlatives enough and I can't sound like less of a joke. It's true. I honestly felt like she was made for me. Meant for me. That's why I had to have her.'

The Prince didn't need to hear more. He knew that Josh would never get over Cushla, that waiting for Martin's return and hoping they could be whole again was useless. Until he had dealt with Cushla. David left the beautiful flat, burnt coffee acrid in the air. He sifted through his new knowledge as he walked back to Stoke Newington. He knew that Cushla had entirely remade herself for both Jonathan and Josh, and now again for Frances. He understood that she could provide the perfect for anyone, that they had no choice but to love her. Both men were right, she was ideal for them, she intended herself to be. David trusted his mother, he understood that by now Cushla had to have at least started to grow a heart of her own and it was the growing of the heart that was causing all the trouble. Simply hurt and wounded, both men would grow the usual broken heart bitterness scab and get over it. Keep a piece of themselves – loving or angry – that was forever Cushla and then make their lives again. But Cushla had made herself The One and she had grown herself in their own desires.

Prince David has no doubt that the reason they cannot rid themselves of Princess Cushla is because she has planted desire deep inside them. They will never be released until she is cut out from inside. Removing the heart in her will remove the longing in them. Because of course, what Cushla had not intended was that stray seeds might fly on unscented winds and plant the tiny garden of desire that is now growing in her. When David cuts out Cushla's heart, when he removes it with a finality of intention, he will also set the others loose. They may still be heartbroken but they will be free.

Here comes the combine harvester.

Thirty-seven

I am soft in this time, gentle with her, gentler with myself. I tire easily, waking already exhausted by the coupling and the unravelling of my plans. I have made myself new and young and fit, but the circumstances of my making will not leave that new body entirely. I am playing for time. I am praying for time. I prick my thumb on the spindle and know something wicked is coming. It is hard to make plans when the possible outcome is inevitably blank. I wind myself up again and go out. I meet her, eat with her, fuck her. She loves it, loves me, our passion is new and already centuries old in its desires. And her skin is easy for me. But it is not enough. I will do this because I must. But now I know that it will never be enough.

In the dark of the tower, new blood wound in my side, I consider that I could give up now, but that I don't know what else to do. I don't know who else to be. And I can't go back to the Palace, not now that I've lived here, played in reality. Besides that, I hate honey and the place is not yet ready for me. I will return, but only on my own terms. So I tumble further into her instead. She is easy to fall against, has soft woman flesh to cushion my harsh new angles. Her body is warm and her passion violent. Brutal empathy is an appropriate combination for a woman. It is an appropriate combination for my current state. It is the state I offered to Jonathan, to Josh. She gives it back to me unasked. Warm holding with white hot sex, her hands alternately heal my aching back and rip apart inside my opening body. I am being serviced and cared for. I will rest here a while. I have healing to do.

The heart of the matter is that this little matter of the heart has surprised me. I feel it swelling inside, touch regrowth with the other blood vessels and cavity walls surrounding what should not be there to be surrounded. I would reverse the growth process but I am not sure of the correct magic. There must be a method for the undoing of a learnt desire, but it was not taught to me. They expected there would be no need. My brilliant education is proving to be sadly incomplete. I was born knowing how to break hearts, I should have been taught how to break my own.

I divide my time between the cold tower where I rip out another heart each time it grows to tiny maturity and the warm therapy rooms where I return for solace. I do not know if she is aware that I chose her. Certainly she knows more than the others did. I am not strong enough any more to screen her entirely from the truth and then, she is also rather more psychic than the other two. I think that maybe she believes she chose me, that I need her. Perhaps she is right. Certainly I need a measure of space. And there is time with this wide woman, long afternoons beyond the early setting sun stretch out to include the holding and the kissing and the curtains are pulled against the outside night, yet we illuminate the room with the pure light of the intense fuck.

There is kicking and biting and scratching and not a mark left on me. There is sucking and touching and tasting and eating and when she is finished with me I am full. She leaves me exhausted. I leave her better than when I came. When I come with her, I am better. This better lasts a short while, but back in the quiet of the tower, the tiny beat waits for me.

I have seen desire in others, watched them suffer with yearning. I have mocked it and enjoyed their suffering. Now I mock my own suffering too, but I do not enjoy it. The playing with Frances takes my mind off Joshua, removes my sexual want for him, but it cannot detach my heart. His presence prompted the first heart into life and each new heart now grows in that fertilised bed. Each heart is born wanting. I could make my flesh self again and again now, but I cannot make myself without the desire. It needs another to take it away. Is this the pain they all suffer here? The love for one that only the next and then the next can take away. A constant yearning that never retreats, is merely unfitting jigsaw piece hidden by the addition of the new lover and then the newer lover and then the newest lover. It is not good enough. No wonder they are so weak.

I am desultory and waiting. I am the bird silent calm before an earthquake. I sense conclusion and am both frightened and relieved.

It's getting closer.

Thirty-eight

Prince David arrives at the therapy rooms shortly after the first client of the day. His visit is not booked but should be an easy consultation, for the purposes of his mission he has dislocated his thumb. Intentionally. A simple but dramatic gesture which he learnt in his seventh week of regulation medical training, left hand lifting his right thumb from its socket and, encased in skin and firm muscle, allowing it to dangle precariously on the edge of bone. As immediate attention-seekers go, it's a winner.

He walks into the reception area at Frances' therapy rooms, silver wind chime glancing off his exquisitely coif-fured head and announcing his arrival. He is not smoking now. It would not be right to start the consultation with being sent outside to dispose of the offending item. The beautiful Prince is all thin elegance and charming insouciance. Except for the thumb. He places his obviously injured hand on the receptionist's *feng-shui*'d desk and asks her, with a pained but genuine smile, 'Sorry to bother you, but you couldn't do anything about this could you?'

This weekend the life-changing workshop was 'Self Analysis for the New Millennium'. The receptionist Shanta, two hundred and fifty pounds poorer and exhausted but laden with an inner spiritual wealth she could not possibly quantify, now understands that she is terrified of ill-health, hence her choice of career. Without knowing it, she was led to be a receptionist in this very building as the concrete manifestation of a subconscious desire to cure her phobia. She is cleverer than she knows. She also now understands that needy men bring out the dangerous mother in her, that she should only consort with men who have already found and conquered their adolescent boy-child, allowing them both to meet in the grounded clearing of adult male and adult female. Shanta has learnt she is more dangerous than she could ever have imagined. The euphoria lasted all through Sunday night and right up until this moment. It is ten thirty on Monday morning. She is torn. The man before her is obviously injured. She could use this as a tool to overcome her phobia. Therefore she should help him. But he's sick and he's beautiful, which makes him needy. Makes him some-one her inner mother rescuer will try to save. So she should stay away. For two hundred and fifty pounds she might have expected a few more answers.

Time passes.

Even David feels pain. 'I'm sorry, but my thumb? Can they do anything for me?'

The receptionist decides retreat is the better part of enlightenment and cowers behind her appointment book. She flicks through scribbled pages and looks as efficient as possible. A picture of complete capability only a little marred by the ladybird tattoo on her cheek and the fact that the wool for her hand-knitted jumper was never quite cured properly – a batch from her sister's first attempt at spinning – and still smells rather strongly of sheep.

Shanta answers, voice catching and betraying her immediately, 'I'll look through . . . the diary. This is the diary. I mean . . . I am . . . You know, maybe we're too busy . . . or something . . .'

Shanta remembers her promise to herself in front of two hundred people on Sunday afternoon, she redefines her terror as power, stiffens the weak and unwilling sinews, stares up at the ideal Prince and opens her mouth to let her soul come babbling out, 'Look. I want to be open with you. To be honest – you alarm me. You are lovely and in pain. There, that's the truth. You disarm me.'

Shanta screws her courage into a ball and throws it with perfect aim into the rubbish bin.

David smiles but this time the ordered charm is cold and purely perfunctory. He is not used to servants stalling him and his thumb hurts like fuck, 'That's as maybe sweetheart. But I've dis-thumbed myself. Isn't there anyone here who can deal with it?'

Then Frances is in reception. She saves Shanta from her own stupidity, takes one look at David and directs him upstairs to the lounge. Frances is not sure why she's come to reception, she has left a woman stretched out on the massage bed, legs and arms slathered in lavender and camomile creams, seven acupuncture needles down each side of her spine. There was no reason for Frances to come to reception just now. Usually if a client needs time alone she will go into the tiny resting lounge, make herself a cup of the strong caffeine-rich coffee so frowned upon by her clients and wait, smoking her cigarette out the window so that Shanta's trained nose does not come running to complain.

But now she is in reception, she is looking at David, she

thinks she recognises him but doesn't know how or why. She leads him to the lounge, rids herself of the client as soon as possible and readies her room for its new occupant. She burns perfumed oil, lights a sacred candle and slugs a large mouthful of pepper vodka from the chilled flask in her bag. She goes to call the tall thin man. She is shaking. Perhaps she should sleep more, perhaps she has spent too many late nights easing her conscience in long lingering sex with her husband, or too many fast-seized afternoons and early evenings fucking Cushla, or maybe she has crammed too much quality time into the spare hours she can grab with her son. There has been no time for herself, no time to relax and simply be. Perhaps that is why she is shaking now. But she doesn't think so.

David looks up as the woman walks into the lounge. Frances is in her late thirties, a handsome woman rather than beautiful. Average height and not slim, she does not fit the classic picture of feminine beauty. Her once-black hair is well cut, short and clearly greying, her smooth dark skin is even darker at the bags under her eyes, her healthy body rounded and soft. She looks fine and vital. But more than her appearance, even from where she stands at the door, David can feel her power. She is tremendously strong. And when she moves a step closer he can smell his sister on her skin.

'I can see you now, if you'd like to come upstairs.'

Frances' statement is not a question. She turns away from the Prince and leads him into her room. She does not bother to ask how or why. He sits opposite her, she takes his injured hand in hers. He feels her heat coursing through his wrenched muscles. This hand has caressed his sister. David can feel the touch of Cushla's skin through Frances. Frances tells him to breathe in and out, in and out, breathe in again, deeper, hold it, and on the exhalation she sweeps both of her hot hands around the displaced bone, lifting and depositing it swiftly back into place. The Prince winces in pain and surprise, sits back in his chair.

Frances barks out another order, 'Don't move it yet. Just wait.'

She leaves him sitting, his hand hanging in the air, crosses to her desk, mixes oils in her palm and returns to him without sound, gently easing the strained muscles back into place.

David could heal his own pain with simple thinking if he wished. But he does not wish. Wishes are rationed at three a day and this would be a waste, he can accept her expert healing and use the time to progress. He is learning from this woman. From her agitation, her concern. He is learning through her skin, he can hear his sister in her breath. The royal children were expensively and expansively educated, they are well schooled in the reading of flesh. Frances has enjoyed his sister, but more than that, her power has fed from his sister's strength. Which means Cushla's force must be waning. Simply from Frances' touch, David knows that Cushla has been experiencing problems. He does not know what exactly, does not know for certain about the little matter of the heart, but he knows she has less strength than he, knows that soon he will be able to accomplish his task.

Meanwhile, Frances is offering a full body massage and David willingly lays himself out.

Thirty-nine

Following his initial massage and the wealth of unexpected extras foisted on him, there was a time of waiting. Two hours until Frances would be finished with her next client. David rested his fine boned and well fucked body on the banana chair in the lounge, smoking with no regard for Shanta's disgust and flicking through health magazines and books on how to heal his scarred and broken life. He rather thought Frances had just given him a pretty good personal tutorial. He did try a sojourn in reception, chatting to Shanta but her conversation was incapable of breaking beyond naïve esoteric psycho-babble and, happily walking on water since he was six, David found her shaky grasp of metaphysics a little basic, to say the least. He was also not in the slightest bit interested in a lecture on the evils of tobacco.

Prince David then, sits alone and takes a moment to study what is happening. The sex with Frances had been enlightening. Here, after all, passion did not come with a reverential deference requiring his lover to leave the room backwards bent in a low bow. Here sex was simply man and woman. It was not that Frances' body had been any sweeter or softer than those David had sampled back at the Palace, in many ways she was yet another perfectly competent lover. Frances was warm and wide and soft, welcoming his cool, thin frame. She held him in her and her in him at the same moment. Strong enough to control and grown enough to know when control gives way to yield. But David did more than fuck Frances, there were hearts beating against each other, warm flesh to warmer, a degree not of deference and respect, but of mutual desire. It was new and David liked it. But beyond the new and the desirable was the goal and in fucking Frances, David touched Cushla. And now he knows Cushla has been here in this room, he can sense her form on the chair where he sits. His fingernail grazed her skin beneath him when he held Frances' heavy breasts. Felt the thin strata of his sister's own flesh laid between himself and the woman he was fucking. He shared twin breath with Frances and knew he touched his sister in the air. For a full half hour the wind chime and the therapy rooms and even the chanting Shanta are silent, and David sits, holding in his narrow torso and long limbs the heat that has flowed between himself and Frances, heat that brands an imprint of his sister on his skin. He can feel Cushla's blood flow, her lungs rise and fall as his fall and rise. He thinks that maybe he can almost feel her heart beat. Feel her almost heartbeat.

Eventually Frances' work is finished for the morning and she takes David to lunch. Even a thin Prince must eat occasionally and His Highness has always found the sexual act gives him a fierce appetite, usually sated by a bowl of boar's head soup, oven-fresh herb bread and a long draft of mead in the Palace kitchens. Or a fried egg sandwich. When you're fucking the assistant meat cook, it pays not to have to travel too far for sustenance. In London however, the local Pizza

Express will suffice. Frances, long rounded and forever watching her weight, chooses Salade Niçoise, shunning the heavy scented yeast of the dough balls. For David it is too much bread and green salad and Frances' discarded dough balls and Pizza Veneziana. He likes the idea of propping up Venice's crumbling foundations with his thin pizza base, extra mozzarella floating in glutinous charitable strings down the grateful Grand Canal. They share a bottle of house white. David would have ordered champagne, but Frances knows she will more easily confine herself to a single glass of house white, than if the choice was of a better quality drink. She also drinks an entire bottle of still mineral water.

Frances' three p.m. client lives hard and fast and her failing body is proof of her post-feminist inclination to do too much. Frances too, is a woman who knows what she wants. Her life is a little better managed though. Before David has finished his cassata and cappuccino, she has used her ever-present mobile to call home and arrange for the childminder to stay two hours later tonight – foot massage and ten quid extra as payment, and she has also cancelled tomorrow's lunch with Cushla. Cushla doesn't know this yet. Frances has left a message, blessing the answerphone culture that relegates personal bargaining to evening and weekend rate calls only.

David doesn't hear Frances leaving these messages, he has escaped to the Gents where he is removing stray spinach from between his perfect teeth. His ideal dentures, willed into existence at the age of three months, the teeth that tore at his mother's full nursing breasts and bit straight through the leather ears of the Palace playroom rocking horse. Cushla's rocking horse, a full grown Shetland pony killed and stuffed for the children to love all the better. The Prince's teeth are strong and white and advertising bright. He smiles at himself in the mirror. There is nothing like pre-lunch sex to quicken the appetite. All the appetites. He is ready now for the rest of the wine, the dregs of his coffee, a good afternoon nap, and then perhaps a little more flesh with Frances. And of course this is all work, he is not really having a delightful time. He is actually just getting on with the job. David takes a subtle check of Frances' pulse and discovers Cushla's tiny heartbeat. He kisses Frances and knows the breath in his sister's lungs. Perhaps this sex will complicate matters for Frances – David does not even acknowledge the possibility. Perhaps it will disturb her marriage, her new affair with Cushla – David is not interested in the maybe. He is interested in his mission. To get close to his sister, to carve a place in her life, to stop the lovers' carnage and to remove the baby heart as proof that it is done. David has been indolent and easy in his mother's land for too long. Now he is involved, he likes it, he has a job, something to do and it pleases him. And the perks of the job happen to be particularly good. Like an executive spending the firm's busy afternoon hours and expense account on a valued client, David can not only get on with the task of dealing with Cushla, he can even eat his passion cake while he's doing so. David washes his already clean hands and douses his finely scented body with still more perfume. He blows a sharp boned, soft kiss to himself in the mirror and smiles. Things appear to be going very well indeed.

Frances and the Prince are going to have an affair. Frances has expressed this determination quite clearly. To herself. Once the first sex was over, Frances made up her mind. She wasn't quite sure what she'd do with Cushla, have the two of them on alternate days perhaps, but she was certainly not going to let this adventure slip from her well worked grasp. After ten years of marriage, eight of them crammed full with motherhood and house buying and business investing, she was more than prepared for a little playing. A lot of playing.

Frances didn't stop to wonder how these two people had managed to come into her life within a few days of each other, or why she found both of them so alluring and then, after she'd tried David, so equally satisfying. It didn't occur to her to remark that both Cushla and the Prince touched exactly the same place in her, reached into a silent part of her psyche, caressing it into life, touching her strangely and wonderfully. And identically. That being in the presence of either one of them informed a layer of her being that she had negated for years. That they were both great shags. She simply took the two people life had set before her and decided to have them. Or rather she took the two people life had set before her, agonized and bit her lip and worried and prayed a bit and then thought more about how she shouldn't do what she knew she was going to do, fought against it for form and protocol and because that's what you do – but knew she was dying to give in all along. Told herself no, told herself bad, told herself couldn't shouldn't wouldn't mustn't. And then decided to do it anyway.

Sleeping the day away in her ivory tower Cushla turns in dream, disturbed by a slumbering sense of stronger force in her world. She has not yet acknowledged the Prince as present, but already she feels his power. She also feels Frances' power. Cushla takes the other woman's strength as a good sign. Their sex is passionate, the romance intense. Frances is an intelligent and interesting woman. Cushla listens to Frances' stories, reads her skin to learn still more. She acknowledges the strength of Frances and Philip's relationship. The bonds of blood and longevity. The tie of the child. She has studied Frances' face to learn of their settled life and unsettled lies, she knows their intention to maintain what they have. She understands how bitterly they both want the new but do not want it to intrude on the old. And that the two of them know it is impossible to have it both ways. And because they both want it all and because there is such knowledge and awareness between them she also knows that the breaching of this couple will be all the more bitter. Cushla wants extremes of feeling, she needs intensity, her circumstances demand that she be full of the present. The past passing holds thoughts too perilous for her to contemplate. Her fear of what grew in the time with Josh means Cushla needs to live in the now so much, that she is in danger of falling into an uncharted future.

She is certainly in danger.

Prince David, officially on a simple reconnaissance mission, had not expected such a welcome reception but, once given, he readily accepted Frances' invitation to enjoy. After all, what was sauce for the goose, might well make a very fine gravy for her brother the gander. He is a very happy little Prince.

His sister of course, is not so happy. Perhaps if David had heard the message Frances was leaving, he might have suggested she treat Cushla with a little more care, be somewhat less cavalier with his sister's feelings. Or not. Frances looks so fine in her black velvet shirt and he quite fancies a late afternoon shag.

When Cushla wakes and plays back her message, she is well fucked off.

Forty

Frances doesn't lie. Ever. She doesn't always tell the complete truth either. But she never lies. Never has. Not small fibs to avoid answering the phone, not friendly untruths about the size of a friend's hips, not little white lies nor great big black racist ones. Frances believes lying to those she loves would be the same as denying herself. And she loves her husband very much. Frances sets herself up for problems.

Frances is at home having dinner with the high flying husband. The son they adore, who drains their energy and soaks up their love, is already in bed and they have three or four precious hours together before sleep beckons. Frances has finished a day of intensive massage, six drop-ins and three hours of work on two regular clients – one of them a six year old with a list of special needs far longer than his stunted body could ever hope to grow. She lunched with David and took an extra hour to fuck the pains of the six year old out of her flesh and then she met Cushla for a brief early tea and lengthy clotted cream passion. This was the first time she'd seen Cushla since meeting with the Prince and Frances noted that Cushla behaved slightly differently, appeared a little less sure of herself. The healer, semi-psychic herself, just assumed Cushla could feel David's presence. Frances will tell Cushla about the other man. The other other man. But not until she has told her husband about them both. She intends to be scrupulously fair about her infidelities. So she sits opposite the man she has been married to for ten years, smiling, waiting. She knows he will ask tonight. She is ready for him.

The dining room opens on to the garden. Ideal for summer lunches or, as tonight, for a winter supper. The table is reflected in the wide uncurtained windows on two walls of the room. Outside the night is crisp and clear, there will be a heavy frost in the morning. An open fire, Victorian original, burns fake gas coals, candlelight enhances the full table prepared by the husband. Butternut squash soup with fresh warm bread to start and then garlic infused root vegetables and roast beef, Scottish and BSE-free. The beef is bloody at its heart, soft and tender. Frances is tender but she is not soft. It is time.

Philip looks up. He loves Frances. He loves her for many reasons. Because he has loved her for so long and now the emotion he feels for her is as usual as cleaning his teeth twice a day. Because she is the mother of his son. Because she supported them through the lean years, allowing him to establish himself in the world of men. Because she is a crap cook and therefore adores every masterchef morsel he puts before her. Because in a world of thin women, Frances has never managed to lose more than a stone and a half and holds in her gentle flesh a cushioning of the vast strength that carries them both. Because she is his best friend. Because she is a healer and a night in her arms sends him out into the bitter world, content again. Because she is beautiful when she wakes. Because she gives such good blow jobs.

Philip pushes his plate to one side, swallows a long draught of the pinot noir and readies himself for her news. 'Do you want to tell me what's going on?'

Frances loves him for the opportunity, loves him for knowing her so well, 'Thanks for asking. Can I finish your parsnip?'

Philip passes her his plate, a half-eaten mound of coriander-mashed parsnip outlined with cold blood from the beef. Frances eats it in four swift mouthfuls, wiping her full mouth as she passes the plate back to her husband. 'I'm having an affair. Or a fling. I don't know yet.'

'Right.'

'Two affairs actually.'

'Or flings?'

'Yes.'

'I see.'

'One's with a woman and the other's with a man.'

'Husband and wife?'

Frances laughs, 'No. They've never even met.'

Even Frances can't know everything.

Philip stands up, pours himself more wine. He walks to the window and looks out at their garden, frost already starting to settle on the manicured lawn. Manicured by the gardener they employ once a fortnight to make their green space perfect even though its only function for the five months of winter is as a backdrop to their equally groomed house. They used to garden together. They used to have time. Now they work all the hours that are required, spend the remainder with their son and admire their garden from afar. Philip sits down again. Picks up a chunk of half-eaten ciabatta, puts it back on his plate. Stands up. Finds himself walking towards Frances and turns back to his chair. Sits down, finishes the wine, looks around for something else to do and, defeated by the empty plates, gives up and turns to Frances.

Frances watches his agitation, 'You can be pissed off you know.'

'Yes. Thank you. I know.'

'Are you?'

Philip shakes his head, 'I don't think so. Not yet. Should I be?'

Frances thinks for a moment, pouring olive oil on her bread, adds salt, a thin sliver of parmesan. She bites off a chunk, makes a brief chewing motion, swallows too soon and feels the hard bread scrape her throat as it descends to her stomach, 'I don't know.'

'Then I don't know either.'

'Fair enough.'

Frances feels the weight of strained polite conversation settle around them. She moves to the painted calico two-seater sofa beside the fire, holds out her hand for Philip to join her. He stays in his place at the table, pulling the cork to pieces.

Ninety long seconds later he speaks again, 'Is it important? Does it matter?' He corrected himself, 'Do they matter?'

'I don't think so. Not yet. It's very new. Both of them are very new.'

'How new?'

'This week.'

'Both of them?'

'Yes.'

'So you could still get a refund?'

'Probably. If I wanted to.'

'Will it make a difference? To us?'

Frances looks up, shrugs and utters a small but terribly important truth, 'I really don't know.'

Philip sits back, stares at his wife. Frances stares back.

Philip doesn't know what to think. His thoughts aren't working, they won't come together in whole sentences, just disjointed images flashing across his mind. Ben's birth. The time he had pneumonia and Frances nursed him. Their first trip skiing, both from families that had never seen France let alone the Alps, they decided that now they could afford to they would do that thing they'd never been able to contemplate before. He and Frances hated it. Ben loved it. Pictures of a ten year marriage and two years of playing together before that. Just looking. Just checking if it was what he thought it had been. Philip couldn't tell anymore. Half an hour earlier they'd been enjoying supper, something was amiss, he'd noticed that much but thought it was probably a work problem or something to do with Ben. Something easily solved over a bottle of wine, something that just took a cool and logical look to rearrange. Or a quick fuck. And now his wife is having two affairs. Flings. Whatever.

The rational side of Philip isn't completely surprised, he knew it had to come eventually. He's had a couple of affairs himself. The first was only an extended fling really. It happened in the first year of their marriage when panic was just setting in, when it was starting to dawn on him that he was in this for life. The woman was a colleague, a new project had thrown them together, they had a two week business trip to New York, Frances couldn't go because of her work, so Philip had travelled alone and made love to Alison every night. They had nothing in common other than a shared love of bagels and lox and their work and the fling very quickly fizzled out after a few days back in the London office. Alison transferred to a larger company with a well hidden ceiling of tinted glass and Philip remembered her every time he bit into a sweet chunk of smoked salmon. But not at any other time.

205

His second affair was a much more serious matter. Spaced over a four year period Philip had periodically made love to his best friend's girlfriend. Made love to, partied with, slept with and after a while, planned with. Philip's plans were strategic flights of fancy, a quick way out of reality and never really in earnest. Claire's on the other hand, were real. Sadly in their long night discussions they never got around to testing the truth of each other's desires. Eventually Claire's scheming became so intense that she decided to leave Michael for Philip. She was prepared to leave her partner of six years and their three-year-old twins for Philip. Or take the kids with her. Whatever he wanted, she would do. But when he was given the choice, Philip confessed to Claire that while he'd happily continue their affair for the rest of their lives, he was never going to leave Frances. Claire came in at a very close second but that was all. He was sorry, he hoped she'd try to understand. They fought bitterly and dangerously through stolen afternoons and phone conversations, horrid threats of truth. Eventually, tired and whisky-soaked and truth-shaken, Claire gave up. Now the families go away for weekends together, the two women laugh at the men's football and real ale closeness and secretly wish they had something more in common themselves, their three children play happily despite the age disparity and Frances has never known the truth. Not officially, not the details.

But Frances did know something had happened. Which is why she feels she can tell Philip the truth about Cushla and David. She has equity, if not right, on her side. And, though he does not want to acknowledge it directly, a part of Philip knows this too. Knows it is her turn. Understands as with all the other compromises of their successful marriage that her tacit knowledge and implied ignorance of his philandering is just another heavily cemented brick in the path they pave together. He is grateful she's never questioned him directly. He is grateful she's taken so long to get around to doing it herself.

However, he is the wounded one in this case and there is always a degree of power to be taken from playing the victim. Philip has one demand. Frances agrees even before he tells her what it is. Caught in the middle of desire and guilt Frances is feeling both so bad and so good that she has no choice but to agree. She waits expectantly for Philip to voice his order. He tells her to invite Cushla and David to dinner. He'd like to meet them. Frances is relieved, he could have asked for so much more and she has no problem with this. She quite likes the idea of seeing the two of them together. Philip intends the dinner to be a test. He will watch Cushla and David talking and eating and drinking. He will allow Frances to have an affair, it is her due after all. But only one. And he will choose which partner she is to have.

Frances and Philip clear the table together, scraping stale bread and cold beef blood into the rubbish bin. She rinses plates and loads the dishwasher, he carefully washes fine glasses under burning hot running water, polishing them dry with a soft cloth, placing them gently upside down in the cupboard when he is done. They move around each other with care and sympathy. They do not touch. They speak little, a brief discussion about Ben's new teacher, a few items for the shopping list. They seem surprisingly calm. The dining room and kitchen perfectly tidy, Frances and Philip then creep upstairs to their bedroom where, with silent mouths for fear of waking their son in the room next door, they punch and hit each other. Carefully and skilfully, blows landed on easily covered stomach and back, upper thighs and upper arms, Frances and her husband beat each other up. She starts it, confused and excited by his reaction to her news, she smacks him, half-naked, in the process of undressing. Punches him in the kidneys, his back to her, and knocks him reeling on to the bed. He comes back just as fierce, angry at the betrayal and enthralled at the prospect of the dinner party to come.

Frances and Philip are equally strong, matched wrathful. She kicks his shins, he pulls her hair, she scratches short but strong fingernails all down his back, he pummels four short jabs into her solar plexus. This is not usual, they have not done it before, it is not the regular concomitant of each night's fuck. It is a physical speaking of all that their nice lives and lovely house and hard-won positions in society mean they are incapable of speaking aloud. New man businessman and post-feminist healer-mother beating shit out of each other because they are too well trained to deny each other new experiences. Because they don't know how else to be. They were born into sixties liberalism, grew up in seventies freedom, became yet more generous through the greed of the eighties and emerged a fully formed couple into the nineties. They are supposed to understand, to care, to be open and loving. They are also supposed to be individually brave and daring and to honour their separate souls, to simultaneously allow themselves both togetherness and freedom. They want their marriage to work. They want to progress as individuals. They know that these are the right things to do. They are just really fucked off that no one ever mentioned that partnership and self-fulfilment are often mutually exclusive.

Frances and Philip go to sleep in a dark room, cotton sheets above and below them, the gentle purr of central heating holding them warm. They sleep with curtains open to the suburban sky, gathering frost reflected on the perfect lawn outside. They lie in each other's arms, exhausted and alarmed. They do not fuck. They are not untypical but they are not a porn movie either. And they have experienced enough physical excitement for one night.

Frances wakes tired and sore, an hour before their son. Philip joins his wife in the shower and they kiss each other's well spaced bruises and are tender and generous and silent. Then they wake their child and enjoy a family breakfast of low-fat cereal and egg-white omelettes and skimmed milk, full caffeine coffee. They all jump into the car, listening to the *Today* programme as they go. Frances takes Ben to school in the new model Audi and drops Philip off at his train and then she drives herself into work where she immediately finds an out of order meter and parks without hesitation in the smallest space she has hitherto attempted. Frances and Philip call each other four times that day and hurry home to rest in each other's arms. They ache together and they are a perfect coupling.

Forty-one

Cushla has an invitation to dinner. She will spend her day in preparation. She knows tonight's dinner with Frances is vital. She feels moment in the air, could touch the import, but she does not know where to look. She dozes uncomfortably through most of the morning, trying to catch up on lost hours. She does not sleep well at night these days. Her body makes too much noise.

Outside, London has already been at work for an eighth of a day. Those that aren't shopping, that is. It is the week before Christmas and the streets are clogged with tired parents and nagging children, spending two hundred hours in preparation for a day and a half of heavily disguised tedium. The streets though, have new purpose. Decorations which have looked out of place since the beginning of November begin to take on a sense of occasion and sparkle despite the six weeks' dust lying on them. Office workers hustle frantically to get through mounds of paperwork before the Christmas break. Their fervour is not simply for the customers and clients who will be so grateful for orders processed before the two week life hiatus that comes with the solstice, it is also because if more work is done this morning then there will be time for a longer lunch of shopping, an earlier finish to catch the shops before they close, a quicker leap into the office party. The ladies toilets are wardrobe sarcophagi for party dresses suffocating three deep in dry cleaning bags around the walls.

Tonight is the night that Janet from sales and Sophie in bookings pile on even more eyeliner than usual and squeeze into tiny dresses that prove they are just as elegant and far more gorgeous than Caroline and Victoria, the senior sales executives who swan in and out of the office on their way to extended lunch meetings. Janet and Sophie are mistaken when they assume they are equal to Caroline and Victoria. Not because their dresses come from Top Shop and H&M instead of Karen Millen and Nicole Farhi, but because though all four women are twenty-five, Janet and Sophie know for a fact that drinking office champagne on an empty stomach will make them very ill before the night is out. They understand the art of preparation. Janet and Sophie nip out at four fifteen p.m. for a quick burger and a shared large fries. And a vanilla milkshake each. Caroline and Victoria however, deny themselves food all day so as to look better in the incredibly expensive outfits they have bought to make themselves feel more equal than the others.

At around eight fifteen p.m. Caroline will vomit all down her new bias-cut satin dress and an hour later, Victoria will split the incredibly tight skirt she wears as she tries to have a drunken pee. Janet and Sophie will simply get pissed, shag someone else's boyfriend each in an empty part of the building – no one bothers with the photocopying room anymore, too hot – and then they will travel home together, giggling

211

on the last tube. All four women will wake up the next morning with splitting hangovers and massive regrets. Only two of them though, will have spent over three hundred pounds each for the privilege. London feasts on inappropriate preparations for the Jesus birthday and Cushla turns in deep and troubled unrest.

Eventually the intrusive dreams recede and she sleeps light enough to wake. It is late when she finally slides from her bed and begins her daily ablutions. First, in the closed curtain room she stands full lit and naked before the mirror. The thin, wiry body shines back at her, the hank of blonde hair massages crooked sleep from her shoulders. She studies her limbs and features for any signs of change. There are none. But, as always in the morning, there is a stirring beneath her left breast. She watches as the tiny motions of a growing heart force her thin skin in and out. She damns her body for the midnight betrayal. Every night the body grows a new heart and every morning she cuts it out again. Cushla can change shape at will, but she cannot change her body's desires. It still wants Josh. Thinks about him on sleeping and waking. He talks to her in dreams and when she wakes she is both saddened and hardened by his absence. She does not love Josh but she feels him. Feels his spirit moving around her, feels his lack beside her. The first little heart that grew for Josh did not have time to grow into love for him. But it lasted long enough to teach the heart cavity, and that which would grow in it, to miss him. She does not want him but she misses him hard, and it hurts.

She studies herself carefully in the mirror and lifts the sharpened knife to her chest. She uses the hunting knife so often now it is routine to sharpen it before she goes to bed. In what has become a practised movement she slits a three inch gap in her fat-free flesh, opens it wide enough to insert two fingers and a thumb and wrenches the delicate beating organ from its place. She is careful not to cut through any veins, their blue paths easily traced under her thin skin. It is bad enough having to do this every morning, cleaning up all the blood from a chance snipped artery would be too much to bear. Cushla pulls on the pumping heart and feels it first dislodge and then come away reluctantly in her hand. The heart roots burrow deep through her body at night and she pulls out a tiny chunk of flesh with unseen far-reaching tendrils. Her entire body curls up to answer the action, her stomach retracts on itself, her back bends away, her legs buckle and drop her to the ground and her cunt pulls up as it is ripped from inside. When Cushla first removed the heart she was relieved, now she cries out as she wrenches it from her and holds it, bleeding and stilled in her hand. The beating stops after a moment and she opens a jar on the kitchen worktop. Inside are nine other dead hearts. She drops in the tenth and places the jar back in the fridge. When she closes the door and the light goes out, they glow a little in the dark.

Then she wipes herself down and begins the magic to cover the seam. Stitches are too messy to perform daily and although the magic is exhausting, it takes less to explain a little tiredness to Frances than a new scar every day. The magic is Latin and alchemical and cabalistic. A mish-mash of remembered potions from the King's study and half-heard curses from the time the Queen attempted to teach her to knit. As magic goes, it is a bit of a muddle really. Cushla knows her tutors back at the Palace would be displeased with her, they have trained her better than this, she is disappointed with herself. But then, Cushla isn't exactly in a position to complain. Fallen princesses cannot be choosy beggars. When the seam is healed and the table cleared she sleeps again. This time there are no dreams. Cushla is throwing her days away to compensate for the past.

She wakes in the late afternoon, feeling much more herself, showers and then, drying her concave stomach, it occurs to her to eat. She goes to the fridge for a snack. There is an old toffee-flavoured yoghurt two weeks past its sell by date, a wrinkle-skinned apple and a large lump of stale cheese. There are also the hearts. It is all healthy red meat, young and tender. It shouldn't go to waste. She could make a good bolognaise sauce perhaps, with fresh basil and oregano and lots of strong garlic. She has plenty of canned tomatoes, juicy Italian plum tomatoes. She is hungry, she really should do something with all that meat. Instead she reaches for the cheese and gnaws on a dry corner. It's a shame, she used to love cooking. But these days, she just hasn't got the heart.

What Cushla really needs is someone to take her mind off Josh. And that's just what she's going to get.

Forty-two

Philip the successful businessman and cuckold is ready. He has spent the morning shopping while his wife cleaned the house. Of course they have a regular cleaner, Rosie, who comes in once a week. A student who's supporting herself with part-time cleaning work. And she's very good at her job. Today though, Frances wanted to make the house her own. So Philip hunts and gathers at the supermarket. He squeezes tomatoes and sizes up joints of beef, he weighs one leg of lamb against the other and with a practised eye knows when the supermarket is shortchanging him by an ounce or two. He returns triumphant caveman, eco-unfriendly plastic bags scattered in his wake. After shopping Philip takes his son to the school football match and then drops him, muddy and elated, elsewhere for the weekend. Philip returns home and begins the long process of preparing the evening meal, Kanye West blaring from the kitchen CD. Philip is a very successful man in his late thirties. He actually prefers new jazz and old blues. But he very much wants to be interesting too.

Philip's wife Frances, healer and adulterer, is ready. She has scrubbed and cleaned her house, baptised dark corners with germ killing fluids and sanctified table tops with furniture polish. She has placed expensive unseasonal flowers in all the rooms their guests will visit, and a couple they might poke their noses into on longer than usual trips to the upstairs toilet. Walking through the different rooms, she has asked herself which one of the two potentials she wants her husband to choose for her. She has stopped at each new dusted lintel and questioned her tense stomach, her clenched jaw. Unusually for one so in tune with herself, there has been no clear answer. Frances does not really know what she wants. But she is enjoying this time anyway. The sexual tension, the constant anticipation. Eventually it grows too fierce. She leaves her duster and polish in the dining room and runs to her kitchened husband. They make love on the butcher's block table, watched by a chilled garden squirrel. When Frances returns to her housework she can smell the strong garlic marinade on her arms and breasts. Transferred from her husband's hands to herself. She will wash it off with care and not a little regret.

Frances and Philip's much loved and occasionally intrusive son Ben has been sent to his cousins for the weekend. Ben loves his cousins, there are five of them, Philip's sister's children, all close to his own age, crammed into a much smaller home than his own, living on top of each other in a re-enactment of the South London Waltons. At their house Ben immediately drops his only-child demeanour of adult conversations and too-soon responsibilities and becomes loud, boisterous and frequently bloody annoying. It's good for him. And Philip pays his poorer sister a daily rate for her pains. Good news all round.

David has prepared himself with great deliberation. He is

looking forward to the evening, he has come into his own and is ready to enter the final stages of his mission. Frances has told him the barest details about the other dinner guest, but he already knows far more than Frances. He does not know if Cushla will recognise him, but he expects she will know him. She cannot possibly miss the shared genetic signals. The Prince is excited. In merely touching Frances he can feel the electric spin of his sister on her flesh. How much deeper the charge will be when the two of them stand together in one room. It has not occurred to David to be concerned about Philip's reaction, he has not thought at all that there might be some other agenda to this evening's meal. The Royal Family are notoriously single minded.

Cushla is horribly nervous. Matters have been taken out of her hands. If there were to be a scene tonight, she would at least know what to do, but she is rightly worried that the couple she is spending the evening with are not likely to regress to traditional patterns. It concerns her that Frances wants Cushla to meet her husband. It concerns her that the husband wants to meet her. This is too much the understanding couple for Cushla, there is no longer a guaranteed outcome. And there is something else happening too. She does not relish the opportunity to spend the evening with the happy couple and an unknown other guest. Cushla's psyche is disturbed, her skin cold, her muscles tense. She has spent the day trying to calm and ready herself. She has taken the time to check precedents. There are none. She has cast runes, spread tarot cards and read the clouds. She is no better informed. When her paternal grandmother indulged in a spot of heartbreaking, it was merely as an adjunct to the courtship ritual she was playing with Cushla's grandfather. It was perfectly normal behaviour for a courting Princess. But it was not a life's work. Unlike Cushla's aims, it did not really matter. Tonight Cushla must improvise, fly blind with her instincts – and therein lies her dilemma. Before the heart started to grow, Cushla could always trust her intuition, she needed no concrete plan, she simply knew what to do, was led by the strength of her chosen path to take the next action. Now however, her body is no longer driven simply by the force of her aims. Tonight Cushla must practise the divorcing of certain sections of her body, separate the newly entwined heart and mind. There are physical precautions which she has already taken. She removed the heart as late as she could this morning, leaving it intact until the last possible minute. Early enough so that the blood has time to coagulate, the magic needs time to seep under the wound's new scab. But also late enough so that the new heart does not grow too knowing too soon. The timing requires skilful judgement and constant monitoring. She thinks she will be safe. As long as Cushla is out of Frances' house by midnight, she should be fine.

Frances and Philip open a bottle of cheap champagne a quarter of an hour before their guests arrive. Philip pours them a glass each. Frances downs hers in one.

David arrives first. He is new suited and delicately scented and specially charming. Delicate and fine on the doorstep, standing back just enough to let the light slap his perfect cheekbones with perfect intensity. Hands over good champagne and pale pink roses on the doorstep, exchanges a quick hidden kiss with Frances and follows to the kitchen to meet Philip. Pre-dinner drinks are always in the kitchen of this house. Whether Frances or Philip is cooking, neither likes to miss out on any part of the evening, so the guests are brought to them. The long room is spacious and well made, elegant lighting at one end protects the guests' features from the halogen ravages of the cooking area at the other. There is a strong scent of garlic marinade in the room. Philip is basting a large leg of lamb, sprigs of half-cooked rosemary float in the mix of blood and fat and rich wine he spoons over the dead animal limb. He places the pan back in the oven, wipes his hands on a tea towel and turns to greet the Prince.

'So glad you could come,' he clasps David's proffered hand in both of his, David feels the marinade seep into his expensively fragranced skin. 'You'll have to take us very much as you find us here. No ceremony on the aperitif front, I'm afraid. Frances? Drinks?'

Frances holds up the bottle of Dom Perignon their guest has brought for her husband's inspection.

Philip approves, 'Good work. We'll finish this other first shall we, save that for our second guest?'

David is happy to wait for the second guest. Five minutes clear of the meeting, he is hot with her closeness. Philip carefully places the bottle in the fridge and pours a glass of the already opened champagne for the Prince. Frances offers Japanese crackers, pistachio nuts, warm ciabatta with homemade tapenade. David refuses food and sips at the champagne, he does not wish to overload his senses too soon. Frances eats ten pistachios in quick succession, choking on the last. David strokes her back gently, the nut is dislodged, Frances' throat closes up in excitement at his touch, a shiver runs from navel to cunt beneath her long silk shirt. The two men watch each other, they play the roles of husband and guest perfectly. Neither knows that the other has plans for the evening and both know that Frances' perfume is too strong. The garlic marinade has done a lot of damage, just as Philip planned. Philip continues with the artichokes, David admires the night-lit garden, Frances finishes another glass of champagne. There is no chance of silence, Kanye West has given way to Billie Holiday, Philip clatters pots and pans, Frances chatters nervously. Two minutes before her arrival, David knows Cushla's taxi has turned into the street. He straightens his back, brushes down his suit, composes his features into taut beauty. The doorbell rings.

Frances jumps up, knocks David's barely touched glass from his hand, spills champagne all down his front. Startled by the noise, Philip drops the basting tray, the leg of lamb rolls out of its dish and on to the floor and two cats appear from nowhere, determined to sear their tongues on its flowing juices. Marinade runs across the floor tiles and seeps into grouting, turning the expensive new white pattern dark wine red. Frances turns from David to help her husband, slips on a slow slick of champagne and oil and slams her head against the open door to the eye level grill. David inches quietly away from the fat cats.

The doorbell rings again, more insistent this time. Cushla is not used to being kept waiting. Cushla is ready and flawless at the door and she has a limited amount of time tonight, just four hours in which to use her perfection to best advantage. David laughs, his well made suit does not show the champagne. He stands and begins to walk towards the front door. Behind him Frances and Philip are silently hissing at each other, shrill blame and accusation about the lamb and the champagne and Frances' drinking too much and Philip's over-liberal use of garlic. Cats scatter beneath the volley of their low-tone fury. Arguing over the pettiness because they are too scared to tackle the real.

The doorbell rings a third time, Cushla's finger just faltering on it as she feels through the wood and window who it is walking towards her. David opens the door. Cushla stands before him. Her regrowth heart leaps and begins to swell inside her. No greeting is necessary, their skin knows all that is needed. They could escape now, would escape now, but before there is a chance to flee, Frances and Philip are behind them, Cushla's heavy wool coat is taken, revealing gold velvet beneath, her light bag is laid down, they are ushered into the drawing room and given drinks and nibbles. They are handled together as Frances sorts out the kitchen mess. Finally Philip too leaves them for a moment. Cushla looks at David. She thin lip smiles. He returns the warmth and reaches out sharp boned to take her hand. They still have not spoken. In the finger touch there is an agony of past and potential. Cushla's heart is smacked with the marvel of his skin. It is like touching herself, only better because she does not know what will happen next. For this reason it is also far worse. They would touch far more but their silence is shattered by a call from the dining room next door. Dinner is served.

Forty-three

The double couple arrangement is never a very good idea for a dinner party. There is too much risk. One of the couples may argue, leaving the other two feeling uncomfortable witnesses to spoken or worse, unspoken but pointed, anger and resentment. Or perhaps if the couples are getting on well within their twosomes there is the greater danger of boredom. He and she are so united that there is no reason for conversation. One he makes a comment and the other he and she reply simultaneously. They laugh out loud at their obvious togetherness, rub in the salt of perfect choice. Then the other couple must fight their way to supremacy in the battle of the dream partners. I know how much she likes . . . I never forget that he . . . on and on with the litany of welded wed. The couple who win of course, are the ones who forsake all first person pronouns entirely. Theirs is the constant we. The constant we that Cushla came here to take apart.

Except that now Cushla is becoming the we. She does not see it yet. Neither does David. She is fascinated by the man she recognises but does not know. He is entranced by the big sister he has heard so much about and followed at a distance, who now sits a scented candle away. Cushla and David could leave now and spend all night, just the two of them, tall and lean matching, touching not talking, being together with no desire to change position other than to study further the beauty of the other. But that would be impolite and Her Majesty has always stressed the importance of remaining at least a couple of hours at even the most tedious state banquet. So they answer their hosts' questions politely enough, both a little surprised at Philip's excessive interest in their lives, a little concerned that Frances is allowing him to probe quite so deeply, knowing as they do the dangers of truth. They eat the salvaged meat and murmur all the appropriate noises of praise, they hear the background music and comment on its aptness. They applaud the room and the house and surreptitiously look at their watches every five minutes. The wine flows across their tongues and begins the slow process of inebriation, an operation continually halted by a half-sipped glass when Cushla breaks off from imbibing to laugh at David's jokes or when David fails to swallow the mouthful he intended to drink because he is too caught up enjoying the candlelight as it shines across his sister's hair.

Philip is not a happy man. His great plan of deciding who his wife can play with appears to be going down the drain as the two possible candidates enjoy each other's company a good deal more than they enjoy his wife's. What's more he knows neither how to speak to David – who is not even trying to reply to Philip's proffered conversation topics of stock market and football and cars and parenthood, nor what approach to use with Cushla. The woman is certainly beautiful but she is having an affair with his wife. So he had assumed at least a degree of lesbian preference and therefore

no need for his masculine wiles. And yet she is flirting out-
rageously with David and practically ignoring Frances. He
attempts first intellectual rigour and then forced jollity and
when neither come close to garnering the slightest reaction, he eventually gives up and storms off to the kitchen,
ostensibly to check on the Winter fruits dessert soufflé, but
really to down two quick glasses of whisky and smoke a
barely soothing cigarette.

Frances follows her husband to the kitchen. She is angry
with her guests for ignoring her, furious with Philip for
orchestrating all this in the first place and more than a little
drunk. As husband and wife they could ally against the inter-
lopers in their dining room. They could join forces to
despise the guests who are here under false pretences. Instead
they take out their bitterness and irritation on the safest
target. Each other. The mortgage is too big, their son too
young, neither of them is going anywhere soon.

'I can't believe you thought this was a good idea.'

'You didn't exactly take a lot of persuading. I expect you
thought it would be marvellous. No doubt you were looking forward to having your harem arranged around you. Just
what the ego ordered.'

'Philip, you're talking rubbish.'

'Frances, you're drunk.'

Cushla and David are sober. She smooths butter on to a
chunk of warm bread, her brother eats it from her hands. His
lips are close enough to kiss her fingers. There is no touch.

'Fuck off Philip, you don't get to be free from blame for
this one.'

'Frances, you talk such a lot of crap.'

David laughs at Cushla's unsaid joke and her baby heart
begins again to swell inside her. She leans across the table and
says still nothing more. But they know it is time to leave.

Cushla stands, silently retrieves her coat from the hall cupboard, David opens the front door and calls goodbye and thank you to their hosts who cannot hear them because they have now progressed to clearly shouting loudly at each other. He helps Cushla on with her coat, she takes his hand and is shocked wide awake by his body heat. He pulls her hair free from the coat collar and his fingers are kissed by the swathe of blonde. There is the sound of smashing crockery from the kitchen. Cushla laughs. Her job here is done. She cannot know that his has just begun. They walk away.

Forty-four

Frances and Philip screamed at each other across a sea of shattered plates and much-too-strong garlic marinade. The elegant kitchen was awash with drunken fury and broken china. Frances threatened with a silver fork and Philip retaliated with a carving knife. They knew they were in a dangerously bloody room and transported their fury to the somewhat safer sitting room where they spat the bitter obscenities of Frances' lovers and Philip's infidelities. They fought with no hands and far too many one syllable words.

Cushla looked at David.

Jonathan visited Sally just one more time. A last desperate attempt to convince her of his new leaf personality. Sally, however, wasn't persuaded of Spring in Midwinter. She shared a Chinese takeaway and two bottles of lambrusco with him, half-dressed and doubly fuckable, before kicking him out of the maisonette and then telling him on the cold midnight doorstep about her lover. All the horny details of the eighteen-year-old car mechanic who was asleep upstairs in the bed she and Jonathan had chosen together. Jonathan went home on the late-night single person's tube and slept in the spare bedroom at his parents' house. The room has racing car wallpaper.

Cushla traced a soft line from David's left eyebrow across his eye teeth sharp cheekbones to the slow smile at the corner of his mouth.

Martin and Josh met on neutral ground in an unfashionable restaurant to attempt a reconciliation discussion. They ordered courses neither of them really liked but hoped their choices would remind each other of dinners gone by. Martin's lobster bisque and Josh's pan-fried Dover sole quickly congealed from potential togetherness into a hasty division of mutual spoils. The dinner was pointless, the prime decision had already been made. Martin had had enough. He had been on retreat and, in full and frank discussion with Father Benedict, had come to a few important conclusions about his future. He had decided to leave Josh, leave London, leave this pathetic meaningless life they'd been living. Martin also left Josh to pick up the bill.

Cushla listened to her heart and was not surprised to hear it had changed its tune. It was no longer pleading for Josh. It was no longer pleading at all. Cushla listened to her heart song and felt too good to remember to be afraid.

Ben woke his dreaming cousins to tell them his parents would be getting divorced. The twins went back to sleep and he lay top to toe in the dark, planning a glorious broken-home childhood with his cousin Stephanie. They would both look forward to the double presents and guilty pocket money. Stephanie and Ben put themselves back to sleep with some childish kissing practice and a dangerously drowsy crunching into the two extra-sour bubble gums Steph retrieved from her bedside table. She'd known there would be an important enough occasion one of these days.

Cushla felt herself incline inwards to David, she could see the tower in the distance. She wanted to kiss his thin soft lips but didn't trust herself. Her heart was in her mouth.

In the Palace garden, high in the disused water tower, a magpie nest quaked to the echoing screams of Her Majesty relayed direct from the South Wing back bedroom. The traditional birthing bedroom, where generations of Kings and Queens had been born. Where Cushla was brought smiling and easy into the world, where David was forced, threat of forceps and suction cups, to leave the comfort of his mother. Mr Magpie flew home laden with five gold rings, two fob watches and a bright shiny new coin. The coin came from a special collection of six thousand, all due to be minted within the next day. The coins would hold the features of the new Palace baby when it was born. The coin in his beak will not make it though. This coin will remain forever faceless and the magpie chicks will use it for stealing practice once they have learnt to fly. Her Majesty cried out again, the land trembled and the people prayed though there was no officially sanctioned religion. The King forced himself to swallow his eighteenth slice of bread and honey that day and ordered another sunflower-seed loaf to be baked. No one thought to ask after the health of Mr Magpie's wife.

Cushla led David back to her tower. They walked or ran or flew through empty dark streets in the no man's land time between Christmas and New Year. She held tight to his hand and when his left index finger moved against her thumb she felt his touch travel through to the soles of her feet.

The Compassion Fairy took a night off. Bottle of Jack Daniel's in hand and sepia photo album on the table, she wept over her long future. A tiny lark flew through the closed window and landed on the table. Gently the old woman picked it up and caressed its talented throat. The Queen wailed again, her primitive regal bawling sent heavy ripples through the forest, across the dark water and right into the centre of the cottage. The Compassion Fairy downed half the bottle and, in her empathetic distress, she snapped the sweet bird's neck.

By the time they reached the tower, Cushla was exhausted. David sent her half-asleep upstairs in the elevator, fortunately cleaned and polished for the festive season. He climbed the hundreds of stairs alone, hacking his way through thick briar and twisted thorn bushes as he went. By the time he reached her door Cushla had woken up enough to let down her long golden locks and pack the spinning wheel into the corner. She had also swept, cleaned and dusted the whole flat, whistling while she worked. She'd laid out fresh coffee and ham sandwiches on the kitchen table too.

Jonathan dreamt of two gay men sitting in the racing cars on his bedroom walls, speeding through narrow, white corridors in an Islington designer home. Martin watched a late-night made-for-TV movie about the bitter breakup of a pair of childhood sweethearts. Frances went to the kitchen and sitting in the light of the fridge ate half a baguette, four cream crackers, a tub of hummus and three walnut whips. The King threw up his twenty-third creamed honey sandwich and called for the Palace hives to be closed. The royal cat discarded a half-eaten mouse at the sound of the Queen's last screams and ran to the birthing room. There is nothing a Palace cat likes so much as fresh royal placenta.

Cushla held David in her arms. She knew and did not know his purpose. They did not speak. She opened the tower windows to the clear night and a freezing north wind swept around the two of them. In the dance that followed,

Cushla held David high above her head and the sweat poured from both of them, they were blindingly hot and ripped clothes from their streaming bodies in an attempt to cool off. When they were finally naked the swirling wind stopped and they heard in the silence a distant baby's cry.

The new little baby pushed and fought its way out from between the Queen's legs, battering a ram's head against the majestic mother's pelvic bone, ripping long healed episiotomy scars from the first birth and the second birth and the agonized Queen loathed her daughter and damned her son and despised her husband and regretted every moment of her life, she cursed her new child and screamed vengeance against the Palace physician. When the baby's head was fully clear of the mother the Palace artists closed in around Her wailing Majesty and started to sketch the child's face, ready for the minting. As the doctor pulled the slippery mess of child free from its mother, the Queen screamed a final expellation of baby and a gasp went up from the assembled dignitaries. The child was brought to its mother so she could see what had caused the shock. The King was sent for and as he came running, the Queen lay back on her bloodied satin pillows in regal triumph. By the time the King arrived the baby had been washed and was displayed naked across its mother's breast. The King stopped in shock and knelt before his exultant Queen. The midwife's magic had been wrong. Perhaps they hadn't needed to remove the lad's appendix after all. The King and Queen had finally done it. All those years of boring bloody bread and honey sandwiches had, after all, been worth it. The special diet had prevailed and His Majesty's sperm was indeed a true miracle. The child was not simply a girl, it was an hermaphrodite. A shout went up across the whole land. It had been achieved! Royal mother and baby doing very well, father proud to announce, Her

230

Majesty the Queen had given birth to a Bouncing Baby Both.

The cat licked its lips. Cushla licked David. David licked her wound.

Forty-five

There was not always a tower block on this site. There were not always people on this site. Before the 1960s the place where the tower block squats was another London street in a long line Victorian terrace mirror. Each little house complete with its one front room and back kitchen and an outside toilet and blooming ceiling roses and ornate cornices and cast iron fireplaces in every room, fireplaces that now fetch an easy grand at auction. Original features were not so highly prized when they were original. They weren't so highly prized when the developers knocked them out with giant steel balls either. Where once stood twenty eight houses, walled yards lying back to back in south facing glory, now there's the deep foundation cement straddle of the tower block. It seems unlikely that the original MFI fittings and concrete floors of this development will ever reach quite the glamorous heights of its Victorian predecessor. Even if it is allowed to last as long.

The houses are no longer there, nor are the fields and forests that lay across this part of the city before the houses, but tonight Cushla is so awake to the possibilities, to the vast what could be, that the whole of what was comes crowding into her consciousness. She opens herself to the Prince's gaze and sees in his eyes countless urchin children playing and scrapping in Dickens' picture streets, sees silent Victorian couples engaging in purely marital eyes-closed procreation, sees stolen youth whispering its secrets to each other behind locked doors and stumbling into guilty sexuality in the long grass at the foot of the old oak. Cushla listens to David as he tells her of his long journey to find her and, listening between the lines of his hurried sentences, she hears the muffled noise of crying children, the anguished wail of the dead baby's mother and the into-his-shoulder scream of the once-virgin. If David hadn't so taken over the touching of her body she could feel their pain too. But he has. And now she can feel nothing else.

Cushla sways along his skin, knocks herself a purring cat against his thin legs, his thin arms, twists and jumps into the lap of his open want. This cat he will allow. The thin Prince is half naked, half over dressed, his narrow torso rib counting bare, his legs encased in trousers and socks and boots with thick laces and too many eyelet holes for the potential of sexual torrent. He tells his stories and she removes the boots, quick as she can but half an hour too slow. He talks of Stoke Newington and Highbury Fields and the tops of London buses and she peels back the socks, uncovers the feet, unused to the long walked distances he describes, footsore blisters blossoming at her touch, she kisses them away, licks back the pain, soothes the tired with her tongue.

Cushla starts to unbuckle his belt, reaches around his wide man's waist and feels the heaviness of his hunting knife. She laughs, uncertain. She senses knowledge of him but would rather ignore the truth for now. All she knows is that she has to have him, will feast on him, needs to taste his flesh, his bones. Her bare fingers land on the hunting knife and through its leather pouch it strikes out at her, the bone handled blade will do its job even if Prince David forgets his mission. The knife cuts and jabs at her, inbred intent and her grandfather's thigh bone following the line of what they must do. Cushla recoils in shock. Blood drips from her gashed index finger and onto the wooden floor. It sits in a red wet pool, slowly increasing in diameter, then slides into the grain. Another drop is about to fall from her surprised hand and David takes the finger, holds it to his lips, lets her blood fall on him and drinks her in. His Highness is thirsty. It has been a long day.

David tastes his sister's blood and the soft iron drops him out of lust delirium into immediate consciousness. His reason returns and the knife prodding him in the back leaps into his right hand. He takes a step back, bows low and introduces himself.

'Your Royal Highness, my esteemed sister, I am truly delighted to meet you.'

Now Cushla knows who he is. Now her brain knows what her skin has known since she first touched him. Well trained in Palace protocol Cushla has half-executed a curtsey when reason catches up with her bending legs. Before Cushla can respond, he has grabbed her by the back of the neck, pulls her to him by the skein of long blonde hair and ripped her shirt open with his knife. The little interloper heart is beating in love and terror. It can smell the blade.

Suddenly Cushla no longer loathes her heart, she would keep it, will keep it. She pushes David away but her fingers love the touch of him, she bites at his face but her teeth offer only kisses. The heart is growing in her breast, swelling to fill the gap left by all the other hearts that grew before it. The

234

heart knows its time is near and yet it still cannot allow her to push him away. It pounds against her, fights inside waiting to get out. It grows with every princely fingerfall. The heart is filling Cushla up, she is choking, there is no room for her lungs, her spleen. The heart is crushing all of Cushla's other organs, she is gasping for air, clawing at David and at herself, running motionless for flight. There is no air left to breathe, nowhere else to go. Cushla is all heart.

David can see his sister dying in his arms. His job is to remove the heart, while it still beats. He can do it now. She is deathly pale, pale as he is and she falls to the floor. He could cut into her easily. She has fallen beside the drops of blood. The pool of blood in the wood grain is starting to spread. Cushla will be dead if David does not act soon. He does not want to remove the heart. He loves its beating, the force of its strength. Every molecule that is the Prince wills life back into Cushla so she can wake and touch him, kiss him, have him. Cushla is unconscious and David is in love. The Queen might have expected more from her only son.

Luckily the knife knows what to do. It directs David's hand, slicing expertly into the flesh. The bulging heart throbs itself through the narrow opening, Cushla screams into awakening, the heart slamming the air, half inside her and half out. David has hold of the heart now, one naked foot on Cushla's chest, he is pulling at it, fat and ready, his hands fully wrapped around the pulsating mess, he pins Cushla down and drags it away from her. Long tendrils wrench their roots from deep inside, her legs and arms curl up, ripped inside out, her back arches to her brother, she laughs and screams in agony and grateful relief. David's hands are encasing her heart, holding it firm and tight, she loves his touch. He pulls harder, she spins on the floor at his feet, wood grains reaching out to pin her down, rip the other woman flesh from the real Princess. He gives it one last vast haul, ripping the final root from her shuddering body, her sex reluctantly giving up its claim on her heart. David staggers back against the wall, covered in Cushla blood and holding the trophy heart high above his head.

Slowly Cushla regains herself. The floor releases its grip, she sits up. She is her true self. Her skin and hair and body are all her own. She is the Princess Cushla and, leaning against her back wall, still beating heart in his arms, is her brother. There is etiquette to be observed, formal rituals of greeting and expressions of good health to be got through. The Prince gently lays the heart to one side, stands, bows three times to his sister's four. She is the elder after all. Cushla hands him a ceremonial box, emptying her costume jewellery from it first. He lays the bleeding and thumping heart on the purple velvet padding and closes the lid. It almost fits. The lid quietly rises and falls with the syncopated beat. He lays the box on the ground by the blood ingrained wood. Then David removes the rest of his clothes to accommodate Cushla's new nakedness. They stand opposite each other and touch their matching birthmarks. She feels for his heart, it is quiet, slow beating, regular. He places his hand over the wound in her side, she would offer him water and wine but he is no longer thirsty. His hand heals her gaping wound and they fall into the bed together, exhausted and bloody. Boy-child and girl-child sleeping in naked innocence.

And waking in carnal want. David wakes before Cushla, thrown by the tower height and the light in the bluegreen room. He turns, tall man in small white bed and crumples Cushla's hair under his arm. In the morning light the resemblance is clear, David kisses his mother's eyes, his father's nose, his own fine lips. Cushla sleeps still but her lips return the kiss. David places a soft hand over her heartspace, there

236

is nothing, no beat, no sound. The wound is fresh and clean, he kisses gentle stitches all along it, healing the scar as he goes. His saliva spreads itself across the wound and then there is no wound and then there is no scar. Cushla begins to wake, her body bends to his, her body knows what flesh it comes from. Cushla feels David beside her and her dreams return to reality. She opens her eyes and looks into the brother eyes that see the same as her. She opens her body to the man that feels the same as her.

When Cushla and David meet in eventual fuck it is coming home for both of them. Not that Cushla or her brother did not have good sex before, we know Cushla did, and the kitchen maids and footmen in the Palace could certainly vouch for the energy of their couplings with Prince David. But this is different. This is the knowing sex that only genetic link can bring, this is the sex of the far away land that is really very close to here. When Cushla holds David tight to her, his heart beats into and out of her heartspace, their bodies not only fit together but his heart can beat for them both. The lust union is momentous and perfectly normal. There will be thousands more like it and yet this is the only one. It is both ordinary extraordinary in a single breath and their skin knows it. Cushla and David join in perfect obliviousness and complete awareness. Their combination has no taint of incest taboo or age concern. The woman is ten years older than him. The man is her baby brother. These considerations are irrelevant in the face of their overwhelming desire and the ultimate correctness of their coupling. Without David, Cushla is a fierce danger. Without his sister, David is ineffectual and weak. Together they are truly two versions of the one whole. In DNA joinery there is just the one umbilical cord, it is silver and twins sibling to sibling, immortally. Plato should have had a sister.

Their coming rocks the tower block and goes completely unnoticed. It tears up the echoes and visions of the closeted Victorians and is no more exciting than the first fuck of the girl next door, back bent to her skinny, pimpled boyfriend, mouth tight shut lest her sleeping mother overhear. They come together not because they are so in tune and adept, but because they have no choice, because he fits her and she wants him and that is all there is.

When they are done Cushla sings her baby brother to sleep. It is the lullaby of the growing love, the song their father sang to them at birth. They sleep for two days. In slumber the Prince returns the heart and ceremonial box to his mother. Places it into her hands and kisses her cold fingers. She takes the box from him and sends him back to the nursery to play with his big sister. Admonishes him not to play with her jewellery box again. The jewels are precious and not for little children. He'll understand at his own coronation. When Cushla and David awake the ceremonial box and the heart have returned to the Palace and where Cushla's blood sank into the wood grain there is a rose bush. The roses are tiny buds and the thorns are six inches long. Cushla cuts one away carefully, when her brother is eating toast and marmite in the kitchen and he cannot see her actions. She has no doubt the long thorn will come in very useful one day.

Forty-six

In the time of rosy glow London senses a possibility of new hope. The New Year is coming. There will be celebration and commiseration and glorious forgetting. New leaves and new choices. A simple decision to call the year by a different name makes the people believe it has all changed. It hasn't. There is no difference from the Thursday night to the Friday morning. A simple last digit has changed but the people are crying out for new. They have all eaten too much and drunk too much and any excuse to begin again will do. Cushla showers and shaves her legs and washes her hair and while she lovingly cleanses her very own body, David whistles around the flat. He changes sheets and makes toast and returns again and again to the steamed bathroom to kiss his washing sister. They listen to Radio 4. There is a warmth, even a thaw. The weather man is pleasantly surprised enough to comment on the unseasonal sunshine during the lunchtime weather report.

Frances and Philip clean up the mess in the kitchen. Slowly wash pâté and winter fruits from the walls. Retrieve knives and forks from behind dressers and drawers. Scrape up congealed egg from the cool slate tiles. They are shame-faced and eventually giggling. Then they are laughing hysterically. They laugh at their own stupidity and their fool-ish desire. Frances reaches her healing hands to hold her husband. To love her husband. Philip is grateful to fall into her arms. They have one more day alone while their son is still staying with Philip's sister. They make the most of it. They love each other and will continue to love each other. Anyway.

Josh and Martin meet on neutral ground to discuss what has been happening in their lives. They agree they are bigger than this. They can get over this. They will get over this. They leave the cyber café and go home together. Martin opens the door and Josh carries him across the threshold. They are gentle and soft with each other. They kiss long and slow on the landing, in the hallway, on the stairs. Martin cooks lunch while Josh goes upstairs and begins a new sculpture. It has to be Martin's head and it will be beautiful. Then Martin returns to his study while Josh makes a candlelit dinner. Martin is working on a new novel. It is about the growth that comes through breakdown, the shared love that grows from suffering and the eventual return to joy. They sleep together and are warm with the windows wide open to winter night.

Sally rings Jonathan. She thinks that perhaps she has had a change of heart. Jonathan is overjoyed, delighted, ecstatic. He rushes round to the maisonette through two red lights and three speed-camera traps. Sally is more than worth the accumulated fines and points, Sally is worth more than Jonathan could say. They shag on the lounge floor then watch a video and order a pizza with extra mushrooms for Sally and double pepperoni for Jonathan. They are delighted to receive their half and half pizza from the well tipped man at the door. Sally pops out to the off licence while Jonathan calls a twenty-four hour flight service and books them two return tickets to Malaga. Malaga was where they were supposed to have their honeymoon. Malaga is where they will plan the rest of their lives. Sally is so pleased she chose not to throw out the wedding dress after all. And in all this strain she has lost half a stone too. What could be better? The first class flights leave the day after tomorrow and Jonathan even dares to book a first class room in a first class hotel. He astounds himself, let alone Sally. Sally and her husband-to-be stay in bed until an hour before it is time to go to the tube. Sally likes the sex very much. Jonathan is surprised at her ferocity. Surprised and not a little impressed. They've both learnt a great deal in their time apart. Sally would almost say it was worth it. Almost, but she's still benefiting from Jonathan's guilt, so it wouldn't do to let him off the hook just yet.

Sally and Jonathan, Josh and Martin, Frances and Philip. Three contented couples, three perfect relationships. They're happy, they're in love and all's right with the world.

Yeah right. What do you think this is? A fairy tale?

Forty-seven

The King and the Queen feasted royally the next morning. For the first time in sixteen years His Majesty was allowed to run free from his sperm selective diet and eat more than bread and honey. He and his wife enjoyed a slap up breakfast of scrambled eggs and crispy bacon, fried bread, wild boar sausages, fresh picked mushrooms, grilled tomatoes, with side dishes of liver and kidneys and heart. Cushla's heart. Which went particularly well with the wild mushrooms the Queen had picked just that morning. The new baby Both had been crying all night and so they'd had very little sleep. The dawn however was so beautiful and the news that the heart box had arrived was so good, that as soon as the first rays hit the distant fields, Her Majesty handed the screaming baby over to the wet nurse and within minutes the Queen was up and dressed and out in the back paddock picking mushrooms.

They didn't eat all of the heart of course, just a token mouthful each. A large sliver was sent to the Palace laboratories for genetic analysis and a smaller chunk dispatched to the Compassion Fairy. To remind her of what she'd done wrong all those years ago. Her Imperial Majesty the Queen can forgive and forget any stupid slight but lateness. Punctuality is the politeness of Princes after all. And the obsession of this Queen.

Following the supremely satisfying breakfast the Queen returned to her rooms to rest with the baby and the King went down to the Counting House. Once he had made certain that the money was all in order, he went up to visit his wife, stopping off at the laboratory on the way. There on the computer was the heart analysis. Its DNA was fifty per cent his own and fifty per cent the Queen's and the great big heart was truly Cushla's. The lab assistant gave him a print-out of the good news and he ran upstairs to his wife with it. The two of them lay on her bed in the afternoon sunshine and thought how lucky they were to have each other. They did not mind that their son had sent a message encoded in the heart, a brief note about how he wouldn't be coming back, he couldn't come back anyway, not now they had the new baby. There was no more need of a son and heir than there was of a daughter and heir. The three of them lay together, a triptych of marital and regal bliss, mother, father and perfect child. The errant daughter could roam the world all she wanted, now they had the new baby they were absolved of responsibility for her and the son too could travel as he wished. They had provided the realm with the perfect heir and who could ask more of a Queen and King?

The Queen was drifting off to sleep and the King kissed her forehead, 'Sleep well my darling wife.'

'I will husband. You too.'

The Queen started to doze, then half-sat up as she remembered the thing she'd been meaning to tell her husband all day, 'Oh that's it!'

'My love?'

'The dustbins – we must remember to put them out tonight.'

'Already done my precious. Already done.'

Her Majesty marvelled yet again that her seemingly stupid husband could be so wonderfully astute sometimes. The baby gurgled happily in its sleep and the Queen leant over to give an afternoon nap kiss to her brother the King.

The three of them fell asleep in happy holy family pose at almost exactly the same time that Cushla leant over her own brother, studied his perfect face, kissed his soft lips and decided to hammer the six inch rose thorn deep into his heart. Cushla laughed. She was sad to lose the chance to continue the relationship they'd spent the night developing, the sex was fantastic as was only to be expected and in many ways, it was what she was born to do. Be his consort, be his Queen. And she wouldn't mind staying here forever either, making a new empire of our land between the two of them. But she was damned if she'd do what her mother did and have to share the whole bloody kingdom with her brother. The whole point of coming here was to rule alone, even the greatest partnership couldn't better that.

She took the long thorn from its hiding place between her breasts. Carefully she slipped her body around David's. He turned his beautiful face in sleep, smiled at her soothing kiss and returned to his dreams. His dreams of loving her. Cushla made her way silently to the other side of the bed. She held the thorn over her own heart space, knew that inside there was no heart to quiver in fear. She drove the thorn into her side and doubled over in agony. The stabbing of her empty place hurt far more than the cutting out of her heart ever had. In the pain she felt Josh's kisses and Frances' sighs and even heard a whisper of Jonathan's tears. She took several deep breaths, then pulled it out again, clean and blood-free. With her own nothingness anointing the vicious thorn, she then pierced her brother with it. Pushing it fast through skin, then muscles, then sinew and finally deep into his loving, gushing heart. Cushla cried as she stabbed her brother. She cried and kissed him and loved him and still she knew it was for the best. For her best.

The Prince woke up briefly, realised what was happening, muttered 'Oh shit' and died.

The King and Queen felt the pain of their son's death in their sleep. The Queen's uterus contracted and she cried out disturbing the King who rubbed at his heartburn, questioning himself as to the wisdom of the third piece of fried bread that morning. The monarchs rolled over dozily to comfort each other, and in doing so managed to suffocate the baby hermaphrodite in the process. In her waking distress at the infanticide the Queen beat her husband senseless and then jumped screaming to her death from the highest battlements of the castle. When he recovered consciousness, the King was successfully prosecuted for the murder of his baby and for faking his wife's suicide. He was beheaded later that afternoon.

The Compassion Fairy watched it all happening on satellite TV and, in a wave of dreadful remorse, threw herself under the tube. It happened to be the tube on which Jonathan and Sally were heading to Heathrow. In the two and a half hours it took to clean up the mess and dispose of the body, Jonathan acted like such a prat, getting more and more angry and resentful, finally abusing the two nuns sitting opposite them, furious at their sanity under stress, that Sally realised how much better off she'd been when she was alone and announced she couldn't be with him after all. She made her announcement, however, just as she entered the departure gate, having kept her own ticket and passport safe and ripped Jonathan's into twenty-seven separate pieces. She'd flushed them down the toilet when she'd popped into the Ladies, claiming the onset of an early period. Had Jonathan understood that Sally's handbag was for tampons and makeup instead of all his tickets and passport and their entire holiday itinerary, he would never have entrusted his papers to her safe keeping and she would never have been able to do it. As it was, Sally flew off to Malaga, happy and single, while Jonathan remained grounded and loveless.

Martin meanwhile confessed to Josh that while they had been apart, he'd had a fairly eventful time himself. In fact, he'd fucked Melissa. Out of pique and jealousy and bitterness and a desire to remember all the fuss about heterosexuality. Melissa helped Martin to remind himself that he was gay. The sex hadn't been wonderful but it had been partially successful and Melissa was now pregnant with his child. Melissa was not interested in being a mother but nor would she contemplate an abortion. She would happily give the baby to Josh and Martin to bring up or, if they weren't prepared to take it, she would give it to her own mother. But she would not keep the kid herself. Melissa had a life to lead. Josh and Martin knew what Melissa's mother was like, they'd seen how Melissa had turned out. They couldn't allow that to happen to another innocent child. Thus two men who'd never wanted more than their private happy coupledom became fathers. Neither of them wanted it, neither of them took to it very well. Their beautiful white and glass home was smeared all over with childish handprints and their perfect life was overlaid with the smell of wet nappies and babyfood and acid, milky vomit. And their work credit rating dropped markedly. Josh learnt that sculpting while holding a colicky baby isn't quite as easy as he might have thought and after three months of sleep-free nights, Martin realised just why his book writing output had been rather more prolific before he became a father. They bickered and fought and almost forgot about having sex for the first five years, but they managed to stay together for the child who, when she grew up to become a born-again evangelical Christian, was somewhat less than grateful to the evil sodomites who'd raised her.

Frances lost most of her psychic powers and had to rely on more traditional massage work for an income. Philip lost a few contracts, bungled a few deals but got back on an even earning keel eventually. Around the time they only had plastic cups left to drink from, they discovered a better way to resolve their differences than smashing crockery. And Ben went into therapy the day he turned thirteen. Other than that they pretty much carried on as usual, neither of them completely satisfied and both of them too scared to ever try alone. They went on being happily/unhappily married and putting up with it. They hadn't exactly been Mr and Mrs Walton to start with.

Cushla returned to the land that is very far from here and really quite close and having graduated from Princess to Queen, she lived and ruled alone. Just as she'd always planned. She banned all the fairies from the kingdom, and put a hundred-year quota on marriages. She made handholding in the streets illegal and enforced heavy fines on those caught snogging on the tube. She had the Compassion Fairy's remains scraped up and placed as perfect manure on the rose bush she brought home with her. The rose bush grew tall and strong and every year Cushla snipped away the tiny buds that never grew to bloom and cut for herself a long, sharp thorn. Then annually, in the full moon light of a late summer night she stabbed herself deep into her heartspace. In the pain of the stabbing she remembered Jonathan and looked on his new life, she kissed Josh and soothed Melissa's baby back to sleep, she held Frances and knew the disappointment of compromise. And as the thorn emerged bloodless from her side she touched her brother the Prince and knew again what she would never allow herself to have. And just once a year she missed him. But that was all. And it was enough.

And no one lived happily ever after. Except Cushla. More or less.